Under a Mexican Moon

Taylor Clark

ISBN: 0990751708
ISBN 13: 9780990751700
Library of Congress Control Number: 2015935565
Perpetua Publishing LLC, Ft. Worth, TX

1

*A*fter a month's absence, John's first day back in the office was a long one, but after ten hours, and with the very able assistance of his secretary, he had put out all the fires and was basically caught up. What's more, the deal, the one that had been of great concern to him, had been concluded in his absence. One might think that his benign neglect had worked where his persistence had failed.

Despite a productive day and some good business news John felt both tired and restless as he followed a waning moon back to his condo. After parking his car in the massive concrete parking garage, he proceeded to the elevator but paused before selecting a floor. His finger waivered over the number that would take him home before selecting another familiar number which would deliver him to the bar in his condo tower. very convenient and with no concerns about having to drive afterward. He took his usual barstool and unknowingly let out a deep sigh. The man behind the bar glanced over his shoulder to put a face to the sigh. He then turned back to the bar and automatically reached for his customer's preferred scotch, poured a shot, added an eyeballed ounce of Perrier to the glass, and covered the contents with crushed ice. A swizzle stick sent it all swirling, and he finished a perfect made-to-order John Sanford scotch and water. He placed a paper napkin under it and slid it in front of John. The bartender was about to turn back when he remembered something.

"Mr. Sanford, you've been away, haven't you?" the bartender asked.

John nodded, and the bartender continued. "Mexico, wasn't it? Did you have a good time?" The bartender paused and studied the face of the patron he had been serving for years now. Sanford had a deeper tan—that was easy to see—his face was more taut and less puffy than he remembered, but that wasn't it. There was something inexplicable about his eyes. They had a faraway look.

"You look different somehow," the bartender said. As soon as he had said the words, he wondered if he had crossed some line between bartender and drinker. He reminded himself that you always let the man on the stool initiate any subject, especially anything personal. The prolonged silence only acted to confirm his error. The drink sat untouched as the man just stared into the amber pool. Finally the tension broke as the man on the stool spoke.

"It's because I am different," he said.

2

ohn's Houston lay in one of nature's most inhospitable environs for human habitation. A megalopolis of concrete, steel, and glass rose out of the hot and humid lowland, with only the southern pine forest to soften its rough edges. Downtown, from the millionaire's mansion to the rough inner-city neighborhood, all shared the same oppressive atmosphere. The marshy land sloped downward and to the east until it met the powdery sand and green waters of the Gulf of Mexico, with its languid sea breezes.

What made it commercially viable was the sluggish Buffalo Bayou, an inland highway for oil tankers. Oil over people.

People came to Houston to make money, and it welcomed all comers. A Houstonian never worried about overcrowding or its effects on the character and quality of life of the city. There, you could build whatever you wanted, wherever you wanted. No one complained. The people knew no other way. They were born in a booming Houston and always knew it as such. Houston was like a perpetually adolescent male with an ever-growing appetite that must be met. If Houston ever stopped growing, it would die. And no one wanted to see that.

Those who didn't need a suburban yard with slender, towering pines could live quite comfortably in the high-rise condominiums that came to dot the city. Pick one close to your work and you could avoid the misery of the commuting suburbanite. You could travel from apartment parking garage to office parking garage without ever having to feel the hot breath of the city in your face. Take your lunch from the building's deli, and your drinks and dinner at the condo, add cable television and perfect climate control, and you could live like you're anywhere else in the United States. You worked hard; you shouldn't have to experience the pulsing city ten stories below, sweating and straining to keep going. Houston, now, was all you knew. It formed you and taught you how to survive and even prosper in the cool, dry, personal biosphere that is your life. Venture out of it at your own risk.

—◦ ◦—

The name on the articles of incorporation read Sanford and Kolenosky Inc., but at his request, that was the only place that Sidney Kolenosky's name appeared. Kolenosky was a reclusive inventor seldom heard from and never seen. He was the patent holder on a device that was required by the Occupational Safety and Health Act on every piece of heavy moving equipment manufactured in the United States. John was the business end and oversaw the production of and marketing of their sole product. Marketing that took him to such glamour spots as Moline, Illinois; Omaha, Nebraska; and Akron, Ohio. But as long as they had a Hilton Hotel, he was at home and didn't care what the view outside his window was.

John had risked all his capital when he agreed to represent a product whose function he barely understood, but it had proved successful. However, things were changing. Competition was entering the market, and he risked losing it all if he couldn't lower his costs. He knew the answer, but it would cost him his Made in America emblem. It hurt his pride and pricked at his prejudices, but business was business. He would have to cross the border.

From John's office window twenty-two stories up, Houston spread out in all directions as far as the horizon. Thanks mostly to an abundance of green growth that battled the concrete daily for space, it was not an unpleasant view from high above. In a conference room dominated by a large, heavy oak table, John faced two businessmen almost identically clad in dark charcoal suits. With their similar dark hair and mustaches, he had trouble telling them apart. It didn't really matter—they seemed to act as one anyway.

Since trade between Mexico and the "States" was opened by the NAFTA agreement, border-town manufacturing plants called *maquila-doras* had sprung up, and with cheap labor, no benefits, and no health insurance costs, they were considerably less costly than the American versions. John needed to shift his production to these cheaper plants. But how cheap were they? These men knew. John could only guess. John wanted to bring them inside the tent, so to speak, as working partners, contributing to the final product and sharing in the profit. They represented the only missing link in his plan for survival.

John's well-prepared presentation had run for twenty minutes before he ended with, "So, what I'm proposing is a three-way arrangement..." He paused as they glanced toward each other and began to speak in Spanish. John could not understand them, but judged that they were speaking in a serious, conspiratorial tone. They looked up and saw the undisguised agitation spreading across John's face.

One of the men—John had already quit caring which one was which—spoke to John in soothing tones.

"Sorry, Señor Stanford. Guillermo," he said, nodding his head to the other man, "was just mentioning that...that we have an early flight tomorrow."

Guillermo now chimed in English but with a slightly heavier accent. "That's right, very early."

John tried to keep his irritation in check and managed to warily reply, "I see." By now the men from Mexico had gathered their papers and briefcases and were making for the door. They stopped to make perfunctory handshakes, and the one who was not Guillermo paused to say, "Well, Señor Sanford, I believe we understand your proposal, and as I said we will be back to you very soon."

5

At this point once again Guillermo chimed in, "Yes, soon, very soon."

As they made their way out, they paused at Margie's desk to have a pleasant chat.

"Como lo hace?" *How did it go?* Margie asked.

Not-Guillermo replied with a noncommittal, "Bueno."

"Vas a visitor su cuynados en San Antonio, durante su visita aqui?" *Are you going to visit your in-laws while you're here?* Margie said in her near-perfect textbook Spanish.

"Claro, siempre. Pero, no yo ellos quieren ver pero sus nietos." *Of course, but it is not I they want to see, but their grandchildren,* Not-Guillermo said. At this he gave a small laugh.

They both shook her hand warmly and parted with, "Hasta luego," to which she replied, "Hasta la vista."

After watching that display, John turned his back and made his way back into his office. Margie heard the familiar sound of him kicking his plastic trash can, and then he bellowed loud enough for anyone to hear, "Margie, get in here!"

Margie knew that he was yelling to her, not at her, but to the rest of the floor this distinction was not so clear. She got up and, for the benefit of those following the drama, made a casual walk to his office. She found her boss pacing his office, squeezing the life out of a tension ball. When he looked up and saw her, he immediately vented his anger. In a mocking, heavily exaggerated Mexican accent he gave voice to his frustrations.

"We'll be back to you very soon," he said, dragging out the "soon." He paused and tried again in a more mature vein. "They didn't even stay to discuss it. I might as well have faxed it to them. Just, 'Adios, muchacho,' and they're gone," he said.

"Did you give them a copy of the prospectus? Maybe they needed time to study it," Margie said hopefully.

"No, I forgot," John admitted. Margie made a mental note to put two copies in the mail for them. John then changed direction and added, somewhat more calmly, "And what's with those matching mustaches? It's hard enough to tell them apart as it is."

"Vincente is the younger, taller one," said Margie. "He speaks English better than Guillermo and does most of the talking. He went to college at Cal Berkeley and has a degree in engineering." She paused when she saw this wasn't helping.

"How do you know all this?" he asked, his suspicion now spreading to Margie.

"I talked to them earlier. Vincente likes to speak English. His wife has some family in San Antonio—"

"He told you all that?" John interrupted. "He didn't give me the time of day."

"Mr. Sanford, I told you. You can't just launch into your sales pitch. These people, any people, need to get to know who they're dealing with. It's impolite to just talk business."

John sat down heavily in his leather executive chair and began to review the fiasco that was his carefully planned meeting.

"Well, what's this business about only speaking Spanish to each other and right in front of me? Is that polite?"

Margie held back. She didn't wish to be perceived as siding with the Mexicans. "No, I guess not."

"Doesn't matter," he said, his ire beginning to reassert itself. "I know what they said."

"You do?" she asked, skeptical.

"I don't know what their exact words were, but I got the gist of it," he said. "Let's screw the gringo!"

At this, Margie started to leave but paused as John changed his tone from a rant to a whine.

"We've got no choice," he said. "We've got to deal with them. They're the answer to our cost problem. But I've got to be on an equal footing with them. I can't be hearing only half of what's said."

"Well, why don't you learn to speak Spanish? That's what I'm doing. I'm using discs. You could borrow mine if you like."

"I could, you know," he said. "I could learn to speak Mexican."

John calling Spanish "Mexican" caused Margie to wince slightly as she slipped out the door.

His outburst attracted the attention of Amanda down the hall who was on her way out. She saw her friend Margie and approached her.

"Margie, why do you put up with him?" she said. "You know, I could get you a better job before the day is over."

Margie found it strange that she still came to his defense. "You don't understand. Underneath all that blustering, he's a scared man. All his success is threatened, and that's a threat to who he is."

"I'm telling you, he's not your problem. When you've had enough, let me know," she said, and then with a shake of her head continued down the hall.

"I'm okay. Thanks, anyway," Margie said, but in her heart she worried about him. That man could be his own worst enemy.

3

The next morning, John arose early with an enthusiasm that, for him, only came from a new deal. When he had a deal cooking, he felt alive with boundless energy. He now had a positive outlet for the frustration his dealings with the Mexicans had brought on. He was going to beat those Mexicans at their own game. He would learn Spanish. He put on his light gray suit and knotted his tie with determination. He took the elevator down to the fourth floor of the parking garage and made for his Lexus. Once inside, he reached for the plastic case holding the discs of Spanish lessons that Margie had loaned him. He selected the disc labeled, "Unit One, Disc One," and popped it into his player. He started the car and made his way down the winding concrete canyon, and by the time he reached the bottom, he and the disc player were beginning on a new venture.

"Buenos días. Repita." The voice on the tape was distinctive, with only a slight accent. John practically sang back, "Buenos días."

"Como esta usted. Repita."

John repeated the phrase with growing enthusiasm.

"Muy bien, gracias. Y ustede?" John struggled with something that sounded like *muy beans, gracias e oostead.*

"What?" he said in frustration, and hit the button to switch to radio, which was preset to a local all-sports station in the midst of giving out the previous night's baseball scores. He listened to it all the way to the office. He parked his car in another parking garage and took the elevator up to his office suite.

There he was met by Margie, who handed him a cup of coffee, black, and he responded with, "Gracias."

She replied, "De nada," *It's nothing,* and followed with, "Como esta ustede?" *How are you?*

He stammered. "Uh, muy beans, okay," in a tone that made it clear that he was at the end of the lesson. "Can we get down to business now? I want the files on the Mexican deal. We need to come up with a formal proposal. I'll need to see sales projection brought up to date from the last quarter."

"Yes, sir," she said as she made for her computer to start retrieving the figures.

By the end of the day, they had a draft of their formal proposal, and John decided to let it sit overnight before he emailed it out. He imagined if the deal went through, there would need to be numerous visits across the border to keep an eye on his partners. He would definitely need Spanish, or he would have to trust them a lot more than he already did, which was not at all.

— ⁓

John left for work in the usual manner but did not bother to activate the Spanish lesson. He looked at the plastic case but could not bring himself to engage with it. It was too mechanical for him, that haughty baritone voice with its clipped tones. It was a faceless voice, and it could not see him or answer questions when he had them. It just didn't work for him. He needed something else. When he arrived at the office and saw Margie approaching, he girded himself for another exam. Sure enough, the first words out of her mouth were in Spanish.

"Como vas la leccion de espanol?" *How are the Spanish lessons going?*

"What?" John asked with undisguised irritation.

"Your Spanish lessons," she said. "How are they going?"

"Oh, great, great," he said unconvincingly.

"Really?" She probed when she should have let it slide.

"Well, no," he said. "I can't work off those disks. That man on there is so irritating. I don't know how you can stand to listen to him. Moooie beans," John said in a mock imitation of him.

Margie laughed. John actually came pretty close to the pretentious voice on the disks.

"I can't work with disks," John said. "I'm a people person. I need a human to teach me."

Margie had to suppress a laugh at John's description of himself. He then looked at her as if he was considering her as his teacher. She reacted quickly.

"Well, I can't do it. Do you want me to find you a teacher?"

"Yeah, do that," he said.

Margie went online to look for Spanish lessons. There were a multitude of classes available, but she opted for a private tutor.

John arrived at seven after a long day, probably not the best way to start lessons. His private tutor was a short, curvy woman from Venezuela named Cecilia. She was cute, funny, and flirty, and she had an enthusiasm that momentarily lifted John's flagging spirits.

"Your problem, John, is you keep using American vowels. They are confusing," Cecilia said. "I don't know when you want an A to sound like an 'ah' or an 'a' or an 'eh.' In Spanish, each vowel always has the same sound. Simple, right? You only need to learn five sounds." She pointed to the letters on the blackboard.

She began again. "Ah, eh, ee, oh, oo."

Cecilia boldly took John's cheeks in her small hand and squeezed, trying to force the vowels out in the prescribed forms. Still they did not come out right. She released it and leaned back, trying to take him in.

She gave him her contagious smile, and he couldn't help smiling back. He liked the way she didn't hesitate to use his first name and he found it endearing the way she mispronounced it, giving the J a Y sound. She had a very forthright way about her that caused John to trust her.

John fumbled through them. "Ah, ee, I, o, uh." He stopped, knowing that they were all wrong, and vented his frustration. "This is ridiculous. Why can't you just do your vowels like us?"

"Why, like you?" she said, breaking out in a tirade that must have been building for some time. "The rest of the world uses them. It is the same for all the romance languages. It is English that is the odd language. We never know how a word is supposed to be pronounced until we say it wrong and somebody like you corrects us."

They both paused and let the room settle down. There was no one else there that night, but she was not allowed to yell at customers. Besides, she found him somewhat handsome. Her tone changed, and she became flirty again.

With a mischievous look on her face she decided to tease John. "Say, John," she said, and the next word came out "chu," but John was used to that, "chu know what you call a person who can speak three languages?"

John couldn't think of the answer, so she said, "Trilingual. Two languages?"

John jumped in with the easy answer. "Bilingual."

"One language?" she asked.

John started fumbling around with the prefix mono-, but she finished it for him. "An American."

She didn't mind laughing at her own joke and John reluctantly joined her but resented it at the same time. It was the truth of the statement that bothered him most.

She then spoke to him in soothing tones. "John, I know how hard it is to learn a new language, and if you want to know the truth," she said, pausing to look around her even though they were alone, "there's really only one way to learn a language. *Total immersion.*"

"Total immersion," John repeated, not being familiar with the term.

"Total immersion," she said definitively. "You go to the country whose language you want to learn, you live there, study, you soak it up like a sponge." Here she puffed herself up to illustrate an immersed sponge. "In thirty days you are speaking it like a native."

"Thirty days!" John said in amazement.

"Sí, only thirty days. Is the way I learned English. I come here from Caracas, very"—it came out *bery*—"dangerous place," she said with a shake of her head as if recalling her former life.

"I go to work for a family, watching the baby while the wife, she works. They very nice people, they help me get my residency here in Houston. That baby and me, we learn English together, lots of Sesame Street." She paused, reflected awhile, and then continued. "I jus' hope I didn't give him my accent." She laughed a little and John joined her. "If a poor girl from Venezuela can learn, a smart educated man like you can, you see. But an hour here, an hour there, is not going to get you anywhere. You go to Mexico, you learn twenty-four hours a day, and then you come back, we can work together. Maybe you call me. Maybe you call me at home, hmmm?" She gave him a smile that held promise if he did as she advised him, giving him further incentive. She also scribbled a local phone number on the back of the business card and passed it to John.

She once again looked around in a conspiratorial manner and then grabbed a bunch of language school brochures from behind the front desk. She gave them to John, who thanked her and then, feeling the same paranoia, stuffed them in his inner suit coat pocket to be viewed once he was clear of the office. He started to leave, but she reached out to detain him, hugging him and standing on tiptoes to give him a quick kiss on the cheek.

"Oh, and John," Cecilia said, returning to her teacher's voice, "look for the language schools in the interior. Stay away from those on the beach. Too many tourists, too many distractions." As he left she called out, "Hasta la vista."

John later looked it up and found that it meant, "Until I see you again," a slightly different, more promising meaning than goodbye. When he got back, he just might look her up. She would be fun to practice with, and who knew...

4

The sun had not yet risen when John walked into work and headed to his office. He paused in the doorway. Vincente and Guillermo were already in there. He was surprised. He was not expecting them. Vincente was actually sitting in John's own chair, and Guillermo stood looking intently over Vincente's shoulder at some papers spread before them. They seemed taller and darker than he remembered, and those mustaches seemed to extend a foot from either side of their mouths. Across the desk from them, Margie sat taking notes as they talked. That Margie was working for them infuriated John even more than them taking possession of his office.

John barged in and yelled, "What the hell is going on here?" No one even looked up. He said it again even louder but got no response. He walked around and inserted himself between Margie and the desk, but she looked past him. Then he noticed that her blouse was nearly undone, and he could almost see her exposed breasts. The lust this filled him with was countered by fury at the thought that she had never dressed like this for him. But she would do it for these Mexicans, who seemed to be taking over. He was getting ready to deal with them, but first he wanted another peek at Margie.

He leaned over and glanced at her open blouse, but before he could see anything, she looked up and spoke to him in a commanding tone.

"From now on we're a bilingual office." She then began to speak to him, but in a language he couldn't understand. They all started talking at once in what must have been Spanish.

He shouted out, "In English, in English!"

Margie finally addressed him and said, "I said we're a bilingual office, but I didn't say the other language was English." At that they all started laughing, their voices growing louder and their faces larger.

He awoke with a start, his fists and jaw clenched. His first thoughts were a mix of lust and anger at Margie. He knew it was only a dream, but he was a man, and he couldn't shake the feeling of impotence that he had experienced with her at the hands of those Mexican men.

He laid his head back down and looked over at the red digital numbers on his bedside clock. They stared back at him, declaring the time to be 6:18—early enough that he could go back to sleep. But he knew he couldn't. He swung his feet over the side of the bed and went into the bathroom. He stood over the toilet, urinated, and then ran cold water into the sink. He doused his face repeatedly in an attempt to drive away any vestiges of the nightmare. He then retrieved the brochures Cecilia had given him and returned to his bed, where he spread them out. He took his other pillow, propped it up behind his head, and started going through them.

The first one was for a school called Solexico, obviously a combination of "sol," the Spanish word for sun, and Mexico. It was at Playa del Carmen, which he recognized as the resort town across the water from the island of Cozumel. The color pictures were of young students sitting on stools around a grass-thatched cabana in the open air. The relaxed atmosphere really appealed to John, but he remembered the warning from Cecilia to stay away from the beach. He reluctantly put aside all the coastal schools and concentrated on those in the interior. Of those, one was in Cuernavaca, and another in a small town north of Mexico City. The latter's brochure was the least enticing, showing an indoor classroom with desks like a high school. It was in the interior, away from the beach and its distractions. He knew his weaknesses and was determined to stay focused.

5

*J*ohn arrived at the office before anyone else. He did not want Margie to be involved in the planning. He did not want her good sense to interfere with his enthusiasm. He wanted to present it to her as a *fait accompli*. He spread open the brochure for the school in the small town on his desk and dialed the number. He remained determined to avoid distractions of a city, or worse, a beach. John was used to making international calls and had no trouble making the connection.

On the third ring a pleasant female voice answered. "Institute de Lenguas, habla Olivia Walker." The woman had identified herself in Spanish, but since she had an American-sounding name, John answered in English. "Hello, my name is John Sanford, calling from Houston, Texas."

"Good morning, Mr. Sanford, how may I help you?" she replied in unaccented English.

John relaxed a bit and spoke confidently to her. "I'd like to enroll in your Spanish course."

"Good. It is for a month," she cautioned him.

"Yes, for the month." He had already committed himself to that.

"Very good, sir," the woman said. "When would you like to begin?"

"I can be there for—" John paused as he ran his finger across the calendar open before him, passing over previous commitments. "I can be there October 7."

"That will work fine, Mr. Sanford."

"Great," he replied, feeling better about this. "Oh, and can you handle my accommodations?"

"Of course, sir, it is part of the package," she said.

"Good," John said. "Now, generally I like to stay at the Hilton, but if that's not available, whatever is the top hotel in town."

There followed a pause, and John wondered if the connection had been lost. Then the woman's voice returned.

"Mr. Sanford, do you not understand our learning technique? It's known as *total immersion*. You'll be living in a Mexican household and speaking only Spanish during your entire stay."

John did not like the idea of staying in a stranger's house, a friend's house, his parents' house, or in anyone's house. "You do have hotels there, don't you?" he asked.

"Yes, some very fine ones, but not for our students," she said firmly.

John paused, and an awkward silence followed. He hoped she would relent. Isn't there another way, say...partial immersion?" This did not meet with any levity at the other end of the line.

"Mr. Sanford, I can put you up in a lovely home. It has a beautiful patio with a swimming pool, a private bath, wonderful meals, and a charming hostess. It runs a little more, but for a gentleman like yourself, I would say it would be well worth it."

When she put it that way, John conceded, but not without some trepidation. They exchanged the usual information to complete the transaction, with confirmation to follow by email. Then she asked a question that caught John by surprise.

"By the way, Mr. Sanford, if you don't mind my asking, how old are you?"

"How old am I?" John thought the question through and said, "Too old to be staying in some youth hostel."

"I understand, Mr. Sanford, that's why I'm recommending this home," she said curtly, not wanting to rehash the issue.

"Okay, my age," John said. "I'm fifty-two."

"Married or single?" she asked flatly.

"Actually, I'm divorced."

She again became the very gracious Ms. Walker and closed by saying, "I'm sure you'll be very pleased with your accommodations. We look forward to seeing you on the seventh, Mr. Sanford."

When she hung up the phone, she wondered about what she had just done. She had made a commitment for a man without consulting the owner of the home—and not your normal college-age student, but a middle-aged man of some sophistication. She closed the management program on her computer and clicked on Google Search, putting "John Sanford, Houston, Texas" into the search box. Several possible John Sanfords came up, but one was associated with a business named Sanford Industries. She clicked on it, opening a website for a Houston-based business. She went to the top of the screen and clicked on "Personnel" and up popped a picture of a tall, lean, good-looking man in a gray suit posing behind a desk. Olivia leaned back, looked at him appreciatively, and murmured to herself, "This could be interesting."

— —

John put down the phone and leaned back in his chair, pleased with himself for taking the first step. He heard Margie coming and started to yell across the room for her. He then thought better of it, got up and stuck his head out of his office door, and said in a normal volume, "Margie, grab a cup of coffee and come and join me." His face flushed with boyish excitement.

"Be right there," Margie replied.

She got her coffee and sat primly in the chair across from his desk with her legs crossed. She wore a dark skirt and white blouse buttoned to the top. He recalled his vision of her from only a few hours earlier. She caught him looking at her in a way she had not seen before, a Cheshire cat smile spread across his face. She ignored the leer and concentrated on the smile. "Okay, what have you done now?" she asked with a mix of curiosity and dread.

"What have I done? I'll tell you what I've done," he said. She knew that boyish enthusiasm meant a new girlfriend, a new business deal, or some kind of crazy scheme. He paused to let the drama build and then exclaimed, "I'm going to language school."

"Oh, you saw the tutor last night, great. What's it going to be? Two, three," she said as he gestured more with his hands, "four nights a week?"

"Wrong! Try 24-7 for a month," he said, and paused to let her absorb this.

"John, what are you talking about?"

"It's called total immersion," he said. "You live it, you speak it, all day long. It's the only way to go. This—an hour here, an hour there, like you do—isn't going to get me anywhere."

"And just where are you going to be doing this?" she asked.

"Well, Mexico, of course. In just thirty days, I'll be speaking like a native."

"Thirty days!" She looked at him with astonishment, the number sinking in where the words had not. She had to hand it to him—when he did something, he did it all the way.

"Oh, don't worry about it," he said. "I'll be in constant contact. I'll set up an office in my room—telephone, fax, Internet, the works."

John spent the rest of the day organizing things for his looming departure date. He and Margie updated the proposal for the Mexicans and asked for another meeting date thirty days out, either Houston or Monterrey, Mexico, their hometown.

"I can't wait to see the look on their faces when I start speaking Spanish," John said confidently. With total immersion, he knew he couldn't fail.

It was seven thirty when they knocked off and a weary Margie left for home. John was still feeling the excitement of his venture and stopped off for a drink at the bar in his condo building. The bartender saw him when he came in and had John's drink ready for him when he sat down.

John spread the brochure for the school in front of him and studied it carefully as he sipped his drink. The bartender leaned over and peered at the brochure.

"Whatcha got there, Mr. Sanford?" he asked.

"Oh, just a brochure for Mexico," John said casually.

"Thinking about a little vacation to sunny Mexico? Take in some beaches, take in some Señoritas?"

"Hardly, Sam. This is no Club Med I'm looking at. This is the real Mexico."

John picked up the brochure that pictured a town perched on some dry hills and waved it at Sam.

"This isn't some beach resort," he said. "This p lace is in the interior. Won't be any bikini beauties where I'm going. Won't be anything but some fat Mexican mamas."

The bartender took the brochure and held it out to look at it. To him, it showed a charming, picturesque, romantic setting.

"You never know, Mr. Sanford," the bartender said. "You never know."

John finished his drink and took the elevator up to his floor. He entered his stylish, modern condominium. He had moved in after his divorce and had it decorated professionally; the place didn't have anything of his own choosing. He did not spend much time there, and he treated the place more like a hotel than a home. He tossed his suit jacket over a chair and made his way into the kitchen, where he opened the refrigerator and leaned in to take a look. He picked up a carton of Chinese takeout and sniffed it. It did not pass the smell test, but instead of putting it in the stainless steel trash can, he put it back in the refrigerator, as if it might improve given more time. He then went to his wet bar and made himself another scotch and water. At the window, with its expansive view of the lights of the city, he made a mock toast. "Wait for me, Houston. I'll be back in thirty days."

6

*I*t was late afternoon and the sun was edging toward the low hills surrounding San Miguel de Allende, casting long shadows across the town. Lourdes de Madrid Rodriguez sat at her small wooden credenza, which, when its lid was pulled up, became her desk. When not in use, it blended in tastefully with the rest of the room. On her nose were perched reading glasses that she wore on a chain of pure silver, locally mined and fashioned. Laid out before her was the same business ledger that she had when she moved into the house some twenty-odd years ago. Here she recorded her monthly grocery bill, utilities, and sundry expenses in the debit column, and the checks for the boarding guests in the credit column. She stopped and exhaled a long breath, thinking about how strange it was that she now ran a very exclusive, small hotel for visiting language students. For students whose parents didn't mind paying a little more, she provided rooms with private baths, excellent dining with an emphasis on freshly made authentic local cuisine, and a beautiful patio centered around a swimming pool.

She took pride in providing the students with an upscale, but thoroughly Mexican, experience. She spoke excellent English, if the occasion required it, but she tried to maintain the total immersion concept so essential, she believed, to learning a new language in one month.

Because she understood both languages, she knew how best to phrase her words to help with her students' understanding at whatever level they were. She saw herself as their teacher when they were out of class and in her care. She made every dinner serve as both a meal and a lesson. She would prepare and present historical and cultural lessons into conversations. None of this, of course, was required of her, but it was in her nature to give her best in whatever she did. But she also expected more of the students in order that they get the most out of their stay.

Her wandering mind was brought back into focus by the sharp knock on her door. During the day, the door was not locked, so that the students had free access, and they were not expected to knock every time they came in. This was to be their home for the duration of their stay and Lourdes was *madre surragate*, their surrogate mother.

Maria, her longtime housekeeper and cook, emerged from the kitchen, wiping her hands with a dish towel as she made her way across the room, but Lourdes waved her off and strode to the door.

She opened the door first a little and then, upon seeing who it was, swung it wide open. With a sweeping gesture, she beckoned her guest to enter. It was her good friend Olivia Walker, who ran the language school and referred students to Lourdes's home. Olivia was about her age, height, and build, but that's where the similarities ended. While Lourdes was dark, Olivia was the picture of the American Midwest, with blond hair, blue eyes, and radiant white skin. They were friends, but there was really only one reason she would be here at this time of day, and that was business. Olivia seemed breathless, as if she had hurried over, but she did not wait to regain her breath, speaking at once.

"Good, I've caught you. I do wish you'd get a phone. It might improve your social life." She spoke with a familiarity that few had with Lourdes.

"My life, social and otherwise, is fine," Lourdes said in the same lighthearted manner. "Sit down, you look frazzled."

"I'm sorry, but I can't stay I have to get back to school," Olivia said. She remained standing, determined to stay on track. "I've come to ask you a favor."

"Of course, anything."

"I've accepted another student at the last minute, and I need a home for placement. It would help me out tremendously."

Lourdes paused and thought of the implications of an extra person. She tried to beg off. "Oh, Olivia. You know I already have two, and they're very nice, but I'm a bit overwhelmed at the moment."

Olivia was determined to have this done and said to Lourdes, friend to friend, "Lourdes, mi querida amiga, my dear friend," she said, switching to Spanish for emphasis, then back to English. "I wouldn't ask if I weren't in a jam. And what's one more? You give him a room and Maria gives him three meals a day. It's only for a month, if he lasts that long." Olivia wished she had not said that last part out loud.

"I...don't know," Lourdes said, but already her tone revealed that she was conceding.

Olivia took that as a yes and continued. "Good. Thank you so much. I've got to run, arrival is sometime tonight."

Olivia was already out the door as Lourdes pondered the last ambiguous part and called out to the quickly retreating figure of Olivia, who either did not hear or chose not to answer, "Wait...what's their name? Is it a girl or a boy?"

Lourdes walked back in and called to Maria to help prepare a room for another guest. As she started thinking of what needed to be done, she sighed and said softly to herself, "Oh well. I am in the business of taking in strangers."

The house already had two paying guests. They were both about what Lourdes had come to expect. First there was Chloe, a bright girl from what Lourdes could gather. She certainly took her lessons seriously and embraced the total immersion concept almost completely. She did, however, seem to have issues with the cuisine. She worked hard and should have a good grasp of Spanish by the end of her stay. She was polite, maybe too polite—she could get on your nerves if you got too much of her. But she respected the rules of the house, and this meant a lot to Lourdes. She could overlook other things, but not that. Lourdes went to great pains to create an environment conducive to the total immersion concept. In that respect Chloe was the perfect guest. Yet, there was something unsettling about her that caused Lourdes to hold her breath until she left the room. Lourdes could tell that she had a privileged upbringing and was used to being spoiled. She had applied to some pretty prestigious colleges, whose names she dropped occasionally, and she said she hoped this study abroad would give her an advantage.

Hayden was more obvious. He had no real aptitude for languages and struggled with his Spanish, but he seemed to try hard. He attended college somewhere in California, but he didn't strike her as the studious type. Unlike Chloe, who at least always acted upbeat, Hayden could be moody and often seemed uncomfortable around Lourdes. She tried to help him fit in, but it just seemed to make things worse. He seemed to be harboring some suppressed feelings, but it was not her job to deal with that, and admittedly she didn't know how young men thought.

—   ~

Olivia Walker ran her school the way she always had, and with consistent success. Foremost was the concept of immersion: no English spoken after the first day of introduction. The school day was divided up into two classes: grammar in the morning and conversation in the afternoon, with a long siesta after lunch. She planned to meet with John—or Mr. Sanford, she hadn't decided how to address him—an hour before the rest of his class to give him instructions on what to expect. Without any way to judge his aptitude for languages, he would go into the beginners' conversational class. She knew every student was different in his natural ability and determination to learn. Language was often a talent; like an ear for music, some had it, most did not. She had had doctors and lawyers who, despite that prior academic prowess, had great difficulty with language. But others with sketchy academic histories took to it easily, the right side of their brain processing the grammar while the left side broke down the sounds into recognizable words and placed them in context. But there was something that she didn't seem to be able to teach. For lack of a better phrase, she referred to it as the seduction of the language. Too many had a prejudice that caused them to resist the new language subconsciously. They would sincerely try to learn it but still kept it at arm's length, as if they didn't trust it. One had to let go and not fight the invasion of the strange and foreign entity that was the romance language.

There was fluidity to class structure. While everyone had the same grammar class, if one student showed some proficiency, he would move up to a more advanced conversational class. If at any time a student merited advancement, it happened immediately, without notice. You could be in a beginners' class one day and advanced the next.

Although she had yet to meet John, she had already developed certain concerns. Her brief telephone conversation with him revealed his reluctance to live in a "residence," forcing him out of his comfort zone. But more than that, she was concerned about his age and occupation. At fifty-two, he was not in the prime years for linguistics. Studies had shown that, but her observations over twenty-odd years were what she relied on. His application contained a lot of blanks that indicated a certain lackadaisical attitude on his part. On the positive side, he would be residing with Lourdes, and that would help. Olivia only had the students for six hours a day, and their home experience was an important part of the learning process. She knew that, although it wasn't her main function, Lourdes treated each meal as a living lesson in Spanish. Most of the other residency homes just provided a bed and three meals and did not interact beyond what was absolutely necessary. This was the reason she maneuvered John into Lourdes's home. That, and maybe another reason she kept to herself.

7

The spires of Santuario de Atotonilco reached up to heaven like antennas to the Almighty. From the high point of San Miguel de Allende, they stood as sentinels, casting their protection and authority over the city like a stern but loving father. There were those who entered the church only a few times in their lives—coming for baptism as infants, and again at first communion, their "spiritual inoculation," as eight-year-olds—but all returned for their funeral masses at the end of their lives. The spires looked down on all corners of the town, but most clearly and harshly on those who sat idly in the central plaza.

At a café table in the plaza, a strategic place for those who wished to see and be seen, sat a group of four women. They met at midmorning almost daily at this table for coffee and gossip. By ten o'clock the people with places to go had gone and made room for the retirees. The pace in the plaza, which was a stroll before, had slowed to a crawl.

The café group ranged in number from four to six. Two of the women came only occasionally, as they were a bit younger and not yet ready to admit that they had nothing better to do. They were welcomed whenever they came, for their new liveliness and new information—that is, gossip. But four was the core group and the number that worked best for the dynamics of the table. Excluding the previously mentioned two whose ages skewed the statistics, the others formed a compact age group ranging from fifty-four to sixty-two, if you accepted Vivian's purported age. No one dared to challenge it, lest they become the subject of inquiry themselves.

They all shared certain things in common: they were second or third wives, or in Vivian's case some undisclosed number over two. They were each at least ten years younger than their husbands and had seen a plastic surgeon within the last five years. At a glance, sitting as they were, they made for a pretty picture, one that could grace the cover of a guide book. With their sophistication, perfect makeup, and rejuvenated bodies, they looked as good now as nature and modern medicine would allow. They had made their last marriage before their expiration dates had run and now battled natural maturity out of a misplaced sense of pride.

They had found their ways to San Miguel from all the major metropolitan areas of the United States. They came to escape crime, pollution, too-hot summers, too-cold winters, the bland sameness of suburban sprawl, and inner-city congestion. The inevitable boredom had more do with themselves than their place of residence. Except for some humble birthplaces in small rural towns far behind them, this was the smallest place they have lived, and they now found it stifling. Not that you could blame San Miguel. Never mind the gothic church and the plaza, the town had more charm in one of its cobblestoned streets than all their previous suburbs combined.

Some dreamed, worked hard, and planned to come here with their husbands after retiring. Others, like Vivian, had never heard of the place before being torn from a condo and landing hard here.

Beverly was fifty-six and probably the most congenial of the group. She had a grown daughter from her first marriage who led a life Beverly didn't approve of, so they had very little contact. After her divorce she found herself pushing fifty with few prospects. She joined a dancing group and met a senior who seemed to appreciate her, a feeling she had not experienced in a long time. She weighed her options; and when he proposed, she accepted, and now she found herself tilting her face toward the midmorning sun in this strange place with these new friends. Things could certainly be worse, she reasoned.

Dottie was the exception, having been married to the same man for forty years. They were close in age, called each other "Mother" and "Father," and seemed to get along well. No good gossip there. Dottie was also a little dotty, but she was pleasant and good natured and always laughed, even if she didn't know why.

Joyce was from Chicago, so she loved the climate in San Miguel. The last thing she did before she left was to get a facelift, which was still too tight. Her husband, her third, had sold his successful car dealership in the Chicago neighborhood of Edgebrook, but he hadn't been able to lose his car salesman personality, which didn't fit in his new environs. People tended to give him a wide berth, which Joyce was painfully aware of, but to which he was oblivious. She and Vivian tended to clash, making Dottie their buffer.

—　—

Lourdes knelt in prayer after morning mass and finished her rosary. Finally rising, she genuflected and blessed herself with the holy water from the font before exiting the church. She emerged into bright sunlight and the teeming of the midmorning town, a stark contrast to the cool, dark sanctuary insulated from both nature and mankind. She strolled toward home and the duties that awaited her. She walked with a grace that was as unconscious as it was beautiful, dressed in a simple elegance that both enhanced and hid a body in the full ripeness of womanhood. The locals no longer turned to watch, for she was a familiar sight, but anyone seeing her for the first time would follow her with their eyes and mourn when she passed beyond their sight.

From their table, the café group had a ringside seat to the foot traffic of the town. All important pedestrian paths converged on the plaza, or as the locals called it, the *jardin* or garden. Often, one of them would make demeaning comment about the locals; the others would be obliged to chide her on her insensitivity before joining in on the fun. But today they all paused when a certain woman strode purposefully across the plaza.

The conversation lagged as Dottie's inexplicable laugh died away. The others followed Dottie's head as she turned to follow a woman making her way across the plaza. They all kept their eyes on her until she passed out of view.

It was Joyce who spoke first. "There's that woman. You know who she is, don't you, Dottie?"

"Yes, her name is Lourdes de Madrid Rodriguez. Or something," Dottie said in her usual confused state.

"She's so...so..." Beverly said, struggling for the right word. "Elegant." The others murmured their agreement, which encouraged Beverly to speculate further. "She looks like she just walked out of a painting by Degas. Anybody know her?" She looked around the table at blank faces.

Vivian chimed in that she didn't know why they were so obsessed over a local woman. Now, if it were a hunky man, *that* she could get excited about. Nevertheless, she shared what she knew—or thought she knew.

"Not very well," Vivian said. "She doesn't socialize much with the American community, except for Olivia Walker, who runs the language school." Vivian paused and gave voice to one of her own prejudices. "And I don't really consider Olivia Walker one of us anymore. Don't we have better things to do than talk about some local woman?" she said, trying to redirect the conversation.

"No, as it happens we don't," Joyce said, not wishing to give in to Vivian's domination. "Is she married?"

"I'm not sure. She has a married woman's name. No one knows for sure about her," said Dottie, but no one relied on it too much.

"Well, she's certainly a hidalgo," Beverly said.

"A what?" Vivian asked, confused.

"A hidalgo," Joyce said. "That's a Spanish aristocrat."

"She looks a little too dark to be a pure Spaniard, if you ask me," Vivian shot back.

Ignoring Vivian's tasteless comment and turning to look at Beverly, Joyce asked sincerely, "How can you tell?"

Beverly shrugged, trying to find the right words. "You can tell by the way she carries herself."

"Is that all it takes?" Vivian said, trying to reassert herself as the center of conversation. She lifted her chin and tilted her head back, trying to strike a haughty pose.

"No, Vivian, it's not that at all," Joyce said, clearly frustrated with her friend. "It's...it's in the breeding. It can't be learned."

"Well, how did she come by hers?" Beverly asked, inserting herself between Joyce and Vivian.

"If I were to guess, I'd say it came from her mother's side—Rodriguez is such a common name," Joyce said, not afraid to speculate about something she knew nothing about.

"Rodriguez? What about Madrid?" Joyce said in confusion.

"Here your maiden name comes last," Dottie said, surprising everyone. "Her married name is Madrid."

"I believe she's right," Beverly said, lending credence to Dottie's answer. "Madrid would have been her husband's name, and 'de Madrid' means 'of Madrid.'"

"Really! Sounds very possessive," said Joyce.

"That's the way it is down here," Dottie said. "It gets worse, though." Dottie now had everyone's attention, a rare occurrence for her, and she paused to relish it before beginning again. "I've heard it was an arranged marriage." She leaned back and basked in the glow of their rapt attention.

"An arranged marriage, in this century? How barbaric!" Beverly said in shock.

"Oh, and I suppose we made better choices our first time?" Vivian said, and they all laughed out loud. Vivian was glad to have regained their attention and was not about to let go of it. "Don't think I don't know what I'm talking about."

"We don't doubt you for a minute," Joyce said, speaking for the group and gladly conceding this dubious honor to Vivian. "Vivian, if it weren't for you, there would a dire shortage of gossip in this town—and don't think we don't appreciate it." They all laughed again, Vivian the loudest.

"Ha. You don't know the half of it," Vivian said, happy to be the focus again.

8

American Airlines had twice-daily flights to Mexico City: an early morning flight, and a midafternoon flight. John chose the afternoon flight, figuring he could square things away at the office before he left. He just ended up repeating the same things he said the day before to Margie. He was nervous and made everyone in the office nervous. Margie was glad to see him go.

Houston had two airports, a national and an international one. John was more familiar with the national from his numerous business trips. The international one he associated with long weekend trips to the beaches of Mexico. He was never one for lengthy vacations. He sufficed with the occasional long weekend. He recalled his last Cancun junket, a four-day package, room, drinks, and meals, at what they called an all-inclusive. You paid it all up front and never reached for your wallet the rest of the trip. Should have been relaxing. The woman, with whom he had gotten along fairly well on dates, had been a real pain on the trip. By Saturday they were no longer sharing a bed, and by Sunday they stayed apart until the blessed hour of the return to the airport. After that he never took another woman out of town. No one stayed overnight if he could help it. He preferred it that way.

These thoughts added to his growing anxiety, but once he was situated in long-term parking, he relaxed a little and considered the words "long term." His car would sit there for a month. In Houston that meant it would get rained on no fewer than ten times. Dust would cover it, get rained off, and cover it again. This would be the longest business trip he had been on by far. He was already having doubts about his decision, but he couldn't turn around now. How would he look?

The tram came to a stop at his terminal, and he got help with his luggage—two suitcases for clothes and a larger case packed with all the electronics he thought he would need to set up his *oficina* at his *residencia*. Margie had supplied him with these new Spanish words. He would be sure to use them when he arrived. That should impress somebody. He imagined splitting his day into work and school, with work coming first.

John was a very frequent flyer with American, and he used his mileage to upgrade to business class. He did not always fly this way, and the flight was only two hours long, but he shuddered to think who might make up the coach cabin. It would likely be filled with Mexican nationals.

He heard the call for his flight, and then for preferential seating. He found his window seat and was relieved when a well-dressed man took the aisle seat next to him. John wore the lightweight gray suit that he always seemed to pick for traveling. The man nodded his acquaintance and then turned back. John watched with some interest as the remainder of the passengers paraded by him. Women with babies, who, if they weren't crying now, would be once they were seated; young, swarthy men with starched jeans and pressed cotton shirts; older couples returning to Mexico, probably after visiting grandchildren. He scoffed at the notion that due to their place of birth those grandchildren held the same citizenship as he did.

Once the plane took off, John glanced out his window at the familiar sight of the Gulf of Mexico. The trip caused John to reexamine things he took for granted, and he pondered the name "Gulf of Mexico." Why not "Gulf of America," or better still, "Gulf of Texas"? He thought, *Shouldn't we have taken the name from them after the last war we won?*

The flight attendant was thin, blond, and professional. When he was younger, John used to flirt with the young ones but had long since given it up and now let them get on with their work. After his seatmate ordered coffee, John hesitated and then asked for scotch. John's seatmate turned to look at him and gave John a broad smile. As the flight attendant passed them their drinks, John, thinking he should excuse his afternoon drinking, spoke before the other man could say anything.

"Better drink this while I can. I probably won't see any good scotch for a while."

His seatmate turned to him and tried to assuage his concern. "Oh, I wouldn't be too worried about that," he said. "Mexico City is very cosmopolitan. You can get anything in the world there."

"Well, maybe, but not where I'm going," John said.

"Oh?"

"I'm going to be in the middle of nowhere," John said. "A place called San Miguel."

"You don't mean San Miguel de Allende, do you?" the other man said.

"Yeah, that's it," John said, surprised that anyone had ever heard of it.

"Oh, it's a beautiful, charming place," the man said. "You should enjoy it greatly."

John didn't know this man but still felt the need to set him straight. "Well, I'm not going there to enjoy myself," he said. "I'm going there to learn Spanish. In thirty days, I'll be able to speak like a native. Then let's see those beaners try and slip something by me."

John, having got that off his chest, turned to the man. He did not like the expression on the man's face but blundered on. "You know what I mean," he said, but without the conviction of his earlier rant. The man didn't respond, and to break the tension John extended his hand.

"By the way, I'm John Sanford."

The passenger responded in heavily accented Spanish with an exaggerated trilling of his r's, "Pleased to meet you, Mr. Sanford. My name is Alejandro Rivera de Ruiz."

John's error was now abundantly clear to him, and he tried to recover. "Nice to meet you, Mr. Reevaro Rueee," he said, the last vowel trailing away. Then John grabbed the first thing he could reach—an in-flight magazine—and held it up to his face for the remainder of the flight.

— ⌣

San Miguel de Allende rose in the morning to receive John, then stood waiting in the midday sun. She paced in the afternoon. She lingered in the long shadow of the setting sun, kept vigilant in the waning evening hours, and still he did not come. But when the full moon showed itself, the town closed its doors and went to sleep. The household of Lourdes de Madrid Rodriquez did not have that option. It waited anxiously past all decent hours, no longer with patience but with persistence. Lourdes worried about any student under her supervision. Even though he had not passed into her care, she felt the same responsibility. Maria offered to stay up and call her when he arrived. But she refused. She would not rest, could not rest, until the child was safe under her roof. She did not worry about San Miguel—no one there was a threat—but she worried about him making his connection and making it out of Mexico City. She refused to change into more comfortable clothes for her wait and still wore the dress she deemed important for making the right first impression. She read for a few minutes, stopped to look at her watch, and then repeated the sequence. Her last glance at her watch showed 11:10. She worried greatly for the child and for his parents.

— ⌣

John deplaned at 8:00 p.m. and found himself in a modern state-of-the-art airport, larger and more up-to-date than Houston International by his quick assessment. His travel agent had arranged private transportation to meet him. The clean, modern setting should have put him at ease, but this was not the friendly tourist-oriented Cancun airport he was accustomed to. This was a place for busy people who knew what they were doing. The signs were in Spanish and the only word he recognized was *Banos*, which he only recognized because of the figure of a man next to it. *Legadas* or *Salidas*—which was the exit? Should he move toward one the many avenues of exits, or should he stay put and let the driver find him?

"How could you trust anyone in Mexico to get things right?" he muttered to himself. His confusion must have been apparent, because a middle-aged man in a suit approached him.

"May I be of assistance?" he inquired politely.

A look of gratitude spread over John's face and he broke into a smile. "Thank God! Someone who speaks English. I'm supposed to meet a driver here, but I don't see him anywhere."

"What time was he expecting you?"

"About twenty minutes ago," John said emphatically.

"Well then, I wouldn't worry about it. Punctuality doesn't have the same meaning here."

"Cheee...what's with this country, anyway?"

"Relax. You'll get used to it."

"God, I hope not."

"By the way, are you John Sanford?"

John reacted with astonishment. "How the hell did you know that?"

The man simply pointed across the terminal to a short man holding a sign with "John Sanford" scribbled across it.

Before John could thank him, the man departed with a wave and, with his back to him, said sarcastically, "Buena suerte." *Good luck.*

In three hours John had seen a huge city pass by, traveled at excessive speed down a superhighway, crawled through winding mountain roads, and climbed in elevation to nearly seven thousand feet to the highlands of Mexico, where strange manlike cacti stood like sentries across the landscape. But by then it was dark and a full moon dominated the sky. He would be getting into San Miguel later than he had planned. He chided himself for not taking the earlier flight. The driver had slowed now and John saw the town that must be San Miguel silhouetted in an all-encompassing moonlight. The driver slowly moved down the narrow street, and John felt the car rumble under the uneven cobblestone pavement. What would become picturesque in daylight was just plain eerie in the moonlight. The driver seemed lost as he paused at every intersection to read the small street signs posted on the corners of the buildings. John felt like he was in a Stephen King novel. John reached into his coat pocket and from his flask took the last sip of scotch, but it was not enough to offset his suspicions. It was now eleven o'clock and he hadn't seen a single person since he entered the town. All he could make out that told him he was at his destination was a huge looming church he recognized from the guidebooks. It was then that the car came to a creaking halt. John looked out his window and saw a stucco wall, nothing more. The driver got out and tested the gate. It was unlocked.

"Estamos aqui," the driver announced.

Did he say something about a key? John wondered if the driver had a key for him. John looked back to the driver, who already had his luggage at the curb. John had paid his fare up front in Mexico but now gave his driver an extra twenty. This was no time to be burning bridges.

The driver had a three-hour return trip ahead of him and was anxious to leave. John was anxious for him to stay. The driver pointed to the number on the gate. John acquiesced but held up his hand for the driver to wait while he went to the door to confirm his welcome. He lugged his baggage to the door and then heard the driver pull away. He watched him disappear and then turned back to face the strange door. He searched for a doorbell and, finding none, took the brass knob and slammed it onto the plate. He paused and wondered if an angry man in an undershirt with a pistol would open it.

—◦—

It was then that a loud clash broke the silence. Lourdes resisted dashing for the door and instead sent Maria while she composed herself and smoothed out her dress before standing and striking a pose that would not betray her anxiety. She thought she heard a loud male bellow but couldn't make out any words. Just when she thought all was well, a startled Maria entered, but without any boy or girl in tow.

"Señora, hay un hombre disconodico Americano en la puerta."
Señora, there is a strange American man at the door.

"¿Un hombre?" *A man?* she asked, momentarily confused.

She recovered quickly and impatiently ordered Maria, "Ve y digale que pase." *Go and ask him in.*

Lourdes waited anxiously until a bedraggled John Stanford entered the room.

John looked at the two startled faces staring back at him and once again bellowed loudly in a bad accent, "Buenas días!"

It was only two words, but he managed to get them wrong in pronunciation and context.

It was too late at night to give him his first Spanish lesson, so Lourdes let it pass and responded slowly, politely, and with feigned enthusiasm in Spanish.

"Bienvenido a San Miguel," she said, pausing to let him absorb the words before continuing. "Soy Lourdes de Madrid Rodriguez." *Welcome to San Miguel. I am Lourdes de Madrid Rodriguez.*

John hadn't understood much but did catch some long, rambling name, so he responded in kind. "How do you do, I'm John Sanford."

Lourdes realized he had followed very little of what she had said. It was late and nothing more could be accomplished tonight, so she allowed a small violation and briefly switched to English.

"Señor Sanford, welcome to San Miguel. I am Lourdes Rodriguez de Madrid," she said as graciously as she could manage at this late hour.

"You speak English." A look of relief spread across John's weary face. "I was afraid I would be stuck without any English-speaking people. I'm John Sanford," he repeated unconsciously. He then extended his hand, which Lourdes reluctantly accepted. She gave him a quizzical look and spoke to him in slow, deliberate Spanish.

"¿Usted es el estudiante de escuela de lengua, verdad?" *You are the student for the language school, right?*

John looked at her with an impatient glare and uttered, "What?"

Lourdes repeated the question, but this time in English. "You are the language student?"

John responded enthusiastically in Spanish, "Sí."

Lourdes gathered what little patience she had left and spoke to him in English. "Didn't Señora Walker explain the process to you? You're supposed to speak only Spanish while you're here," she said, finishing the sentence with an undisguised sigh of exasperation.

John, too, was at the end of his patience and thought the conversation was getting ridiculous and expressed it in his tone. "I don't speak Spanish," he said in deliberate, clipped words. "That's why I'm here." He paused again to let the words sink in. "To learn Spanish. Then I can speak it. I can't speak until I learn how. Cheee..." he said, not bothering to hide his frustration. "I do have a reservation here, don't I?"

"You're still speaking English," she reminded him.

"All right, you tell me how to say it in Spanish, and I'll say it," he said in conciliatory manner.

"That's not how it works. You are supposed to figure it out."

"With what, some kind of Mexican magic? Wait, you speak both languages. You had to learn somehow."

Yes, she had, but she wasn't going to get into that with him now.

"The two of us arguing in English isn't going to help." Here her voice dropped down to a more mellow tone, but her cheeks still flared red in exasperation. "Comienza escuchando con sus orejas." *Begin by listening with your ears*, she said as she placed her hands behind her ears.

"Okay, I'll give it a try," he said earnestly.

"You're still speaking English," she reminded him.

"So are you," he countered.

At this she threw up her hands. Lourdes wanted to lecture him on the total immersion concept but then thought better of it. It was late, the poor man looked exhausted, and she knew she was tired, too. Tomorrow everything would work out. She would give in this first night and break the Spanish-only rule, but only tonight. Tomorrow the rule would be firmly reinstituted.

She now spoke in a soothing voice. "You must be very tired. Maria will show you to your room. If there is anything you need, let Maria know." Of course, Lourdes knew Maria did not speak any English, but let him find that out, she thought, savoring a small victory. She then turned to Maria and spoke in rapid Spanish, "Maria lleva al Señor Sanford a su cuarto, por favor." *Maria, take Señor Sanford to his room, please.*

Maria was also not pleased with the situation. She could not follow the exchange in English but could tell by the tones used that things had not gone well. She took an instant dislike to this Señor Sanford. She did not like the way he had talked to the señora. She moved to pick up his bags, but John refused to let the small woman carry the load. He gathered up his things and followed her up the stairs. At the top of the stairs she motioned with her forefinger to her lips to proceed quietly. John realized that there were others in the household asleep at this hour.

Maria stopped midway down the hall before a solid oak door and opened it, then stood aside. John entered and set his heavy bags down with a rather loud thump. He winced at the noise he had just made. He immediately reached in his pants pocket for some bills to give Maria for a tip, but when he turned around he realized that she had already departed. *Oh well*, he thought as he shoved the cash back in his pocket. Only then did he pause to take in his surroundings. The room was clean but sparse, containing only a bed, dresser, chair, and a small desk, all made out of the same heavy, rough oak, with black wrought iron handles. Other than the entry, there were two closed doors. He opened one immediately. It contained a closet. The second was the private bath he had been promised. Had there not been a bathroom behind that door, they would have had a problem. What the room did not have was a television, an outlet for modem a telephone, or even—and he searched hard before he was sure—a thermostat. Instead, he found a window partly opened and a cool night breeze that filled the room. In addition to the usual bed covers, a heavy woven blanket lay folded at the end of the bed. The room was chilly and John considered whether he should shut the window. He walked over to it and was drawn by the full moon that was perched just above the hills. With the curtains drawn back, it illuminated the room in a soft light. He gazed at it, and it looked back defiantly. For some reason he thought of it as a Mexican moon, different from the one back home. In the clear, thin mountain air, it seemed larger, brighter, and more dominant in the sky. It spoke to him and said it was older, wiser, and would watch him come and go on this earth like all others before him. It gave John a strange feeling of being drawn into its control.

John turned his back and felt its powers wane as well as his own. John was overwhelmed by the events of a day that had seemed to last a week. It had been too much to absorb in one day, and to top it off, that confrontation downstairs with that strange woman. He wondered if he had made a mistake coming here. He stripped down to his underwear, went into the bathroom, brushed his teeth, and then climbed into the bed. Its sheets were stiff and cold. He reached for the heavy blanket at the end of the bed, pulled it up to his chin and laid his head back on a feathered pillow. He had not felt a feathered pillow since childhood. It was as if he had not just crossed hundreds of miles, but hundreds of years. In the morning, things would look different, he told himself as he fell into a deep sleep.

9

*L*ourdes stood before the mirror in a full slip. The sun had not yet reached the second floor window, but there was enough light for her. She picked out a dress of bright colors and slipped it on, hoping it would brighten her mood. Only then, fully dressed, did she move to the corner of the room where a crucifix was hung. She crossed herself, knelt, bowed her head, and prayed in the hushed tones of a well-rehearsed ritual. Midway through, she glanced down at her watch and resumed her prayer, only now at a hurried pace. She then rose quickly and crossed herself before hurrying out the door.

Hayden heard the first stirring of the house coming to life. He had slept well. The natural cool of the night uninterrupted by an off-and-on thermostat suited him. It was 7:30, according to his alarm clock. He reached over and shut it off before it reached the designated time of 7:45. The alarm had not been needed again, but he felt insecure without it. This was one place where oversleeping would not be looked on kindly. Lourdes ran a tight ship. He slipped out of bed and went through his morning routine. He brushed his teeth even though he knew he would have to brush them again after breakfast. He did it for her. He shaved even though he could skip once in a while, but he wanted to look good for her. He brushed his hair into place, then ruffled it a little to give it a casual look. He didn't want to appear to be trying too hard. He slipped into khaki shorts and his Mexican huaraches sandals worn over wool socks. Mornings began chilly here. He gave more thought to his shirt. The tight, navy blue nylon pullover clung to his chest and biceps in a way he hoped would please her. It was still early, but he wanted to go downstairs in case she was already there.

Chloe's alarm went off, sending her reeling from a dream that disappeared without a trace. She paused and wondered what it had been, and where it had gone. The room with its open window was cold. Why couldn't they regulate the temperature here like they did at home? She went grumbling into the bathroom. She would need every bit of time to get ready. Heaven forbid she be late for breakfast. She didn't have any appetite in the morning anyway. She would just as soon take her tea in bed. But she was expected, as was the entire household, including that gross old man in the wheelchair, to make an appearance. She found the whole household routine set up by Lourdes a little oppressive. Probably the hardest part of the whole total immersion routine was this home experience. It wasn't anything she actually said or did, but the woman had a manner about her, a formality that made Chloe feel uncomfortable. The way she dressed made Chloe uncomfortable, too. Chloe preferred wearing her shorts and sweatshirts. Señora or Señorita Lourdes, whatever she was, never appeared in anything but dresses. For God's sake, it was just around the house. Lighten up. And what was with that name, Lourdes? It certainly fit her. There was nothing warm and fuzzy about it. As far as Chloe was concerned, Señora Lourdes was what became of women who didn't have a man in their life. Had she ever? She was, or could have been, an attractive woman for her age, Chloe imagined, but no man was going to be interested in her the way she was.

All the bedrooms in the house were upstairs except for the Old Señor's. He had awakened earlier but had to wait for the women to come help him. Lourdes arrived at his door at exactly 7:30. She found Maria already waiting. She gave a formal knock on the door, as she always did, and waited a prescribed thirty seconds before the two entered. As was their routine, they both said almost simultaneously, "Buenos días, señor." He grumbled something back and then they began their routine, the same as they did every morning. Lourdes helped him to the bathroom and then left him until she heard the toilet flush. She placed him back in his wheelchair, gave him a sponge bath and a shave, combed his sparse hair and wheeled him back into the bedroom. There Maria had his clothes laid out and together they dressed him. From the knock on the door to the last button on his shirt, twenty minutes. Maria then left for the kitchen, and Lourdes wheeled him into the dining room. There he took his customary and ceremonial spot at the head of the table at exactly 7:55.

John had had no trouble getting to sleep after his exhausting travels. He did not even have his alarm clock unpacked, but as the light began to fill the room he glanced at his wristwatch on the table. It read 7:38. John thought that he would be better served by an extra hour of sleep. It was his first day, and he needed a day to acclimate himself to this foreign place. He would need to unpack, set up his office, and generally settle in. In his mind he made a mental list of his tasks. He realized he did not even know what the room looked like in daylight, but that would have to wait. He pulled the spare pillow over his head.

The breakfast table had been beautifully set by Maria. There were flowers in a traditional Mexican glazed vase in the center. The tablecloth was a local product in bright colors. Sliced fruit in a ceramic bowl gave off a fragrance that competed with the hot bread and fresh coffee. Scrambled eggs and thin slices of ham awaited any hearty eater. With two young people dining, Lourdes wanted to make sure there was plenty, and, of course, there was the new gentleman, Señor Sanford.

Lourdes swept through the room and approved of the table. She heard heavy steps on the stairs that she knew belonged to Hayden. A nice boy as far as she could tell, well-mannered and respectful of the house and its routine. Lourdes knew that she did insist on a strict schedule for the house, but it was all for the benefit of the students. Most were here for only a month, and part of the education happened in the home. Lourdes saw herself as their teacher away from class and sort of a parent. Hayden didn't seem to mind, but she couldn't be sure of Chloe. She was harder to read.

Hayden stood at attention as if waiting for her to sit first, or seeking permission to sit. His politeness could sometimes be annoying. But she had duties that came first before she could have breakfast. She addressed him in the customary way she did every morning, "Buenos días, Hayden. Asientese, por favor." *Good morning, Hayden. Please be seated.*

"Buenos días, señora., esta muy bonita esta mañana." *Good morning, señora, you are very beautiful this morning.*

Telling a woman that she was very beautiful was a bit forward for a boy his age, but since he was only trying to use his limited Spanish, somehow it seemed innocent to her.

She replied, "Gracias, Hayden, usted eres muy amable." *Thank you, Hayden, you are very kind.*

Hayden went further. "De nada, ademas, es verdad." *You're welcome, besides, it's true.*

Lourdes always encouraged conversation with the students, but this was getting out of hand, and she was glad to see Chloe appear at the table.

Chloe opened the conversation with words she had prepared on the way down. "Buenos días, señora. La mesa esta muy bonita, esta mañana." *Good morning, señora. The table is very beautiful this morning.*

The table was arranged the same every day, but Lourdes knew that Chloe was also trying to make use of her limited Spanish. Chloe looked appreciatively at the food and once again spoke unnecessarily to keep the conversation going. "Yo tengo hambre." *I am hungry*, she said, even though she intended to have only herbal tea and possibly a roll.

Lourdes noticed that neither had begun to eat and were waiting for permission. "Por favor, no esperan. Ustedes necesitan comer antes de la clase." *Please don't wait. You need to eat before class.*

Lourdes looked around and saw that Mr. Sanford had not come down. She looked at her watch and saw that he was going to be late if he didn't get down immediately. She turned to Maria, who had a concerned look on her face. This was not a situation she was used to. Every morning everyone came down on time, no exceptions. He was told the time for breakfast last night. Finally, Lourdes called Maria over and spoke to her in a hushed tone in Spanish. "Maria, vas y ve sí Señor Sanford esta lista." *Maria, go and see if Señor Sanford is ready.*

Chloe and Hayden looked at each other but avoided looking at the señora. Chloe suppressed a slight amusement. Someone had dared to disturb the routine of the household. Good for them, whoever they were. She chanced to glance up at Lourdes, who seemed a little more piqued than someone should be over a little tardiness. Chloe felt emboldened to test the limits, while Hayden vowed never to be late.

Lourdes turned back to the students, who were dispatching their breakfast with an eye on the time, and gave them a faint smile. They were curious about this Señor Sanford. Why was he referred to as *Señor*? They lingered over the last of their breakfast as they waited for things to develop. There was so little going on in the household and school that they welcomed any diversion.

Hayden glanced at his watch and then moved around the few remaining scraps of what had been a hearty breakfast but avoided eating them. Chloe, who had no appetite in the morning, toyed with the remnants of her roll and homemade marmalade.

Finally their patience was rewarded as Maria returned and, instead of reporting confidentially to Lourdes, announced loud enough for anyone to hear, "El Señor todavia esta dormido."

Given the context even the beginning students recognized the verb *dormir*, to sleep. Chloe looked at Hayden and mouthed the word *sleep,* and he nodded back knowingly. Chloe failed to suppress a small giggle, which got the attention of Lourdes, who turned to her with a serious expression. She then changed her face to a smile and spoke to them gently.

"Niños, ahora el tiempo para la clase." *Children, it is time for class.* She followed this with a shooing motion with her hands. Hayden had just been referred to as a *niño* or child and had been shooed. This did not sit well with his manhood.

They quickly rose from the table, gathered their backpacks, and made for the front door with only a quick *adios* before departing.

Once in the street, Chloe, who was about to burst, didn't bother with Spanish and blurted out in English, "So, who's this Mr. Sanford?"

Hayden started to chide her for using English but didn't want to be hampered with Spanish either and replied in English, "Just some jerk who can't get his butt out of bed in the morning." He tried to sound non-chalant but his irritation showed through.

Chloe wouldn't let the subject go and continued. "So why does she call him Mr. Sanford but refers to you as a niño?" She was trying to get a rise out of Hayden and wasn't disappointed.

"She calls you a child, too." His comeback betrayed his irritation more than he wished to. He tried to gather his wits about him and came up with the Spanish phrase to express it. "Basta!" *Enough!* He said it with such finality that Chloe did not respond, and they walked the rest of the way in an imposed silence.

As soon as they were out the door, Lourdes turned back to Maria and spoke with alacrity. "Esta no importa, disperete lo." *It doesn't matter. Wake him up.*

Maria shrugged and headed back up the stairs. She did not want to disturb this man in his sleep. She cooked, she cleaned, she even helped with the Old Señor, and she did not complain, but this should not be one of her duties.

If it happens again, I will say something, she vowed to herself.

She approached his door, gathered herself, and knocked firmly twice. She waited but heard nothing. She knocked again with the same force—any more might be interpreted as angry or aggressive, and she did not want that. She waited. She did not wish to disturb this man in his bedroom, but neither did she wish to confront an already impatient Lourdes.

Finally she opened the door a bit and did not enter, but in a moderate tone called out, "Señor, señor." When no response came, then and only then did she fully open the door. She found the señor sprawled across the bed with the spare pillow covering his head. He was as she remembered him, tall and lean with light brown hair sprinkled with gray. She realized that it was wrong to watch him without his knowing. She must do something. She tiptoed silently across the room before she realized how silly an act it was when she was going to rouse him from his sleep anyway. She took him by the one shoulder that protruded from the covers and shook it gently. He moved with a jerk and made an incomprehensible sound, possibly in English but more likely only a groan. He tossed the pillow aside and stared up at her.

He saw a brown face bearing a concerned look. His stare had no malice, no judgment behind it, only bewilderment. Once he realized who she was, he deemed her no more than a human alarm clock, a low-tech hotel's wake-up call. He had had numerous hotel wake-up calls in his life. The voice always the same, gentle but terse, and once finished, it moved on to the next guest without any further responsibility. But she did not disappear like the voice in the bedside phone. She lingered in an apprehensive state. Maria would not return without a response she could relay to her lady.

First fucking day here and I'm supposed to fall into some regimentation, he said to himself. He looked up at Maria and knew that she did not want to be there any more than he wanted her there. It was that other woman. He wanted to say something to the maid in Spanish, but finally fell back on the universally accepted phrase.

"Okay, okay," he said, and raised his hands in mock gesture of surrender. Only then did she depart with a slight bow as she backed out the room.

John disappeared into the bathroom, and when he emerged, he stepped into the pants he had worn the day before and put on his wrinkled shirt. He made his way to the stairs, and his senses were aroused by the smell of coffee, fresh-baked bread, and some kind of pork. As he entered the dining room, he was met by the stare of that woman from the night before. Apparently she worked the day shift as well as the night. He smiled at her, and in return he got what he judged to be fake smile.

He then tried his most charming Spanish. "Buenas días, señorita. Something smells really good."

He was back to speaking English again. She would speak firmly and directly to him and for the last time in English.

"Señor, por favor, you must maintain the total immersion concept at all times. For the duration of your stay you are to speak only Spanish."

"Huh...it's a little early in the morning for Spanish, okay? Let me get a little coffee in me first."

"Señor Sanford, we take total immersion very seriously in this household. The other students are, as I am, very serious about maintaining a pure Spanish atmosphere. Please do not speak English in their presence."

"Oh, I think they overdo this *total immersion* thing."

"Total immersion means total immersion, nothing less." Even as she said it she knew that she was violating it. "You need to make more of an effort," she said with finality that she hoped he would accept.

"Yeah, I'll give it a try. I just need a little more time to acclimate to these rustic surroundings."

Lourdes was very proud of her home and did not like it being characterized as rustic. She did not wish to get into an argument with him, especially one in English. So she tried again in Spanish, very slowly and distinctly.

"Señor, ya esta tarde. Es la hora para su clase." Surely he must recognize the Spanish words *tarde* and *clase*. She gestered to the clock its hands on eight and sixteen, she paused and waited for some recognition. Instead she saw that he hadn't been paying attention.

He just looked up and said, "Huh."

This time she was not going to budge. She stood with her hands on her hips and stared him down.

Finally, he spoke in exasperation, "Look, I told you I don't speak Spanish."

Lourdes conceded this round and reverted back to English. "You're going to be late for class." She was ready to hand him off to Olivia and let her deal with him.

"Oh, right," he said.

John gulped down the remainder of his coffee and poured himself a second cup, which he took with him.

"Be right back," he said, and bounded up the stairs. Lourdes had only a moment to compose herself before Maria wheeled in an old heavyset man in a wheelchair. Lourdes now shifted her attention to him. She prepared him a plate of scrambled eggs and melon cut into small pieces.

John had now reappeared and stood before her. She continued to attend to the old man while John waited patiently.

Finally, she looked up at him and asked with slight irritation, "Yes?" She then chided herself for having slipped into English again.

She continued to look up at him until he muttered, "I don't know where the school is."

Lourdes gave out an audible and undisguised sigh and turned to Maria, who had come in and taken her place beside the old man. Lourdes stepped out of the room, returned with a sweater, and headed for the door while John stood by watching.

She turned back to him impatiently and spoke sharply. "Venga." *Come.*

John did not know the word, but its tone was definitely a command, so he followed her out the door.

Lourdes walked with a determined stride as John hurried to keep up with her, his footing uncertain on the cobblestone streets. They passed through the square and climbed slightly until John saw the old building that served as the school, only differentiated from all the similar-looking buildings on the block by a sign affixed to its stone facade, which read, "Institute de Lengua, San Miguel de Allende, established 1992."

John noticed that the architecture of the town had a certain sameness to it, making it difficult for him to tell one place from another. Lourdes did not pause but walked right in and boldly entered the first open room. John had tentatively followed her and now stood uncertainly behind her, feeling like a child whose mother had taken him to his first day in school.

Olivia sensed that something had happened to divert the class's attention, and she looked toward the door to see her old friend Lourdes with a tall, middle-aged man. Over the years, Lourdes and Olivia had become friends as they worked together to house the students. She saw now that her friend was giving her a hard look. Olivia may have misled Lourdes, slightly, about the age of this student. Since she had handled the registration over the phone, she knew his age, but she had not communicated it clearly to Lourdes. Olivia found it somewhat funny, but the look on Lourdes's face indicted that she did not. Olivia decided to try defusing the situation with a little humor. She walked over to her old friend and stood close so that they could have a private conversation.

"Pardoname, profesora," Lourdes said, "pero tengo su estudinate nuevo, Señor John Sanford." *Pardon me, teacher, but I have your new student, Mr. John Sanford.* Lourdes spoke coolly through clenched jaws.

There was no mistaking the edge to Lourdes's tone, so Olivia tried to share a little joke with her. "Es un chico grande, verdad? No?" Olivia said. *He's a big boy, right?*

This did not get the desired response from Lourdes, so Olivia tried to play innocent. "Lourdes, mi quierda amiga, no tenia idea que era un hombre adulto." *Lourdes, my dear friend, I had no idea he was a grown man.* She paused and looked John over, saw a nice-looking, unshaven man in rumpled clothes, and continued. "No es mal parecido, pero se ve un poco mal esta manana." *Not bad looking, but he looks a little rough this morning.*

Lourdes stared daggers back at Olivia until finally saying in a low voice, "Despues hablaremos de esto." *We'll talk about this later.*

Lourdes turned on her heels and departed, leaving a befuddled John standing alone before the class. Olivia gently took him by the arm and directed him to a desk in the front of the class, where she could keep an eye on him.

John looked around the room. It was lit with sunlight from open windows. The plaster walls were white, freshly painted, with travel posters depicting scenes from Mexico, Spain, and South and Central America. Some he recognized, like Sugarloaf Mountain overlooking Rio de Janeiro, and the Alhambra in Spain—the rest looked like third-world Latin America to him. He scanned the rest of his classmates: predominately girls, some young men, average age about twenty, all probably attending college. *Not my demographic,* John mused. At least the teacher seemed to be his age—an attractive woman who, with her strawberry-blond hair, didn't look at all like a Mexican to him. He looked up and saw that Olivia was saying something in Spanish and then acting it out.

"Levantese," she said loudly, accompanying it with an upward sweep of her hands. The class stood up in unison, with John following afterward.

"Sientese," she said, and the class sat back down.

She stopped in front of John's desk to involve him in the exercise and spoke directly to him. "Señor, camina?" She saw he needed help understanding, so she demonstrated by parading by him with her hands on her hips, taking pronounced strides, and then repeated, "Camina." *Walk.*

When John did not react, she took his hand, got him to rise, and began walking around with him. She pointed to herself and said, "Yo camino, señor camina, tambien."

Olivia took his hand again, and they strolled across the room. She said to the class, "Nosotros caminos." John was allowed to sit down.

She called up another student, Roberto, who took a few steps and announced, "Yo camino." To another student, Olivia asked, "¿Quien camina?" *Who walks?* The student dutifully answered, "Roberto camina."

John tried to process the lesson and looked to the blackboard to see if he had missed something, but it was blank. Olivia continued with the lesson format, substituting different verbs. When she felt that everyone had gotten the lesson, she paused before John to make sure and asked, "¿John, quien camina?"

John looked panicked, leaned forward to speak confidentially, and whispered, "I don't really speak Spanish. Don't I get a book or something?"

Olivia said loud enough for the entire class to hear, "Despues. Primero, usa sus ojos y sus orejas." *Later. First, use your eyes and ears.* She touched her eyes and ears to make her meaning clear.

To John's relief, she then moved on. She addressed the whole class, slowly and emphatically, the message intended especially for John. "En este clase, hablamos solamente in espanol." *In this class, we speak Spanish only.*

After John had passed from Olivia's gaze, John leaned toward the young, pretty girl next to him and whispered, "You understand what's going on?"

Expecting sympathy, he was disappointed when she said brusquely, "Habla en espanol, por favor," and turned back to the class.

"Yeah, right," John said, pouting.

—　⁃　—

After his harrowing morning class, John received a textbook and a workbook, which he found comforting. He had planned on taking them up to his room and studying them like a business proposal—in an organized fashion, not like the dog and pony show he had been thrust into that morning. That was no way to teach. Didn't the woman have any training in education? Learning began with a book. Anyone knew that. Next time, he'd be ready for her, he vowed to himself.

He was just about to head up the stairs when he heard voices coming from the patio, speaking Spanish, but not the rapid machine-gun patter of the natives—a more deliberate cadence. He went through the partially opened french doors and spotted two college-age kids he recognized from class. More importantly, he saw that they were sitting around a small oval swimming pool. They had on swimsuits, and the girl wore a large, floppy straw hat. She had a nice enough body, but he didn't concern himself with that. The boy was shirtless, and you could tell he spent a lot of time working on his pecs and biceps. A couple of Greek letters were tattooed on his triceps, no doubt signifying his fraternity. John had been in a fraternity at the University of Texas, and he finally sorted through his Greek alphabet—to pledge in any fraternity required it be memorized—and recognized the tattoo as an alpha and a kappa. *An Alpha Kappa*, John thought. *Just one more reason not to like him.* He moved on.

John went to his room and dug through his bag until he found the swimsuit he had tossed in as an afterthought. The size 34 was only one size larger than he had worn when he was their age. John's body wasn't pumped up like the kid's, but he had a natural athletic leanness with long, ropy muscles. *Not too bad*, he thought to himself. He put on the Mexican guayabera shirt he had bought on one of his Cancun trips, leaving it unbuttoned, and headed back downstairs with his textbook.

He emerged onto the patio and, without saying a word to the kids' surprised faces, dove into the pool. He surfaced at the other end, ran his hands through his hair, and finally said, "Hey, kids, how ya doing?"

They recognized him as the man in class who had struggled so badly that morning. And now here he was, not even trying to speak Spanish. Hayden scowled at him.

John sank back down into the chilly water, launched himself across the pool, and then hoisted himself out of the deep end. Chloe watched his muscles flex under the exertion. *Not bad for an older man,* she thought to herself. *Not like Hayden, but good in a different way.*

John found a lounge chair and settled himself in. He was going to do some intensive study, when he realized an iced drink might be helpful. He saw the maid from the night before and, remembering her name, called out to her. She dutifully came over and stood before him.

"Can I get a drink around here?" John asked. "Scotch on the rocks." He turned toward Chloe and Hayden and said, "I'm ordering a drink! Can I get anything for you two?" He thought this was the perfect icebreaker.

Chloe was surprised John would assume that a private home would have a poolside bar. Where did he think he was—some Cancun resort hotel? She hesitated, but Hayden curtly answered for both of them. "No, gracias."

Maria still stood staring at John, an eyebrow raised. She had actually understood some of his English but did not want to play barmaid to him. She decided it would be better to hide behind her supposed ignorance.

John saw that he was not getting through to her. In frustration, he appealed to Chloe and Hayden. "Say, you two are always speaking Spanish," he said. "Order a drink for me." Maria, afraid that they might actually do that, escaped to find Lourdes.

Hayden, said, feigning politeness, "Perdoneme, señor, hablamos espanol solamente. Nosotros no comprendemos Ingles." *Pardon me, sir, but we speak Spanish only. We don't understand English.*

John gave out an audible sigh and muttered, not caring if he was heard or not, "Oh, be that way." He was through trying to get along with the smartass kid. Hayden leaned back in his chair, savoring John's predicament, but sat up sharply as Lourdes appeared, looming over John.

"Maria said you asked for something," she said in English. She was not going to lecture him on total immersion in front of the others. She planned to get this over with in as few words as possible.

"Yes, I asked Maria for a drink but I don't think she understood me and those two," he motioned with his head towards Hayden and Chole who were watching intently, "were no help at all," John said. "Anyway, scotch, if you have it."

"I am sure we don't. We might have some wine. I could look."

"Oh, never mind," he said thinking he had ended the conversation but Lourdes remained till the others were no longer watching and then leaned uncomfortably close to him.

"Senor, por favor, it is bad enough when you speak English to me but," here she paused and spoke emphatically, "please do not use English with the students. They are here to experience a "total immersion" environment. Do not rob them of this opportunity!" She then straightened up and with her hands on her hips said with authority, "De acuerdo?" *Agreed.*

She stood her ground and waited for his response with a withering glare. Chloe and Hayden could not hear her words but it was not hard to read her body language and they had seen that stare before. She meant business. Chloe felt that the Mexican woman had over stepped her boundaries, while Hayden was almost jealous of the rapt attention Lourdes was giving Sanford.

John tried to consider it a compromise. She had not forbidden him from speaking English just not to the kids. He would let her have her way this time. So in the most non-chalant tone he could muster he answered back with a shrug , "de acuerdo." Lourdes turned sharply on her heels and John looked down at his book, while Hayden watched the departing figure of till she was out of sight.

10

The many churches in town were deemed colonial treasures. They now existed as much for the tourists as for the people. But the business of Father Morales took place far away from the beautiful churches, the quaint shops, and the nice restaurants that clustered around the jardin. Father Morales worked out of an old colonial building on the road heading west out of town toward Dolores Hidalgo. The building was designated as a Mexican national monument—not unusual for San Miguel. But this one had no ornate columns, towering spires, or picturesque carvings. The structure, with its low walls surrounding a large courtyard, had been built for function and not show; even the chapel was a structure without adornment. The former army garrison now housed children. Father Morales was in his seventies, and though the spirit was still with him, his body was crippled by arthritis. The cold morning made it a struggle to get out of bed. He looked forward to the day when he would rest with his savior, but until then, he would have to force himself to rise every morning with increasing difficulty. The town's warm afternoons provided only temporary relief.

He worried further that there was no young priest waiting to take over this thankless but vital service. They all wanted to be surrounded by gilded walls, not crumbling adobe. But Jesus had said, "Suffer not the little children." At present the number was a manageable twenty-two, but when conditions in the country worsened, their numbers would swell.

Some came by the time-honored way of the doorstep, left by a young girl with no one else to turn to. Some came by way of the police after both parents were killed in a traffic accident—the curvy mountain roads were littered with memorials, a testament to bad roads and cars navigating nights without headlights. A few were left because of congenital illnesses or incapacities that were beyond the means or patience of their parents. They would rather put their efforst toward their healthy children, who someday could be called upon to take care of them. Disturbingly, a growing number were left behind while the parents tried to make some quick, illegal money in northern Mexico, never to return, and most likely dead in the Chihuahua desert.

From the outside, the Church of Mexico looked rich, with its ornate gold facade, but behind that they were as poor as the people they served. The orphanage didn't even have a facade; it was simply as it seemed. A few of the locals helped out with clothing, food, and money. Lourdes's family had been generous supporters in the past, but since they lost their wealth and position in society, they essentially no longer existed. Lourdes, as the sole surviving member, carried on the tradition as best she could, with her service but little money.

Sister Guillerma, trained in Mexico City as a nurse, was the no-nonsense woman who ran the clinic. A disciplinarian when she had to be, the children, even the teenage boys, did not cross her. She did not seek this role but had to compensate for the doddering figure that was the Padre.

— ⁓

Something moved in the shadows. It caused Lourdes to pause. She blinked twice; it was still there. Her first thought was that it was a small animal, a dog or perhaps a coyote. But as she cautiously approached, she made out the form of a small child wrapped in a rough woolen blanket shivering in the early morning chill, or perhaps out of fear. It would not be the first time she saw a child standing by that gate. He looked to be about seven years old, or perhaps a malnourished ten. His limbs were long, but so thin they barely held him up.

She squatted down until she was level with him and gave him a warm smile but took no other action. She waited patiently while his large brown eyes took her in fully before extending a hand. She could feel that he wanted to accept, but he held back. She waited and then stood and began to turn as if she was going to walk away. It was then that he moved after her, and without looking back, she put out her hand and felt him grasp it. His touch alone told her he was sick, not just weak. She took him straight to the clinic, where Sister Guillerma found him a bed. But first he had to be bathed. The nun led him to the bathroom and drew the hot water. He stood aside, looking at the steaming water like it was some medieval torture device. When the sister tried to remove his clothes, he shrieked and held them tight as if he thought she meant to steal them. He stopped struggling when Lourdes entered the room. The nun resented his attitude toward her and was ready to deal with him forcefully. .

"He needs to learn how to behave," she said. He was just one of many here, and he would have to learn to conform if he were to stay. She could physically strip him bare—he was much smaller and weaker than the hefty nun. Sister Guillerma believed discipline was best learned the first day.

The boy had backed himself into a corner and looked like he was going to claw at her if she came closer. She pushed up the sleeves of her habit and was moving toward the confrontation when she saw that the boy's eyes were no longer on her but looking past. When she turned around she saw Lourdes.

She respected Lourdes and the work she did for them, but this was her responsibility, and she did not want any interference. After all, she was the one who would have to deal with the boy on a day-to-day basis. She did not want her authority undermined. Lourdes understood the situation she was creating and knew the nun was the authority here, but this child was not ready for it yet. First, he needed to be cared for. If asked to leave, Lourdes would have acquiesced—but she was not going unless asked to. The nun turned to Lourdes, and shaking her head as if to say, "You're making a mistake," she handed the sponge to Lourdes and stalked out.

Lourdes did not confront the boy but drew up a stool and sat down, making herself seem smaller, less threatening. She sat and waited patiently for the boy to calm down.

Finally, she said, "¿Estas listo?" *Are you ready?*

He nodded, and she left the room to allow him to undress. When she heard the splash of water, she entered the room and looked down at the figure of the naked boy. Without his clothes, he was even thinner than she expected. He sat up in the steaming water but did not move, his hands clasped over his genitals. She moved the stool next to the tub and sat down with soap and sponge in hand. She had bathed children before, but never this old—and yet she knew, if left up to him, it wouldn't get done. It was if he hadn't ever been in a bathtub.

He watched her intently as she dipped the sponge in the water and then rubbed it with the bar of soap. He sat still until the sponge touched his chest—he flinched as if scalded. She handed the sponge to him, but after holding it silently for a few moments, he passed it back to her, and she began again. This time he held still as she scrubbed his face. He held out his arm, laying bare his groin, as she passed the sponge up and down his thin arms. She then moved it across his chest and stomach. She thought she heard him moan as it reached his lower abdomen. Lourdes went behind him and did his back. When he was scrubbed clean, she took the boy's hand, helped him climb out of the tub, and wrapped him in a

thin, scratchy towel. In a cabinet she found a pair of wool pajamas that looked like they might fit. The boy put them on and she led him to a bed with freshly starched sheets. He ate soup and bread and fell fast asleep for eighteen hours. Lourdes watched him breathe with some difficulty. She knew he was not a well child. Which was probably the reason for his abandonment.

She left the boy in the care of the nun but knew that she would still be responsible for him. Lourdes went to the chapel office and sought out the Padre. Before she left she had committed herself financially to the child. She did not know how she would meet this new obligation, but she knew she had to try. She had also made a commitment to God to look after his emotional welfare.

The next day she came to see him, he clung to her as if she were his own mother. The nun looked at her and said in resignation, "El es suyo ahora. Conteste su nombre?" *He's yours now. Ask his name?*

Lourdes drew close to him as if they were going to share a secret, "¿Como se llama?

The boy spoke softly and only to Lourdes, "Mateo."

"Su appelido." *Last name.* The nun interjected not as a question but as an order.

The boy looked at Lourdes but only shook his head out of shame.

—　—

That was five years ago. Maybe because she was the first to find him, or because he was so needy, he became so special to her. In the first years he seemed to grow stronger and eventually reached a delayed puberty. Over the next year, he grew a little taller if not stronger.

Mateo turned out to be a bright child. He learned to read quickly and because he tired easily he sought refuge in his books. He seemed to accept his limitations and found joy in his world of fantasy. While sister Guillerma did not approve, Padre allowed him comic books filled with the exploits of men of extraordinary powers. He got along with the other boys but without ever becoming one of them. He wasn't sturdy enough to for their rough-and-tumble world. He instead tended to spend his free time with the old Padre. In studying his catechism, he asked profound questions and saw the application of faith and love in his life. Sometimes Padre would marvel at how Mateo, impoverished in so many ways, could have seen through the hardness of the world and found goodness and hope. Mateo was the very definition of an "old soul."

— —

Then, about six months ago, something went wrong. His afflictions returned, cruelly robbing him of his impending manhood. The local doctor tested him, but after many months of trying to eliminate various benign possibilities he suspected the worse but did not wish to guess. Any definitive answer would require expensive lab work.

Mateo woke before sunrise. He his bed clothes were soaked in sweat though the morning was still quite chilly. He felt an ache deep in his bones and his breath was short and laborious. He tried to rise but fell back again. He would prefer to stay in bed but the Padre would be rising soon and they had their work to do.

He knew the Padre bones ached and he tired easily too, but the Padre was an old man. "I am young but I ache like an old man. If the Padre can get up then so can I," Mateo reasoned but still he remained in his bed.

"Why should I feel like an old man?" Mateo wondered to himself. He watched the boys his age chase the soccer ball across the yard. They run effortlessly but I now creep around like the Padre. "Am I an old man or a boy?"

But even more than the boys he found himself watching the girls at play. Some were very pretty and some had started to develop breasts. Not large mounds like Sister Guillerma but small round balls that bounced as they ran or jumped rope. They paid little attention to him preferring the boys with muscles, who could run fast and kick the ball hard. They treated him with kindness but borne of pity.

He could not get those girls out of his mind. At mass he would look across the aisle at them and imagine what lay beneath their white starched

blouses. What would it be like to touch them? It gave him a strange feeling in his groins.

— ~

Lourdes found the Padre and Mateo in the chapel. Any other child would have been sent back to the classroom, but Mateo's education was no longer a major concern. The Padre's focus on Mateo had shifted from studying for the future to contemplating the hereafter, thoughts a boy of his age should not have to deal with. He spent his days tagging along with the Padre, assisting him in his duties. Always asking deep questions of the Padre but receiving only trite Bible quotations in return.

When Lourdes entered the chapel, Mateo stopped his work and tottered across the room to hug her. He had grown taller—his head now came to her chest, and he rested it against her bosom. She gently pried him off and said to the Padre, "¿Padre, puedo tener Mateo por un poco tiempo?" *Padre, may I have Mateo for a little while?*

"Sí, claro," the priest said. *Yes, of course.*

She took Mateo by the shoulder and led him into the sunshine. Weak or not, she thought Padre kept him indoors too much. Leading him into a courtyard, she opened a satchel and began to remove books. One was a picture book with sights from around the world, the other a book about outer space, planets, and stars. Space had become both a scientific and spiritual place of wonder for him. He would often contemplate the eternal questions of our place in the vastness of the universe. But while the philosopher Mateo looked at them with interest, the boy Mateo turned back to make sure there wasn't anything more. Reluctantly, Lourdes withdrew three comic books. He beamed when he saw them. In comic books, he could escape his weakened body and live through his heroes and vicariously experience their power.

Lourdes left him left him to enjoy the diversion and went back inside the chapel to talk to the Padre. Speaking in Spanish, he said, "We have the blood test back from Mexico City. It was just what Sister Guillerma had said: leukemia. We could put him in the hospital for treatment, but they say it would only prolong his suffering."

Lourdes nodded in agreement. She had observed Mateo's growing weakness and had already accepted the inevitable. "Voy a empiezar a preparer la alma del nino," the priest said. *I will begin to prepare the boy's soul.*

Lourdes thought this ironic; the boy's soul was pure—it was his blood that was tainted. But the Padre would do what he knew. She hoped the priest would spare the boy this knowledge, at least for a little while longer, but she wasn't going to tell the Padre his business. Sister Guillerma had given him a month at most and Sister Gullerma was rarely wrong.

Each week that followed, Lourdes witnessed his decline. He still wanted to be useful, but he could no longer manage even the easiest chore that the Padre could find for him. The next week he went to his bed, and the wait began in earnest.

11

*L*ourdes was definitely a person of habit—habits that had served her well for many years, habits that kept the house running smoothly, that kept her body running smoothly, that keep her life running smoothly. She went to bed at ten and, after reading for an hour, turned on her left side and awoke the next morning at 6:30 a.m. She kept her curtains pulled back so the sun would wake her instead of a startling alarm clock. When the other residents' alarms went off, she would already have been awake for some time. She had certain outfits that she wore on certain days, and always with sensible shoes. It all worked very well for her. She enjoyed the comfortable routine. The lodging business she had fallen into, with help from her best friend, Olivia, had given her what she cherished above all: her independence. Life was good.

In her business, one day was the same as another. Clean rooms, beds made everyday, healthy home-cooked meals, and a little discreet supervision of her students. She did consider them her students; she was their teacher when they were not in class. She conducted all contact with them in simple Spanish, choosing her words carefully to fit each student's level of instruction. She knew Olivia's lesson plan and saw that it carried over after class. Other student residences did not go to this trouble, but

Lourdes always gave more than was required. She also felt responsible for their welfare and tended to look after them as if she were their mother. Since her residence had the best reputation and was always in demand, Olivia only referred Lourdes her best prospects. That meant no heavy drinkers, vulgar talkers, smokers, or bad-mannered students. Rarely did Lourdes have any trouble with her house rules.

The only break from her routine came on Sunday. On Sundays she rose a little later, and she and Maria went to Mass in shifts. The lunch was formal and served in the afternoon, after which the remainder of the day was given to rest. A glass of wine and a good book were her only companions.

Walking kept her in good shape, and while she no longer had the figure she had when she was twenty, she'd worn the same size since she turned forty.

In her spare time, she loved to read good literature, alternating between Spanish and English. Her reading glasses were her only concession to middle age. Tonight she had lain in bed with a copy of Barbara Kingsolver's *Lacuna*. At exactly eleven o'clock, she turned on her left side and fell asleep. Life was good.

— ~

Lourdes did not like to make exceptions, but she had this time. The exception was an eight-year-old boy named Pepe. He was Maria's nephew, her younger sister's child. Her sister Juanita and her husband had had to leave San Miguel. It was not an uncommon situation. San Miguel was a great place to live if you had money, but a hard place to find work. Maria knew how lucky she was to have found a job with Lourdes and did not want to do anything that would jeopardize it, but Juanita and Pepe were family. Juanita's husband had been promised a factory job that was opening up in Monterrey, and they had to move fast to secure it. They would be living rough until the first paycheck and didn't want Pepe to experience that kind of hardship. There would

be plenty of time for that in the future. They would only be apart for a few weeks.

Maria had set up a cot in her own room for the boy, and, except for lunch, he took all his meals in the kitchen. He was expected not to be seen, and especially not to talk out of turn. For a naturally outgoing boy of eight, he maintained a surprisingly low profile and knew his place in the household. He took a breakfast of cocoa and rolls in the mornings and then left out the back door for school. He returned for lunch, where he was allowed to sit at the table but then was not seen again. In his spare time, he scurried around the house like a mouse, doing simple chores for Maria. Lourdes was secretly fond of the boy, even though Pepe was an extra mouth in a household run on slim margins.

— —

John came down late for breakfast but unconcerned about it. He considered this trip to Mexico a working vacation, and he was trying hard to relax while he was there. Houston was plenty hectic, and he needed this time to unwind and not to punch some sort of time clock. He, like everyone here, felt the pressure to stay on the schedule that the lady of the house tried to impose, but he wasn't going to give in to it. He was the guest here, and she could stand to be a little more flexible. He would learn Spanish, but at his own pace.

As he entered the dining room, he could see that the college kids were just finishing. The girl was all right, if you didn't mind phonies, but the frat boy got on his nerves. All swagger, living off his parents, pretending to be a man. John knew his type: drove a muscle car his father had bought for him, took it all for granted, no clue what real life was like.

He decided to play nice, greeting them with exaggerated politeness. "Buenas días, Chloe. Buenas días, Hayden," he said.

Chloe was the first to respond. "Buenos días, Señor Sanford."

She had called him "mister," which warmed him to her. "Hey, call me John," he said.

"Buenos días, *Juan,*" Hayden said, sneering.

John was glad when they left for class, leaving him to relax with a cup of what was actually some pretty good coffee. Maria, who had been waiting for the students to leave, wheeled in the Old Señor and was not pleased to see Mr. Sanford still lingering over coffee. It was too late to wheel the Old Señor back, though, so she took him to the table and helped him with his breakfast—a task she would have preferred to do alone. John noticed her discomfort and looked away discreetly. A small Mexican boy slipped in and took a roll off the table before anyone could say anything. John watched in confusion and then noticed Lourdes had silently entered.

John pointed a finger at the retreating figure of Pepe and asked, "What's the deal with...uh..." He waved his outstretched finger in the direction the child had gone.

Lourdes filled the blank in for him. "Pepe."

"Pepe," John said. "Is he an orphan or something? You know they have places for kids like that."

Lourdes raised an eyebrow at John. How dare he question the way she ran her house! "I know what an orphanage is," she said, her voice low. "He is not an orphan. His parents had to leave San Miguel to find work. They left him in my care. They will call for him when they are settled."

"They're probably in Houston right now," he said indelicately. "Man, you'll take in anyone."

"Apparently," she muttered.

"Oh, by the way," John said, "There's not a telephone in my room. And does this place have Wi-Fi?"

"There's not a telephone in the house," Lourdes said.

"Well, how do you...oh, never mind," John said. Under his breath, he said, "It's a wonder anything gets done in this country."

"There's a Larga Distancia in town on Calle Benito Juarez," said Lourdes, "and an Internet café next to it. They can place your call for you."

"How convenient," he said with undisguised sarcasm.

Then she looked at the clock and said in Spanish, "Es la hora de su clase." Then repeating in English. "It's time for your class."

"All right," he said as he gathered up his book and left.

Lourdes stayed in her spot, fuming at him, and Olivia Walker.

❦

After his afternoon conversation class, John remembered what Lourdes had said about the long-distance call. He found Calle Benito Juarez and the Larga Distancia. When he entered, he found a large room broken up by booths supplying a modicum of privacy for its patrons. He was surprised to find the occupants consisted mainly of middle-aged women. While waiting for a booth to open up, he overheard a conversation:

"Pablo, tiene mucho cuidado en Houston." *Pablo, be careful in Houston.*

At the word *Houston*, John's ears perked up. He tried to pick up more of the conversation, but the woman spoke Spanish even faster than most, probably due to the charge per minute. Finally, a woman approached him and pointed to an available booth: number twelve. He gave the woman the written number he wished to call and, since numbers are universal, had no trouble.

He waited until he heard her call out, "Numero doce llamada para Houston."

John picked up the receiver, and after a couple of rings, he heard Margie's familiar, comforting voice.

"Hello?" she said.

"Margie!" he cried.

"Mr. Sanford, is that you?"

"Of course it's me. I haven't developed an accent, have I?"

"No, no," she said. "How are you?"

"Surviving," John said, "and that's no small feat down here. You wouldn't believe what I've had to go through just to make this call. Anyway, what's going on at the office?'

"Just the usual. We still haven't heard back from those Mexican gentlemen."

"I'm not surprised. It takes these people forever to do anything. It's amazing anything ever gets done. When I get back, I'll get them moving. I'll talk to them in a language they can understand."

Margie was silent for a moment but then said, "How is your Spanish going?"

"Great, great. Absorbing it like a sponge. It's sink or swim here. Total immersion, you know. It's the only way to go."

"I'm envious," Margie said. "You've probably already passed me up."

"It's a matter of survival down here."

"Entonces, es necesario a hablar en espanol, para vivir. ¿Verdad? Margie said. *It's necessary to speak Spanish to live. Right?*

John didn't understand a word she said. "Look, I better get off," he said. "These must be the only phones in town."

"John you're not on your cell phone?"

No I can't get any reception here. This place is just west of the middle of nowhere."

"They must have wifi there," Margie paused and thought this through and then continued, "John have you changed your settings to wifi?"

When he didn't answer she knew he hadn't. "John, go to square that has an icon of a cog wheel, scroll down to Wi-Fi and press it. That should allow you to make calls and acess the internet."

John realized how lost he was without his Margie but didn't want to admit to her.

"Sure I take care of it and check back in a few days. Adios."

John emerged into the street, feeling at loose ends. He did not want to go back to the house just yet, so he wandered about the town, aimless, turning down streets he had not taken before to delay his arrival. As he walked, he unconsciously read the names of the businesses, learning new words as he went. He passed a place and read the sign above the door, and then paused to read it again: "The Gringo." A pejorative Spanish term for an American, actually probably peculiar to Mexico. Wondering who would brazenly display such a sign, he turned back to investigate.

12

Jose—his real name was Ramon Gutierrez, but the patrons of The Gringo never called him that—saw John's face poised halfway through the door and smiled invitingly at him. The Gringo, owned by an absentee businessman in Mexico City who kept a weekend home in town, had gone through a name change as well—it was originally Los Vasqueros, a tourist bar meant to give its owner a tax write-off for his vacation home, which he listed as his "office" on tax forms. Los Vasqueros had been listed in guidebooks and hotel brochures as a good place for tour buses to unload for restrooms, beer, frozen margaritas, and spicy peanuts.

But eventually, American expats found it and transformed it to their liking. American beers were displayed next to the superior Mexican selection. Hot dogs and microwave pizzas stood alongside a nacho dispenser. The two televisions placed high on the wall carried continuous CNN and ESPN, and the jukebox was stuck in the sixties. The average age for male patrons was past sixty, and the women were invariably stuck at "forty-nine." Golf made the men tan, but not fit. No joggers, weight-trainers, or early-morning lap swimmers frequented The Gringo, as it was renamed. The average man's waist came in at about thirty-eight inches. These, at least, were the observations of the long-suffering Jose.

But it really was better, Jose thought. The retirees were an easy bunch to handle. He could keep long-running individual tabs all night—he knew the names of all the regulars, and they looked out for and monitored each other. If one of them had too much to drink, or became too outspoken about his political view of a country he no longer lived in, the group would come together and tend to him, like a lost sheep. He would get home safely and return the next night in good stead. Plus, one look at the clientele discouraged younger, livelier guests from entering, and they'd take their business, and trouble, to another place.

Encouraged by what he saw, John entered and looked around attentively. He paused, tuning his ears to what he was sure was American English. A couple of guys at the bar immediately spotted him and waved him over. John approached, but cautiously. He'd seen Mexicans pass as American before.

"Sorry, I couldn't help but overhear," John said. "You speak English?"

"All the time," one of them answered.

The second man said, "Lonesome for the old native tongue, are you? English is spoken exclusively here at the Gringo."

"Sort of an American enclave," the first man said. "All of the American community passes through here sooner or later. Sort of like Rick's Café Americain."

John, confused, said "Huh?"

"You know, like the movie *Casablanca*."

"*Casablanca*? Sounds Mexican to me," John said. When this did not elicit a response, he changed subjects. "Tell me, what brings you gentlemen to San Miguel?"

"We live here."

"You live here?" John could not disguise his surprise.

"Sure, we're retired," one of the men said.

"We like the climate," said the other.

Total immersion, John thought, and then said, "You must speak Spanish pretty well, then."

"Don't know two words," the first man said. "Just enough to get me in trouble, if I tried." He lowered his voice. "That's why we like it here at the Gringo. This is like the American embassy. It's American territory. Everything is like back home—American people, American television, American food." He gestured to the TV screen and the hot dog rotisserie. "You need your passport to get in here."

John patted his pocket, but the man waved his hands, saying, "Just kidding—but seriously, we have one rule: no Spanish spoken here." He turned to the bartender. "Right, Jose?"

Jose replied as if on cue, "Sí, Señor." The men on the barstools chuckled.

John turned to the bartender. "Jose," he said, like he'd known him forever, "a scotch and soda on ice, and a round for my amigos. I mean friends," he said, correcting himself.

"Thanks," said the older of the two men. "I'm Bill, and this is Jake," he said, motioning to the man on his right.

"Pleased, to meet you both. I'm John Sanford."

"Well, John, what's your story? What brings you to San Miguel?" Bill asked.

"Oh, I'm going to the language school," John said. "Learning Spanish." Bill and Jake nodded in admiration.

John continued, saying, "Yeah, I'm in business in Houston and have dealings with Mexico. Today, to conduct business internationally, you have to function in more than one language."

"So how's it going?" Jake asked.

"Great. I'm absorbing it like a sponge," John said. "By the end of the month I'll be speaking like a native."

"Sounds great," Bill said. "I probably should learn some. Afraid I'm too old, though. Old dogs, new tricks, you know?"

"Pshaw," John said, waving a derisive hand at Bill. "It's all in your attitude. You can't allow yourself to get set in your ways. Have to remain flexible. Mind you, I have to stay on my toes to keep up with the kids in my class."

"Well, my hat's off to you for trying," Bill said. He held up his glass in a toast to John and, smiling, said, "Salud."

John did not realize the toast was in Spanish and said, "Cheers."

Jake bought the next round, then it was Bill's turn, then it came back around to John, and when it came back to Jake's turn, Bill and John realized that at some point he had gone home unnoticed. They flipped for the round, and John lost good-naturedly. He then remembered a joke and tried it out on Bill.

"Bill, you know what you call a person who can speak three languages?" John said.

Bill grinned back blankly.

"Trilingual," John said. "Two languages?"

Bill confidently blurted out, "Bilingual."

John paused, building up to the punch line. "One language?"

"Monolingual?" Bill asked, uncertain.

"No, an American!" John said, and he and Bill doubled over in laughter.

"Ain't it the truth. Ain't it the truth," Bill said, shaking his head.

John, inebriated, suddenly turned a little serious. "No! No, it's not. I'm living proof of it. We can learn their language if we put our mind to it. Remember, we Americans put a man on the moon. I'll show 'em," he said, winding down. "I'll show 'em."

Bill placed a reassuring arm over John's shoulder. "You show them. You show them what we Americans can do."

Leaning on each other for support, they made their way out into the street singing the only Mexican song Bill knew—"La Cucaracha."

John made his way back to the house and stumbled through the front door, where he was confronted by an impatient Lourdes. He smiled blearily doing a semi-rumba, singing, "La Cucaracha, la Cucaracha..."

"Señor Sanford, this is a respectable house," Lourdes said.

"Oh, sorry," John said, his dance slowing. "I learned a Mexican song tonight. Like to hear it?"

"No! It is not a song I care for."

"Have it your way. See you in the morning, bright and early," he said, making his way upstairs, still humming.

—　～

John sensed the morning before he felt it. The house was still, his room more dark than light, but he knew day couldn't be far away. In lieu of the digital alarm clock he had left at home, he wore his wristwatch to bed. When he lit up its small face, it read 6:58. Too late to get back to sleep; it was time to assess his condition. A massive hangover loomed over him, but he didn't feel it yet. His mouth was dry and sticky, and he spied a bottle of purified water on the dresser. He propped himself up on his elbow, and his head gave a warning throb. Rehydration was the first step to recovery, so he embarked upon the ten-foot journey between him and the bottle and held it up to his mouth, drinking deeply. Cool refreshment washed over him. He carried the bottle with him to the bathroom, where he removed an economy-size bottle of aspirin from his toiletry bag. He shook out two tablets, then two more. He made his way back to the bed but was careful not to lie back down and instead sat up and waited for the medicine to do its work. This was far from the first time this had happened, and John took a perverse pride in not letting it stop him from carrying on. He likened himself to the athlete who plays hurt—though this injury had been self-inflicted. The aspirin started to work, and John's optimism was on the rise. Maybe he could sneak downstairs and grab a cup of coffee, or even the whole pot, and take it back to his room. He didn't want to make any decisions before his coffee. He found his robe and pulled it around him and, in his bare feet, made for the dining room.

He smelled the coffee before he saw it and hoped that Lourdes had already left the house. He poured himself a cup and then took the unnecessary risk of sitting down at the table.

Despite his meager precautions, Maria had heard him and entered with his breakfast. She was shocked to see him—robe hanging open, bloodshot eyes, hair in disarray, unshaven face a sickly pale—but set down his plate as if nothing was amiss, then turned to leave. John looked at his plate. The eggs were slightly overcooked and the smell made his stomach, already acidic from alcohol, aspirin, and coffee, revolt. John shoved the food away and took deep breaths to help settle his churning stomach. The nausea passed and he felt confident enough to return to his coffee, but it was only a trade-off. With each sip his head improved, but his stomach rebelled. There would be no quick fix this time. If he took it easy, he thought he might recover in time for afternoon classes.

He was staring down into the inky darkness of his cup, a perfect metaphor for his present situation, when he sensed a nonmetaphoric shadow hanging over him. He both recognized and dreaded her presence and stared at his coffee all the harder, thinking that maybe if he didn't look up, the early morning angel of death might yet pass over him. But it was not to be. In any waiting game, he was going to lose, so he turned his sickly head and faced her.

Lourdes, in her dark blouse and skirt, with her hands on her hips, struck an imposing figure. Despite her scowl, despite his nausea, despite his current situation, he still couldn't help but notice how attractive she could be, in a domineering sort of way. He felt like a troll under a bridge compared to her majestic presence.

She moved the plate back under his nose and, in a not-quite-accusatory tone, said, "Señor, you need to finish your breakfast."

"I'm not very hungry this morning," John said, straining to mask his disgust at the eggs' stench.

"You will be later," Lourdes said. "Eat and get ready for school."

"I'm not going to class this morning," he said with as much defiance as he could muster.

"Oh, yes you are. Hurry up and eat and get dressed," Lourdes said.

John fell back on the one thing he thought would be indisputable. "I don't feel well. I think I might be coming down with, you know, *tourista*."

Tourista is known to all Americans and Mexicans as the intestinal bug that comes from drinking water or food not up to US purity standards. Considering he had eaten mostly in her home, Lourdes naturally was insulted. John could practically see her patience wilt.

"How dare you try and pass the blame onto us! I know what is wrong with you. I have seen it many times, and it is no excuse. Now get moving!"

John may have been in a compromised state, but he had his pride and was outraged that she would question his lies. No one had spoken to him like that since he was a kid, and that was just a sadistic high school coach.

He wanted to stand up to Lourdes, remind her he was a guest there, not a servant. Retorts ran through his head, but in the end he realized he did not feel strong enough to match her anger. That, and—though it was less important to him—he didn't exactly occupy the moral high ground. The best he could do was to slowly rise from the table and, with deliberate care, pour another cup of coffee before announcing, "I think I will go to class." Now that the decision was made, he felt a little proud that he would go, even with his hangover. But Lourdes had embarrassed him, and he would not forget it. He would wait for an opportunity to settle this score.

With determination that came from anger, he showered but skipped shaving and dressed in the clothes that he found sitting out, reiterating his vow that he was tougher than any hangover. Many times in Houston he had stayed out all night and then kicked ass in business deals the next morning. *He* was the master, not the hangover.

— ᵕ

John felt every cobblestone jostle his head. He stopped along the way at a small bodega and bought two cans of Coke—he appreciated the way they made it here, with plenty of real cane sugar. That was one thing they did better than the United States. He opened one of the cans and took a deep drink. The carbonation shot through his sinuses and exited his nose like a puff from a cigarette, a habit he had broken with great difficulty. The combination of sugar and caffeine worked on his head while the carbonation eased his stomach. He discarded the first can as he entered the classroom, only slightly late. No one noticed or cared—the novelty of the grown man in class had worn off—and he moved into his seat without incident. Once there, he tried to tune his mind into Spanish. He heard the students respond to commands and looked around. They were working from the textbook, which was good because John preferred the written word to the spoken. He leaned over to the young girl on his right to find the page number. He still reeked of the night before, and she leaned away in disgust while extending her open book toward him.

John resented her obvious display of distaste but still said, "Gracias."

He settled in, popped open the second can, and took a sip before returning his attention to his book. Alert and running, feeling a little sugar high, he was beginning to feel glad he came. *I'm here, I'm alert, might as well learn some Spanish,* he thought. He scanned the page in front of him. *Open your mind,* he told himself, *let go, feel the rhythm of the language. You don't need to do anything. Don't fight it and the language will come to you.*

The sugar and caffeine started working overtime. He took another drink from the can, hearing words, recognizing words—he was feeling the beat, he was in the groove.

In the groove? When was the last time he had heard that? His mind wandered back in time, away from San Miguel. Women from his past popped into his head, disappearing before he could fully identify them.

His head slipped off his cupped hand and he saw the desktop rushing towards him. He jerked up suddenly and saw that the others were all looking in his direction. Laughter scattered across the room before the teacher could redirect the class's attention away from John and back to the lesson.

How long had he been asleep? Had he been snoring loudly? He felt the can of Coke—it was no longer cool to the touch. He sat back and wished he could disappear.

～ ～

As soon as class was over, Chloe and Hayden rushed out the door. They looked at each other, waiting to see who would begin first. Finally, Chloe burst out, not even considering speaking Spanish, "Did you see him fall asleep in class?"

"Of course I saw him!" Hayden said. "I heard him snoring and had my eye on him when his head hit his desk."

Chloe laughed with abandon.

"Man, he must have a huge hangover," Hayden said with delight. "I give him credit for showing up at all."

"I bet she shoved him out the door this morning," Chloe said.

"She should throw him out altogether," Hayden said, no longer joking.

"Oh, he's not that bad," Chloe said, flapping a hand in his direction.

"The hell he isn't!" Hayden said.

"I find him entertaining, the way he messes with her," she said.

"She shouldn't have to put up with him," Hayden said.

"Well, it's not just him."

"What do you mean?" he asked.

"Well," Chloe said, and paused to choose her words with care. "You don't find her a bit...haughty?"

"I think she has a certain dignity."

"Well, that's putting it mildly. Hayden, the woman is a stone-cold bitch. I like the way John puts her in her place."

"I don't think it's his place to put her in her place—it is, after all, her place," Hayden said awkwardly. "And I don't find her that way at all. I think," he said, choosing his words carefully as well, "that she has a certain charm and I find it attractive."

"Attractive?" Chloe said, barely masking her jealousy. "Attractive in what way?"

"Well...in the same way any man finds a woman attractive," Hayden said, his voice trailing off. He wished he'd put it differently.

"Hayden, do you know how old that woman is?"

"No, do you?" he shot back.

"Too old for you," she said.

"Well...I didn't say I was interested. Just commenting on how a woman can have be attractive at any age," he said, crossing his arms.

Their quickly spinning conversation had taken them all the way to the house. They had each revealed more than they would have liked to and now felt uncomfortable in each other's presence. They split up immediately upon entering the house.

Chloe went to her room and slammed the door a little harder than she intended to. She hoped that Hayden hadn't heard it and interpreted it wrong—or right, whichever. She didn't know how she felt. Was she jealous of that haughty middle-aged woman? Who cared?

Besides, if there was an attractive older person in the house, it was John Sanford. She had seen him shirtless by the pool—he had a certain Clint Eastwood hardness about him, and she loved the way he didn't bow to Lourdes's tyrannical running of the house. No one pushed him around. She just hoped that when Lourdes finally blew up, she would be there to witness it.

When Chloe's mental rant finally subsided, she was upset with herself for letting marginal people in her life get to her. It wouldn't be long until her and Hayden's time in San Miguel was up and they'd be returning home, and then back to college. She shouldn't concern herself with these people. They were just passing through her life, and she would never see them again. She had hoped that maybe something between Hayden and her would develop, but he was too distracted by that Mexican woman.

Hayden felt embarrassed that he had lost control and spoken his thoughts openly. He was afraid Chloe might tell someone what he had said. Though there was really no one she could talk to, unless she said something to Sanford. The thought of that happening sent chills through him. She wouldn't, unless she was really jealous. *Maybe I should pay more attention to her,* he thought. *Act interested in her.* He leaned back in bed to think of a plan. He wouldn't have to put up with any of them much longer—they had less than a week left.

John arrived shortly after Chloe and Hayden, went straight up to his room, stripped down to his underwear and promptly fell asleep.

Lourdes returned home from running errands and was relieved at how peaceful the house seemed. She decided that, with everything in order, she could afford to go to her room and lie down for a while.

13

Maria had been living in this house since she was a young woman. Her short marriage had ended with her as a childless widow, her husband a victim of a mining accident. She had been afraid she would have to move to Mexico City and seek work with millions of others. She was afraid of the city. The largest in the world, some had said. She had always thought she would live the life of her mother and grandmother and all women in her family: wife, then mother, then grandmother. She had no skills other than domestic. The city would swallow her up. When her husband died, she was young enough to marry again, but she had never been the type of woman likely to attract very many men. And, as a widow, she was used goods. She had not enjoyed her short marriage, and with her husband's death she felt a loss of security more than love. Her next match, if she could have arranged one, would have been even less favorable. She dreaded the prospect, but feared the city more.

Then one day, just before the meager insurance settlement ran out, she was offered a job taking care of the fine house of an absentee owner. The house had a remodeled kitchen with all modern appliances, and it took Maria some time to learn how to use them. She brought with her a large cache of recipes from her mother and grandmother—some written down, some stored in her heart and mind. When the owner came, he did not care for her traditional cooking and wanted only grilled beef with potatoes fried in lard. But mainly he drank, and when he drank he became abusive. At times like that, she learned to make herself as small as possible—a lesson she vividly remembered learning.

Maria never considered herself pretty—she was just a plain girl—but at that age she still had a slim waist and an ample bosom, and that was enough to get the Señor's attention when he was drunk. First it started with the name calling: *puta*, whore. The abusive language was a form of foreplay for him. Then he'd call for her to bring him something and grab for her as she went by. She learned to move quickly, and he would be too drunk and sluggish to catch her. She would place a full bottle of tequila on the side table and then remove herself from the house until he had drunk himself into a stupor; only then would she slip back in and go to her room.

Still, sometimes he would rouse himself in the middle of the night and bang on her locked bedroom door, calling her names, listing the vile things he was going to do to her. She remembered from her marriage how men, when they drank, thought of women as possessions, free to use without asking or caring. She tolerated it as part of marriage, but this was just a job. Still, if all she had to do was take care of the house, cook a couple of meals a week, and take only verbal abuse, then she preferred this life to marriage.

The next day he would sleep until noon and rise hung over and hungry. He would eat a breakfast of eggs and sausages and grumble at her. Then without saying a word, he would depart for the ranch in his Cadillac. He only came once a week; the rest of his time was spent at the ranch or in Mexico City. She supposed that the house served as midway point between the two destinations. She had no idea what he did in Mexico City, but he always seemed like he needed the rest that the house in San Miguel afforded him. He slept a great deal of the time when he came, and that suited her fine.

She wondered why he didn't just stay in one of San Miguel's fine hotels until one day he arrived with a woman from the city. She was young, only slightly older than Maria, pretty in an obvious way, and very so-phisticated. She was fair-skinned with blond hair and blue eyes, a rare combination, but not unheard-of in Mexican women. She brought with her a great number of bags. It was evident that she intended to stay. Maria wondered if she would last a day—or rather a night. Did she have any idea what he was like when he drank? But Maria was in no position to come to her rescue. She was not going to jeopardize her job.

That night after a dinner in which he consumed about sixteen ounces of undercooked beef and the woman had only salad, they retired to the salon where he kept a fully stocked bar. They had drinks—or at least he did. Maria wasn't sure if the woman drank like she ate: only enough to be company. Maria knew what would come next, but did the city woman? Maria worried about her, but the woman was moving into the house—surely she understood the obligations that carried. But did she know what form his sexual perversions took?

It took about an hour for him to reach the state of inebriation where he was at his best, or worst. Maria busied herself in the kitchen, but her fear for the woman was foremost in her mind. If she cried out for help, what was Maria's obligation?

Then it began. He bellowed out in a voice so loud there was no doubt that he meant Maria to hear, too. "Consuelo, venga." *Come.* He used the form of the verb one would use when calling a child or a dog. Maria drew near the closed kitchen door and waited, afraid of what would follow.

Consuelo sat across the room from him and made no effort to rise from her chair. She took a small sip of Jerez sherry and gave him a non-chalant smile, sitting impassively as he undid his pants. He was not a bad-looking man and was probably considered handsome in his young-er days. He certainly had a virile quality about him. His swarthy, fleshy face was slightly puffy from years of hard drinking. He was tall for a Mexican man, over six feet, with a chest that was large, expansive, and powerful, but only slightly bigger than his stomach. He had a full head of black hair with only a few strands of gray. It was his mouth that gave her pause—it was a cruel, hard mouth that betrayed him for the sadist he was.

He pouted and spoke in a mock pleading tone. "Venga, por favor, tengo algo para ti." *Come, I have something for you.* Maria could guess what that something was.

Maria heard her scream the last words, "¡Nunca! ¡Puerco!" *Never, you pig!*

Maria froze. She felt that she should do something. But what could she do? At best lose her job and at worst become herself a victim of his savagery. Maria listened. She heard furniture move. A lamp crashed to the floor. She expected to hear the sound of feet stomping, or him dragging Consuelo toward the downstairs bedroom, where the door would slam and mercifully all further sounds would be shut off. But instead, she continued to hear their voices and noises clearly.

She then heard the woman cry out!

They had not left the salon but were going at it there in the open. Animal noises flowed forth. Maria pictured the room. There was a sofa he could make use of or even the table. It seemed to last forever to Maria, trapped in the kitchen, only feet away from the action. She could hear the sound of a hand slapping against firm flesh. She tried not to picture the visions that came with the sounds.

The male grunting was clear enough and familiar, but what was the woman doing? She made sounds that were not like screams of pain, but primal passion mixed with disgust. Maria did not know what it meant, but the sounds continued to grow louder until the woman confused her by shouting, "Sí, sí! Mas, mas." Then all went quiet.

━ ━

The next morning, the woman surprised Maria by appearing in the kitchen and helping herself to the coffee Maria had made but not put out yet. She had on a silk robe and looked not the least bit embarrassed. After she got her coffee, she went to the front door, where a copy of the Mexico City paper was waiting. Maria immediately began to set the table for one, knowing that the man would not be up for hours. They would be alone for a while.

The woman smiled and accepted the fresh rolls Maria had made and said in a kind, gentle voice so different from the coarse, crude sounds of the night before, "Gracias, Maria." Maria welcomed the words, which were so much nicer than those of the Señor. But what the woman said next frightened Maria.

"Por todo." *For everything.* Maria realized that her role as voyeur was a planned part.

There was also a clear understanding between the two of them that, despite the role she played last night, this new woman was now the lady of the house.

14

Vivian woke late to find Bill had already left. Her alcohol-soaked brain ran through several clues and then deduced that it must be Wednesday. Bill would be having his weekly golf game. She lay back, not knowing what to do with herself. It was nine thirty—no way was she going to be able to get back to sleep. Nevertheless, she slipped on her black sleep mask to keep away the light and settled her head back on her pillow. She wished she could close her eyes and then find it was lunchtime. She did not want to deal with the thoughts she went through every morning. Vivian hated San Miguel. She hated its cobble stoned streets, its quaint shops, its small town feel. She missed the American city, her own car, the malls and more than anything the freedom of anonymity. Here she was known and whatever she did was soon known. It formed a picturesque prison and she was serving a life sentence, if not her life then at least Bill's. Bill had rescued her from a life of 9-5 office drudgery to leave her with a life of 24 hour monotonous leisure.

San Miguel suited Bill fine; he was sixty-eight. . She was only fifty-four years old. What kind of life was this for her?

This town was fine for a relaxing vacation, but not for a home. She had her friends, they had their coffees, their luncheons, and Tuesday was their golfing day. But it was not enough. And worse, it turned out that Bill was not enough. She needed some excitement. His sexual level no longer matched hers. The frustration built daily, but there was no way she could have an affair, not in a town this small. Everybody drank, and everybody talked. She couldn't risk it, even if she knew someone who might be amenable and discreet—and she didn't.

She reached into her nightstand drawer and removed a prescription bottle of Valium. It had been prescribed to relieve anxiety, but she found it helpful for boredom, too. She washed it down with her ever-present bottled water and put her head back, hoping for the oblivion to wash over her. Maybe later she could manage lunch out with the girls. Right now, she had to get past the morning blues.

<hr />

John came downstairs and noticed a sweet aroma coming from the kitchen, the smell of baked sugar. A smell that took him, in a flash, across time and space to his grandmother's house and her fresh-baked cookies. He took a deep drink of his coffee, and the memory vanished; he was back in central Mexico. Was Maria changing up the breakfast menu to include some sort of sweet roll—maybe a cinnamon roll? *Now that would be good with this coffee,* he thought.

When Maria emerged, she had the usual hot crescent rolls with homemade strawberry jam. *Still good, but what had all that sugary smell gone into?* He wondered as he spread jam across the bread.

Lourdes proceeded across town, following Canal Street to the road leading west to Dolores Hidalgo. In her left hand she carried a basket of small iced cakes that Maria had made earlier in the morning. As she entered the gate to the orphanage, some children recognized her and came running—they knew she always brought sweet treats. On ground where soldiers had once drilled, the earth was now beaten down by a multitude of small feet. Grass had never had a chance to regain a foothold on this patch of earth. They came running in order of age, the youngest sprinting, the older ones walking.

Soon she was surrounded by children ranging from five to fourteen years old. The youngest had no inhibitions about jumping up and down like puppies begging for a treat, but the teens, especially the boys, hung back with feigned indifference. In the end, all accepted their treats with graciousness. Lourdes held on to one cake with special decorations on it, and protected it as she made her way across the yard and entered the building.

Padre was still in his room, trying to gain strength from a cup of strong, bitter coffee. He became aware of the ruckus in the yard and guessed its source. He rose with difficulty and, taking his cane, proceeded on tottering legs out the door. He made his way across, disguising his discomfort, and greeted his old friend and benefactor.

"Lourdes que bueno que venistes. Ya sabes que me los vas hechar de pedir a los ninos." *Lourdes, how good of you to come. You know, you spoil the children.*

"Y cada uno ellos hacen lo mizmo a mi cada uno a su manera," *And they, in their way, spoil me.*

They began to stroll across the yard, in what might have appeared to be an aimless manner, but they both knew their destination was the clinic. Unspoken, but understood, was that she was there for a certain patient. Before they reached the door to the clinic, she reached out and held his forearm, and he paused to look at her. They both knew the purpose of her visit, so when the question came, it was short and direct.

"¿Padre, como esta?" *How is he?*

The Padre hesitated and tried to weigh his words. "Esta comodo por el momento, pero el doctor dice se puede ir a qualguiere momento. Le dara mucho gusto verla." *He is comfortable enough for the moment, but the doctor says he could go at any time. He'll be happy to see you, though.* Lourdes nodded in understanding and released his arm. They proceeded through the door.

Mateo lay in an iron bed, not a proper hospital bed. To prop him up to eye level, they had stuffed pillows behind his back. The Padre left them and proceeded out the door, wishing it was he who would soon be dead. Didn't he deserve the gift of death just as much? A release from a life that now offered only pain? He asked forgiveness for his malingering in the face of despair and went out to sit in his chair that faced the morning sun, hoping for some relief for aching bones.

The boy was thirteen years of age, but because of his lifetime of illness, still looked like a child a few years short of puberty. But even in his weakened condition his eyes lit up at the sight of Lourdes. She took the chair next to his bed, last used by the doctor and pulled it even closer. His eyes darted from her to her basket and back again.

Lourdes looked at him and then at the basket and said, in a slightly mocking manner, "¿Soy o es la canasta que mas te interesa?" *Is it me, or what's in the basket that you're more interested in?*

He smiled back weakly and she saw with how much difficulty he held himself up. She would tease him no longer. She reached into the basket and took out a small cake with red frosting and his name, Mateo, written across it in white icing.

His own name in writing meant more to him than even Lourdes could have anticipated. It meant that he was someone, that he was recognized, and as much as he wanted to eat the frosting he could not bear to see his name obliterated. He took the small cake in both hands and held it out, looking at it with great pride.

Lourdes had expected him to thrust it in his mouth immediately, as the other children had done. Instead he placed it on the bedside table and admired it, as if it were a trophy that proclaimed him an individual.

⁓ ⁓

John walked the streets aimlessly. In Houston he had never walked anywhere, but here he had begun to enjoy it. Eventually, he knew that he was going to end up at The Gringo. He didn't want to get an early start, nor did he plan on staying late; it was easier to control his time there than his consumption, and he didn't want a repeat of the last hangover. He was trying to pace himself so he could last the month. He considered leaving the school and moving to Cancun, where he could find modern technology and wait out the rest of the time. No one back in Houston would need to know. But that woman—that dorm mother, that warden—she would know that she had beaten him. Who was she, anyway? Just some Mexican. *Back in Houston, she would be cleaning my condo twice a week,* he thought.

All right, he was in her house, in her country, but he was paying her. That's what it came down to: money. She took his money, so she worked for him, end of story. His arrangement with her was no different from the dozens of hotels he had stayed in during his business travels. Her job was to make him comfortable, not to judge him, and certainly not to talk to him as if he were a child.

His anger had made him thirsty, and he wanted to head to The Gringo for his first drink of the day. He hesitated; it was too early. He would wait. He sought out a park bench on the plaza beneath a shade tree that he couldn't identify but knew it was different than those at home. The sun was going down, and the church cast long, spiky shadows across the open space. John looked up and saw a child, a small boy, staring at him. He wore long pants and a T-shirt with the name of a Mexican soccer team emblazoned across it. He looked to be no more than ten years old, but he could have been older—down here, they tended to run smaller.

The boy's shiny, brown face looked up at John hopefully and spoke to him in English. "Shine, mister?" The boy had a wooden box with a footrest on top. On the side of the box, painted words read: *$5.00 US.*

John looked down at his dusty brown Gucci loafer and said, "Sure, go ahead."

The boy squatted before him and went to work with vigor. At the end, the boy took his oily cloth and pulled it back and forth, making a squeaking sound with his mouth as if it were coming from the leather. John found this entertaining and reached in his pocket, deciding to reward the boy with ten dollars. By now, however, the boy had maneuvered his shine box to show the reverse side, which read: *$20.00 US.*

John and the boy engaged in a staring match, the boy's finger pointing to the stated price. John didn't know how to handle the situation. After all the embarrassing things that had already happened, he didn't want to be seen arguing with a small boy in the central plaza over a few bucks. He knew the boy would point to his sign until the next morning if he needed to.

He got me, John admitted to himself as he dug out two tens. *Five dollars for a shoeshine, and fifteen dollars for a lesson.* It will make for a good story at The Gringo. The boy gave John a small nod and disappeared across the plaza.

John entered the Gringo and found Bill and Jake sitting at the bar. John took the seat next to them and Bill looked up at him.

"Never guess what I just went through in the plaza," John said immediately. "This kid comes up with a shoeshine box—"

"First he shows you the five-dollar side, then afterward switches to the twenty-dollar side?" Bill asked, grinning.

"Yeah, I guess it happens to every new American."

"You didn't pay him the twenty, did you?" Bill asked.

"No, of course not," John said, hoping he sounded convincing.

Bill took a long, appraising look at John. "John, old boy," he said, "you doing okay? You look a little bushed."

"I'm okay," John said. He turned to the bartender and caught his eye. Jose nodded and set to preparing John his usual scotch, splash of soda, and ice. John marveled at what great rapport he seemed to have with bartenders. Why didn't he get along that well with the rest of humanity?

Jose placed the drink in front of him, and John turned his attention back to Bill, who continued his counsel. "You know, John, you shouldn't let me keep you up so late. I'm retired, you know. Got nothing to do the next day."

"I'm fine. I can handle it," John said. "At home, I'm used to long days."

John glanced over at Bill's newspaper, *USA Today,* and saw it opened to the sports section.

"Hey, where did you get the newspaper?" he asked Bill.

"There's a little newsstand off the plaza. The only English language newspaper they carry is *USA Today*—only by the time we get it, it's *USA Yesterday.*"

"I'm starved for some news of the outside world."

"Here," Bill said. "I don't really care about the news anymore. I just try and follow baseball."

Bill passed the unread front page to John, who found it as absorbing as his scotch. After a few undisturbed minutes, during which John reassured himself that the world was continuing on in his absence, he turned back to Bill.

"Bill, it doesn't bother you that the stock market could crash, and you wouldn't know it until two days later? This place is like living in a time warp."

"I suppose," Bill said, "but you get used to it. I actually find it comforting. When there is bad news, it sort of softens the blow when you realize that it's already said and done by the time you hear of it."

"Man, you've been down here too long," John said.

"Maybe, maybe you're right. I don't know. I—I just don't think I'd want to face that fast-paced world again," Bill said.

"How long did it take you to get that way?"

"Don't worry, John. It takes longer than a month."

"Thank God for that!"

Each took a section of the paper—business for John, sports for Bill—and read for a while. John, satisfied that his investments were safe as of yesterday, turned back to Bill.

"How are the Astros doing?" John asked.

Bill summed up the sports news like a professional broadcaster. "Let's see. Lost 3–2 to Oakland, giving up seven hits. Their chances of winning the series don't look good." He looked at John to see if this had had any impact on him.

If John were still in Houston, he would have followed the series closely, but here it didn't seem to affect him. He merely shrugged, and Bill knew what that feeling of disconnect was like.

When Bill continued, a note of sadness had crept into his voice. "That's what I miss about home. We get some games on satellite, but it's not the same."

John was somewhat taken aback. "You're living in this third-world country, and that's all you miss?"

The conversation grabbed onto baseball and didn't let go of it the rest of the night. The American League designated hitter rule took up two hours itself. Bill tended to romanticize the old days of Mantle and Maris, while John said they couldn't play an inning in the times of Josh Hamilton and Alex Rodriguez. Which led to a heated discussion of steroid use and whether all steroid-influenced records should be thrown out. On that subject, Bill lost his laid-back demeanor and went into a full tirade.

"To hell with them all," Bill said, winding down.

"Yeah, you're right. To hell with 'em. Who needs 'em?" John echoed, slurring his words.

Bill drained his drink. "Let's go home," he said.

"Yeah, home sweet home." John laughed as he and Bill staggered out the door.

15

It was October 12, an official holiday in Mexico, as well as other parts of Latin America. In the United States it was Columbus Day; here it was a little more complicated. Over five hundred years ago, Columbus had landed somewhere in the Caribbean, and in the ensuing years Mexico had undergone drastic changes. First the conquest and subjugation of the Aztec empire by Cortés and his five hundred Spaniards. Then disease, which eradicated nearly 90 percent of the native population, and finally Christianity to replace a culture now all but lost. But from the ashes of the Indian empires arose a new people, the mestizos. Today in Mexico, it was no longer the arrival of the first Europeans that was celebrated, but the birth of the new race. The celebration was called Dia de La Raza—Day of the Race, or Day of the People. This birth was not metaphorical but could be traced to an actual event. Gonzalo Guerrero, a Spanish conquistador, shipwrecked off the coast of Cozumel in 1511, became the father of the Mexican race by marrying a Mayan princess. Their children, mestizos, are considered to be the first Mexicans.

Tonight Maria would prepare a special dinner, and Lourdes would give the students a small talk on its meaning to Mexicans. It was a touchy subject and would have to be handled delicately. Festivals were part of the students' cultural experience during their stay, and she meant for them to enjoy it, but she worried about them, too. She knew all she was required to do was provide them a bed and three meals, but she couldn't help but take an almost motherly interest in their welfare. Dia de la Raza could be a precarious time to be an American in Mexico.

She felt the children would exercise good judgment, but Señor Sanford was another matter. Maybe his lack of proficiency in Spanish could work in his favor. He, hopefully, would not engage the locals, who might get contentious, in conversation. He might not even be aware that it was Columbus Day. Lourdes hoped he would sit out the night in the bar with his American friends, but if he got drunk and wandered onto the plaza, there could be trouble.

She was miffed with him and with herself. He was a grown man, and she was not his guardian. She also included her good friend Olivia as an object of her discontent. *How dare she place that man under my roof? What was she thinking?* She fumed as she went about planning her talk with the students.

Chloe and Hayden came back from their afternoon dialogue class through the plaza. A bandstand was being set up, and vendor tables were appearing. A photographer had set up a burro on which children could have their picture taken, and people were streaming in, wearing colorful, traditional Mexican clothes. The sombreros the men wore seemed to be a yard across. Merchants arrived early to grab choice spots for their food stands. A variety of finger food called *antojitos* would be prepared at home and kept warm.

The two students gave each other a conspiratorial look, and Hayden said, in English, "Columbus Day? I can't see what they've got to celebrate. Cortés and a few hundred men defeat the entire Aztec empire. Embarrassing, if you ask me." He looked a little proud of the vicarious accomplishment.

"I guess they got Christianity out of it. Better than their religion of human sacrifices," Chloe added.

"Suppressed by the Spaniards *and* the Catholic Church—what a bargain!" Hayden had strong opinions on authority and was not shy in expressing them.

When they entered the house, they could tell that Lourdes had something special planned. The table had a decorative setting that always meant a lesson with dinner. Chloe and Hayden, when they walked by, saw a Lourdes they had not seen before. Her hair was moist and hanging down from the heat of the kitchen, and she wore blue jeans. Her long-sleeved white cotton shirt had splotches of red chili sauce across it. Chloe found it amusing to see even a single hair out of place on the fastidious woman. Hayden appreciated how the snug jeans outlined her hips, and the tautness of the cotton shirt made her breasts more pronounced. She glanced up and saw him looking, and he turned away in embarrassment.

For Lourdes cooking was the easy part. The harder part would be to make sure Señor Sanford was present and not disruptive of the evening she had planned. She was too busy to wait on him, so she decided to leave a note in his room. She sat down at her desk and took out her stationery. In her often-outdated fashion, she still liked to send notes to people. She preferred the more personal touch, and the delicacy this message required would be better served on paper. She paused to gather her thoughts, then began trying to strike the right balance between formal courtesy and insistence. And, of course, it must be in English or he'll pretend he didn't understand.

> *Señor Sanford,*
> *We are having a special dinner to celebrate Mexican Dia de la Raza. I would like very much for you to attend. It is a chance for you to learn something of our history and culture and experience an authentic meal. Please try to be present promptly at seven o'clock. Thank you very much.*
> *Lourdes de Madrid*

She went upstairs and pressed the paper firmly through the gap in the door, resigned that she had done all that could be expected of her. She would just have to wait and see. She still had much to do before seven.

Promptly at seven, Lourdes came from the kitchen dressed in a knee-length skirt and a colorful blouse. Hayden couldn't keep his eyes off her. Maria appeared behind her, but she was small and of no consequence to Hayden. His eyes followed Lourdes across the room, noticing her every move, every expression. Their age difference was too great for him to consider anything, but still, he couldn't help admiring her. But, then again, if she didn't mind, he certainly didn't.

Maybe Lourdes's grace and dignity came with age, or maybe she'd always had it. She had something that someone like Chloe could never have. Chloe's looks—and she wasn't bad looking—like her character, were all on the surface. What Lourdes had was an enigma to him. What was a woman like her doing running a boarding house for language students? She was obviously so much more than that. He caught himself staring at her, and he looked away. He had to accept that she was of another generation. Lourdes was unattainable, but there was still Chloe, and he knew how she felt about him. Better take what was available. But his heart wasn't in it. He didn't want cute; he wanted exquisite.

The table had a glass vase with small Mexican flags pointing in all directions. The plates were colorful ceramic. Chloe had bought a Mexican blouse for the occasion, and was in a festive mood. Hayden wore jeans and a polo shirt, no different from what he usually wore. They took their regular seats at the table and waited. It was obvious that Lourdes had something planned, but that she was waiting on something, or someone, before commencing.

There was a sweaty pitcher of fruit punch called *ponche* that gave off a sweet fragrance. While they waited, Lourdes poured each of them a glass. She looked down at her watch and, with a sigh, was about to begin when she heard footsteps on the stairs. Lourdes paused and was relieved when she saw John rounding the corner. She had prepared a short story about the occasion and was anxious to begin before she lost everyone's attention.

"Señor, asientase por favor," she said to the looming figure of John Stanford. To Maria, who was standing in the doorway with the first of the dishes, she nodded as she said to the others, "Esta noche tenemos un comida especial para ustedes."

Chloe was always wary of special dinners—strange sauces covering up God knew what meat and weird chilies. She wished Lourdes, or Maria for that matter, wouldn't bother. A veggie pizza would be fine with her. Hayden, she knew, would act as if he appreciated the native cuisine just to please Lourdes. *Anything for Lourdes,* she said to herself. What was it with him and that middle-aged woman?

John probably wouldn't bother. He would just go into town to eat American food. She had to admire his independence; he just did whatever he wanted.

Chloe moved the food around her plate, eating the rice but avoiding anything she didn't recognize. Hayden made a display of relishing every bite and complimenting Lourdes on it. Lourdes ate little and seemed preoccupied.

Finally, when she saw that Hayden and John had finished, and Chloe was never going to eat any more, she addressed them.

"Ninos y Señor," she began. She wished she had a better term for them, but to her, that's what they were. She would speak in Spanish, but would keep it very simple so there would be no misunderstanding. "Esta noche es un dia muy especial en todo de hemisphere occidental. En los Estados Unidos se llama Dia de Columbus en Mexico se llama Dia de La Razas." They nodded, the message was so simple even John was able to follow it.

"It's Columbus Day today? Guess I lost track down here. I haven't missed Christmas, have I?" John said, kidding. Chloe burst out laughing, not just for the joke's own sake, but because John had undermined Lourdes's solemn presentation. Chloe regained her composure, and John adopted a feigned contrite look.

Lourdes did not wish to continue the breach of total immersion, but she could not let John's statement go unchallenged.

Wanting to answer in as succinct a manner as possible and be done with it, she said, "It's called day of the races for reasons I'm about to explain." She regrouped, and began again. "En este dia la raza Mexicana nacio y la gente se llaman meztios, asi como yo." *On this day, the Mexican race was born and are called mestizos, like myself.* She gestured with her spread hands turned inward touching her chest.

Chloe, more than Hayden, had followed Lourdes's words. Lourdes had proclaimed herself a mestizo and had acted proud of it. Should she tell Hayden? Did he already know? Would he care?

Lourdes dragged out the dinner with a special dessert, filling time so the students wouldn't go to the festival, but eventually the music outside was so loud that it could no longer be ignored. Lourdes would have liked to close the window, but that would only draw more attention to it. Chloe started humming the music, and Hayden went to the window to listen more closely. Finally Lourdes realized that they couldn't be expected to ignore a festival right outside the window any more than if there had been war raging in the streets.

She looked at their faces and relented, speaking solemnly to them as if they were her own children. "Deben de ir a una fiesta durante su tiempo en Mexico, pero tengan mucho cuidado. Guedanse juntos. Hay muchas borrachos este noche. Entienden." She told them they should attend the festival, but should stay together and watch out for drunks. Hayden nodded knowingly. Lourdes was entrusting him with Chloe's safety, although she was worried about his too-macho attitude. Chloe ran upstairs to get a jacket while Hayden basked in the trust that Lourdes had placed in him. Soon they were both out the door and headed for the plaza. John lingered at the table and saw the concerned look on Lourdes's face.

"Don't worry, I'll head down there and keep an eye on them," he said, but that gave little comfort to Lourdes. John pushed away from the table and headed out the door.

— ~ ~

John started walking toward the plaza but reconsidered. He needed a drink first. When he got to The Gringo, he was surprised to find it closed. He did not know if it was closed for Columbus Day, or that Raza

Day—maybe Jose just wanted the night off. He shrugged and headed back toward the plaza.

Chloe and Hayden had cautiously approached the plaza and stood off at some distance. Hayden found a perch on a low wall and stood, his arms folded across his chest, and observed the native festivities as if he were an anthropologist studying a primitive society. Chloe was a little more adventuresome and moved closer to the action as she swayed to the music.

She turned back to Hayden and said above the music, "Vamos un poco mas cerquita." *Let's go a little closer.*

Hayden, satisfied with his viewing position and distance from the locals, answered, "Usted va." *You go.*

Chloe warily made her way a little closer to the crowd and soon found herself immersed in it. She swayed to the Latin beat and started to let go a little. Hayden had lost sight of her and stood on his toes to get a better view but was unwilling to merge into the brown sea of humanity.

Just as Chloe was starting to feel one with the crowd, a young Mexican man approached her. He had a swarthy face that shone with sweat from dancing.

He doffed his sombrero and made a slight bow before he said politely, "Señorita, quisera bailar."

The word *bailar,* to dance, was familiar to Chloe since her first day of class, so she knew that he had, quite politely, asked her to dance, a normal thing to do at a fiesta. She looked into the boy's expectant face and then turned back find Hayden, but she couldn't see above the surging, joyous crowd. When she looked back, the boy was still there waiting patiently, smiling broadly, his white teeth gleaming.

When she did not reply, he asked again more slowly, gesturing with a sweeping hand to the dancing couples. "Ustede desea bailar, Señorita."

Chloe realized she was on her own, that Hayden was not going to appear, and that she would have to handle this on her own.

She put an innocent look on her face and, with a phony smile, said, "I'm sorry, but I don't speak Spanish." Without further explanation, she turned and made her way through the crowd to resume her place next to

Hayden. She did not say anything but inwardly seethed at Hayden for his lack of concern for her.

John had entered the plaza and found a vendor with a metal cart on wheels, cooled by a large block of ice, and bought himself a Modelo beer—the perfect accompaniment for the evening. John looked to his right and saw three Mexicans looking in his direction. They were short, heavy-set men dressed in jeans and starched shirts unbuttoned to their mid chests. John turned away from them, took a deep gulp of his beer, and pretended to be interested in a young girl performing a traditional folk dance. When he felt he had given it enough time, he looked back and found the men's gaze was still on him. *Drinkers are the same all over the world,* John thought. *What would I do if I were in the States?*

He raised his bottle and, in a voice loud enough to carry over the other noises, called out to them, "Viva Mexico!" When they smiled back at him and raised their bottles, John felt much better, turning up his bottle and draining it in relief. He sought out the beer vendor for a second bottle and then had a bold idea.

"Cervezas para los Señores," he said to the vendor, who removed three cold bottles from his cart, walked over to the men, and gave them the beers.

The men's smiles broadened further, and they raised their bottles to John and said, in near unison, "Gracias, señor!"

They maintained their distance, but there was no longer a glare crossing their space. John casually finished his beer and approached the expectant vendor to buy another round, but the three Mexicans raised their hands and rushed forward, saying as they crossed the short distance, "No, señor."

John paused and watched with some apprehension as they converged on him and repeated, "No, señor."

As they drew closer John got a better look at them. They appeared to be in their mid-thirties, with thick torsos balanced on short, bandy legs. Their sleeves, rolled up just above their elbows, showed the strong arms of men who worked hard for their living. John wondered what they had been so vehemently protesting, when he saw one of the men produce from the tight confines of his back pocket a well-worn wallet, crammed with currency.

They recognized it was their turn to buy. The evening progressed, each man taking a turn to pay, lest their pride be slighted. It wasn't long before John's turn came around again. The men now seemed very interested in John's story. In a mix of his Spanish and their broken English, they managed to converse. Like the intoxicated person who is emboldened to sing, John was eager to speak Spanish and was surprised at how well it seemed to flow. Of course, when he did not know a word, he would merely use its English equivalent with an "o" added to the end, which in his mind Latinized it. He told them of coming from Houston to "estudiar espanol," and that he "vivo en la casa," all at which they nodded in approval.

After a while, the men took John by the arm and led him away from the main square and down a darkened street until they came to an alley. They ushered John down the dark passage until they reached a point about midway.

Even in his inebriated state, John was aware of his situation and considered dropping his wallet and running as maybe the best alternative, but then the three men turned away from him, faced the wall, and began urinating. Relief flowed from John's mind and body as he, too, faced the wall.

Back at their spot, another round was procured from the vendor, who ended up joining their group, and even contributed the next round. The tallest of the three Mexicans reached up and hooked a beefy arm around John. Feeling like he should reciprocate, John raised his bottle and said, "Amigos!"

"Amigos!" said two of the others, raising their bottles as well. But John noticed that the one with his arm on his shoulder had not joined in—rather, John felt the hand on his shoulder tighten, as the muscles on the man's arm tensed. John tensed, too.

An uncomfortable silence followed. John searched the men's faces, but the two not holding John seemed just as perplexed as he was.

The silence came to an abrupt end as the larger man attached to John said, in a grave voice trembling with emotion, "No! No somos amigos." *No, no, we are not friends.*

The intervening seconds passed slowly, and the noises of the fiesta seemed to still, as if they, too, became part of the ensuing drama.

"No somos amigos," the man repeated. "Somos hermanos." *We are not friends, we are brothers.* The tension broke, and all four men embraced one another and, with arms interlocked, walked around the square singing in Spanish.

Hayden and Chloe had given up standing and were now sitting on the wall, watching the parade of departing people pass by. They heard loud, raucous laughter and drunken male voices. Chloe got to her feet and stood back on the wall to clear a path.

"Cuidado, vienen algunos borrachos," she said. *Careful, here come some drunks.*

They stood back as John and some Mexican men passed by with their arms interlaced, singing loudly. Chloe put her hand to mouth to try to suppress her laughter at the sight. Hayden's resentment couldn't be restrained.

"Wouldn't you know it? It's that son of a bitch Sanford," he said.

As they passed by, the Mexicans cried out in unison, "Viva los mestizos!"

John, caught unaware, could only think to respond, "Boo, Columbus!"

16

Chloe sat at the edge of the pool, her feet paddling in the water. She wore a sky-blue two-piece swimsuit that accented her blond hair and blue eyes. She wished she was thinner, but at her age it all looked good. Hayden noticed, John noticed, and she noticed them noticing. Hayden jumped in the pool and dragged her in with him. The water was always cooler than she would have liked, so she shrieked and got out, bundling herself in a towel. Hayden climbed out, and she appraised his body—a frat boy's body, well developed but with a layer of beer bloat.

John, on the other hand, had a hard, lean, sinewy body. Sure, he drank a lot, but he had an edgy energy that seemed to keep the fat off. He was a businessman, he had an office with a secretary, he drank scotch; in other words, he was her father—only sexy. He would be experienced. He would know how to make love to a woman.

Frat boys didn't know squat, in her experience. She had been with plenty of *Haydens* before—they couldn't make a move until they were drunk, and then didn't know where anything was. She looked up at Hayden, but his gaze was elsewhere. When she followed his eyes, they led her to Lourdes, who was standing in the doorway, not doing anything except watching them. She caught John looking in the same direction.

Lourdes had stolen their attention from her without even trying. Chloe wondered if even dropping her top could get them to look away.

Chloe took in her adversary. She was attired in a long dress that came below her knees. She wore a pair of black flats on her feet, not even sandals or open-toed shoes. The outfit couldn't have appeared plainer. Yet there was an understated elegance about it that gnawed at Chloe. *She's just a landlady. Just a Mexican woman running a boarding house. Where does she get her pretensions? What can Hayden possibly see in her?*

Even now, his attention had been diverted from Chloe's bikinied body to Lourdes in her stodgy old dress. Had Hayden seen the lines around her eyes and mouth? *He might be blind, but I'm not*, she said to herself. The woman was old enough to be Hayden's mother. *That's it. She's some sort of Madonna s to him, a Virgin Mother figure.* Chloe crossed her arms. *Well, wake up, Hayden. She's just a middle-aged woman with a middle-aged woman's body.* Chloe looked at Lourdes and wondered why Hayden couldn't seem to see her thick waist, the slight bulge under her chin.

Why doesn't she put on a two-piece and join us? Chloe concluded she must be afraid to compete. She flung her towel on the ground, leaned back, and pushed out her chest. *This is what you're up against, Lourdes*, she thought, and pushed harder.

Lourdes caught Chloe's posturing and harsh glare and turned back and entered the house.

—◦—

The evenings could run cool in San Miguel, and the open window brought brisk, fresh air into the house. Chloe and Hayden were seated at the dining room table, doing repetitious homework out of their workbooks. Hayden had been working steadily for about two hours, while Chloe's attention waned.

Finally, she shoved the workbook away and said to Hayden in a low, conspiratorial voice, "I've got to get out of here."

Hayden looked up and grinned, shrugging his shoulders as if to say, "Why not?"

"How does a cold beer sound to you?" she asked. As if he needed any more encouragement.

"Great," he said enthusiastically.

"Good. Let me handle it," she said.

She left the room and found Lourdes at her desk, sorting through receipts.

"Necesito algunos cosa in la puebla. Siento mas…" she said, fumbling for the right word, "…mas cuidado, sí Hayden va conmigo." *I need some things in town, and I'd feel safer if Hayden came with me.*

"Sí, claro," Lourdes replied, not looking up from her receipts.

"Regresamos en dos horas," Chloe said. *We'll be back in two hours.*

"Bueno. Tengan cuidado." *Good. Be careful.*

Chloe returned to the table, grabbed Hayden, and said, "Vamanos!"

Once they were out the door, Chloe let out a breath that turned to mist in the cool night air.

"We've got two hours," she said, shedding her Spanish for the evening. "Let's make the most of it. You got any ideas?"

"No. Let's just stay out of the touristy joints."

"What does that leave?" she asked.

"I don't know. We'll find something."

They headed toward the plaza, more out of habit than design. Once there, they started working the side streets. They passed a couple of places but rejected them as either too touristy or too dangerous.

It was Chloe who spotted it. They had walked past it when she paused and ran the two words through her head. The Gringo—a strange mix of English and Spanish. She stopped and turned back. Hayden followed. They paused in front, and she was trying to size the place up when an impatient Hayden said, "What the hell," and entered with some trepidation.

Despite the bar's amusing name, Chloe was apprehensive about entering. What she saw took her breath away. It was as if they passed through some sort of portal and had been transported to Anywhere, USA. There were neon signs of popular American beers, all in English, and it was definitely English everyone was speaking. Chloe scanned the faces of the clientele and saw only middle-aged Americans.

"Do you feel like you're in a *Twilight Zone* episode?" Chloe asked. "One of those where they cross over into another dimension?"

"Yeah, weren't they all like that?"

"Yeah, I guess so," she said.

Hayden said, "Maybe this is senior citizen night. Two for one, if you're over sixty."

"Well, at least it's safe," Chloe said. "What do you think?"

Hayden did not want to waste any more of their precious time looking and said, "We're here. Might as well get a drink."

The bar was lined fairly solidly with men, while the tables and booths held what appeared to be old married couples. A jukebox played hits from the sixties, but not too loudly. They took a booth, but when no one came to wait on them, Hayden got up to go to the bar.

"I'm having a beer," he said. "What do you want?"

"Mmmm, a frozen margarita," Chloe said in a coy tone that Hayden found annoying.

Hayden found a gap in the line of men, squeezed into it, and leaned over the wooden bar counter. Jose saw him, moved down the line, and greeted him in only slightly accented English.

"Good evening, what can I get for you?"

"A Coors and a frozen margarita, por favor."

The bartender threw the margarita ingredients into a blender, poured the slushy mixture into a wide, salted glass, popped a bottle of Coors, no glass, and placed the drinks in front of Hayden. Hayden had not had a beer in weeks and immediately tilted the bottle back and took a long draw. It was ice cold, and its effervescence felt good on the back of his throat. He was just about to pull away when he heard a familiar voice.

"Well, I think it's all a bunch of crap. What part of *illegal* don't those liberals understand? And I don't buy calling them 'undocumented workers.' They're illegal. It's not as if they have documents they just forgot and left them at home. They don't have documents because they're *illegal aliens*, period. It's not up for debate." Hayden leaned back over the bar and caught a glimpse of John Sanford at the other end.

Hayden didn't disagree with John's sentiments, but he resented that the loudmouth deemed himself the spokesman for the conservative view. He lingered, not knowing whether he wanted to hear more or not. The dripping margarita glass reminded him that Chloe was waiting, but he took another long draw on his beer before he left the bar.

Chloe saw the look on his face when he returned and wondered what could have gone wrong. Her margarita, in its wide-rimmed, salted glass, looked delectable. She also noted that Hayden's beer was half gone. He placed the sweaty glass before her. She took a sip and looked back at his contorted countenance.

"Do you know who I saw at the bar?" Hayden asked.

Chloe did not wish to provoke him further, so she merely shook her head and murmured, "No."

"It's Sanford. He's at the bar, shooting his mouth off about immigration—like he knows anything."

"Of all the gin joints, in all the towns, in all the world, he had to walk into mine," Chloe said, approximating a man's voice. She let out a small chuckle, but Hayden was unmoved. She was not even sure he got the reference.

"*Casablanca*," she said. "Bogart."

Hayden continued to glare at the backs of the men at the bar.

"Oh, let it go," she finally said.

He did not answer but instead took a final gulp from his beer, got up, and headed for the bar. He got another beer but did not immediately return to the booth. Instead he stood still and eavesdropped on a friendly, lively conversation between Sanford and an older man. Sanford was adamant in his opinions, while the older man was more conciliatory.

When he returned to the booth, his second beer was already half gone. "You can hear him from here," Hayden said.

"What do you care?" She started trying to draw his attention away from the bar and toward her. She slid next to him and put an arm around his waist. "Come on, we're here to relax," she said, although she was anything but relaxed. She was tired of his little-boy tantrums and the way he ignored her.

He lifted the bottle for a drink, but it was already empty, so he nudged her to move.

"Slow down, we've only been here half an hour," she said, consulting her watch.

"Let me out, please," Hayden said, barely controlling his anger.

She sighed and slid over, and he bounded out. When he returned he had two beers, both for him. He worked on them as she played with the slushy margarita. Eventually she finally pushed the glass away from her and announced in a hurt voice, "I'd like to go now."

Without taking his eyes off the bar, he answered, "Not yet."

She slumped back, crossed her arms over her chest, and tried to melt into the soft leather seat. She waited quietly, and when he had drained the second bottle she sat up quickly. "Now?" she asked.

He looked back and gave her a cockeyed smile. His eyes wandered over her body, which she would have welcomed if he hadn't been drunk.

Finally he looked her in the eyes and said, "One more round, then we go. You ready for another?"

She shook her head and scooted over to let him out, lingering at the edge of the booth and reminding him firmly, "Last round."

He nodded back and repeated, "Last round." She let him out, sitting back down on the other side of the booth. She was not in the mood for any physical advances.

He returned with a bottle of Coors in his left hand and a shot of tequila, wedge of lime, and salt shaker in his right. He proceeded to make a production of taking a sip of tequila, licking the salt off his hand, biting into the lime, and washing it down with beer. He repeated the process, but each time he got the procedure out of order. Finally, he finished, got up on tottering legs, and started toward the bar. Chloe stood up to block his path and said, in no uncertain terms, "We agreed. Last round."

"Just going to hit the ol' banos," Hayden said.

She stood aside but kept her eyes on him until he entered the bathroom. When he emerged, she was relieved, and she gathered up her purse to be ready to help him out the door. Everything appeared to be going well until he paused at the bar behind John Sanford and said, in a voice loud enough for everybody to hear, "Hey, Sanford, just so you know, we're leaving so we don't have to listen to you anymore."

John turned and was surprised to see the kids from Lourdes's house. *What the hell are they doing here?* he thought. The kid stood as defiantly as he could on swaying legs. John watched him closely, in case he had any ideas about following up on his statement, but Chloe appeared, spun Hayden around, and said, "We're going." She gave a quick nod to John before she shoved Hayden towards the door.

Later that night as Hayden lain in his bed his head spinning from the alcohol he thought of the woman just down the hall. *Just down, just down the hall, with only a thin wooden door separating us.* Before he could act on his desires the god Morpheus mercifully intervened and sent him into a deep and dreamless slumber.

17

The harsh sound of brass on brass broke the lull of the late afternoon. It resounded through the house, as unexpected as it was unwelcome. It was not a good knock, everyone knew. The young man standing outside was too timid to slam the knocker down again. It was too soon to knock again, but it was harder to do nothing. He took the knocker in his hand and counted to twenty before bringing it down again. He did not know why he was there, but he knew his mission was urgent—the Padre had told him so. He had run all the way, and his breath came in short bursts and sweat gathered on his forehead as he waited.

Inside, Maria had put down her duster and was moving toward the door when she was intercepted by Lourdes, who, with a look and a quick word, told Maria that she was expecting this. When Lourdes opened the door, she faced a teenage boy who was breathing heavily and his face shone with sweat. He was of the age when machismo was of great importance, but he was unable to contain the quiver in his voice as he spoke to the lady.

"El padre quiere que señora venga rapido al orfanatorio." *The Padre asks that the Señora come quickly to the orphanage.*

Lourdes did not speak but nodded back in understanding. She grabbed the sweater she kept on a hook next to the door and slipped it on as she made her way to the street, setting a fast pace to the plaza. There she found a taxi, opened the back door, and motioned for the boy to get in. He hesitated; he had never ridden in a taxi before, only the back of a pickup truck. He had assumed he would be walking back. Lourdes gave him a gentle shove into the taxi, and he slid to the opposite side.

Lourdes gave the driver the address and they started off. As they made their way through the town, the boy looked out his window, hoping to see someone he knew so he could wave to them from the back seat of his taxi.

The taxi pulled to a stop, and Lourdes quickly paid the driver and walked purposefully through the gate. The boy lingered, making the most of the stares of the other children, who were watching him exit the cab. He stopped and spoke to the driver as his friends looked on. All he said was, "Thanks," but he hung his face in the window long enough for the others to wonder what business he might be conducting.

The Padre stood beside Mateo, scripture and holy oil in hand. Sister Guillerma stood off to his side, helplessly watching as he performed the rites. Throughout the procedure, the boy had acquiesced to all that the Padre had hurriedly said, but with little understanding. When the Padre looked up from the book and saw that the boy was looking past him toward the door, he quickly finished his routine and stepped aside, letting Lourdes take his place. He nodded to Sister Guillerma, and they slipped out of the room.

To Mateo, the priest's words had sounded serious but were spoken at him more than to him. He now turned to Lourdes for the truth. He tried to rise to meet her, but when it was apparent that he was too weak, she leaned over the bed and brought her face close to his. The smell of impending death hung over him, but Lourdes pushed past it and kissed the boy on his forehead. It radiated little life force but as her chest brushed against his, she saw his face redden, and a weak wave of warmth passed over him. She pulled back and sat down but carried his hand to her lap and allowed it to remain there while they spoke.

"¿Señora, que esta pasando?" Mateo asked. *What is happening?* "¿Que es lo que dice?" *What did Padre mean?*

Lourdes knew she must deal with the boy gently, but honestly. She let out a sigh and said, "Mateo, el Padre quiero confesarte, por ultima vez porque la hora ha llegado, la hora dela que hablamos de morir." *Mateo, the Padre wanted you to confess your sins one last time. Because the time I told you about has come. You are going to die.*

Mateo looked up at Lourdes with fading eyes. In a gesture meant to bring comfort to him she took his hand in hers and held them against her chest. It was only then that he felt the courage to ask her the question he had not asked even the Padre, "¿Señora, que pasa cuando me muero?" *Señora, what happens when I die?*

Lourdes paused, taking her eyes away from the boy, gazing upward as if seeking guidance. She knew she was on her own—the Padre was incapable of deviating from his script, and, at any rate, he and the sister were gone. Lourdes lowered her eyes until they were level with the boy's and began.

"¿Mateo, recuerda antes que te enfermaste, habia noches cuando te quedabas viendo peliculas en el tele? Pero usted creza demasiado cansado y te quedas dormido en el sofa." *Mateo, can you remember before you took to this bed? Some nights, you would try to stay up late with the Padre to watch those movies on the television downstairs. But you would grow too tired and fall asleep on the coach.*

"Sí," Mateo said. He vaguely remembered that.

Lourdes continued. "Mateo, la hermana te llevaba por la noche de arriba y en la manana te despirtavas en su propia cama. La muerte es como quedarse dormido, solo que esta vez, cuando despiertes vas ha estar en el cielo con nuestro Señor." *Mateo, the sister would come for you in the night and carry you upstairs, and in the morning you would awake in your own bed. Death is like falling asleep downstairs, but this time your heavenly Father will come for you, and when you wake up, you will be with him in heaven.*

Mateo brightened a little, to Lourdes's relief.

She took him in her arm and held his head to her chest. She could feel his shallow labored breaths and knew his end was near. Lourdes then felt Mateo's small hand begin to stir in hers as he desperately pushed his weak hand up until it reached her breast. She let it remain there but then he started to clutch at it. Her first reaction was shock, and she took firm hold of his hand but continued to let it rest against chest. She had forgotten that, despite his immature body, he was on the cusp of manhood—a manhood he would never reach. He would die, never even knowing the feel of a woman's breast. She paused for only a moment and then unbuttoned the top of her blouse, picked up his hand, and slipped it inside her bra, allowing his small hand to pass over her flesh until his fingers grasped her nipple and held on to it for a moment. Then his grip weakened, and he let go. Lourdes gently removed his lifeless hand and placed it back in her lap.

She then leaned over and kissed his pale, dead lips and said softly to him, "Vaya con Dios." She stood, buttoned her blouse, and smoothed out the front of her dress. When she turned, she was facing the Padre and Sister Guillerma, who had come forward. Remembering her job, Sister Guillerma moved to the bed and placed a finger to his neck, checking for a pulse. She gave the Padre a meaningful look, and he descended upon the corpse with more words and gestures. When he finished, the sister pulled the sheet over Mateo and looked around the room to make sure that Lourdes had departed before speaking.

"¿La viste? ¿La viste? Se fue con sus ojos seco totalamente!" she said. *Did you see? Did you see? Her eyes were perfectly dry.* Sister Guillerma wiped her own eyes, as if to emphasize her point. "Toma muy bien la muerte," she said, with a mix of resentment and admiration. *She handles death very well.*

"La muerte si," the Padre said. "Es la vida la que le da problemas." *Death she can handle, it is life that gives her a problem.*

—　—

Lourdes left the orphanage without looking back. The walk back to town would be a long one but she needed the distraction of the repetitive steps and the time alone. The boy had passed on, her role was over. She tried to distract herself by thinking of the things that needed to be done when she got home but the spirit of the boy followed matching her step for step. She was determined not to morn his death. To her it was not untimely tragedy but a blessed transition from a cold harsh world to a place of peaceful repose. Mourn for the living, the dead are no longer in need of it. She believed this and held to it. It was not just her Catholic upbringing but her own life experience. She did not expect fairness in this world. She did not feel herself entitled to happiness or fulfillment. She had expected it once and had seen how quickly it could be snatched away. Life was to be endured with dignity if possible but endured for however long was ordained.

If she had helped ease him through that final struggle then she was not ashamed of what she had done. "I have nothing to confess," she vowed to herself.

18

Lourdes wore the vengeful mask she reserved for late sleepers. She entered the dining room to find Chloe and Hayden, as expected, sitting quietly at the table. Her eyes scanned the table where she found the usual fare: fresh fruit, bread, and, for Hayden, scrambled eggs and a plate of roasted potatoes. A vase of fresh flowers adorned the center. She watched as Hayden piled potatoes and eggs on his plate. It gave her satisfaction to watch him dig into a hearty breakfast—he seemed to appreciate the work that she and Maria put into meals, and he was always eager to experience the local cuisine. The same could not be said for Chloe; the girl never said anything, but Lourdes saw how she avoided new foods and had even brought along her own herbal tea. But for breakfast, everything was as it should be—except for the one place that was empty.

Chloe and Hayden saw the look in her eye and the scowl on her face. They wanted to linger to watch the fireworks, but it was getting late. Chloe liked it when things did not run smoothly for Lourdes. She enjoyed the monkey wrench that was John Sanford. Hayden just found her angry face very provocative.

Lourdes saw them waiting in anticipation and said, "Ninos, es la hora de sus clases." *Children, it's time for class.* Hayden wished she wouldn't refer to him as a child, but he got the message, and he and Chloe gathered up their backpacks and headed out the door.

With them out of the way, Lourdes could turn her full attention to the perpetually tardy Señor Sanford. She didn't bother with Maria this time but strode up the stairs to his room. She knocked firmly, but only once, and then burst into his room, where she found him still in bed. Suddenly she realized how embarrassing it might have been if he'd been undressed. But that was not the case, and she felt justified in pulling the curtains back to let in the harsh, judgmental sunlight.

In a loud and sarcastic voice, she bellowed, imitating his bad accent, "Buenas días!"

John rolled over toward her, his hand shielding his eyes from the sun, and mumbled, "What the hell?"

In a musical but sarcastic tone, Lourdes said, "Levantese!"

John, befuddled, could only say, "Huh?"

Lourdes said, "Get up," without humor, and turned to leave. As she shut the door, she saw John's feet land on the floor. His hands rubbed his face.

Moments later he entered the dining room, reasonably dressed but unshaven. As he sat down and reached for the coffee, she placed a plate of food before him.

Before taking a sip, John looked up and, managing a slight smile, said, "Look, I'm up, I'm eating!" He gulped down the too-hot coffee but left his plate untouched. After looking at his watch, he rose from the table, stuffed in his shirttail, and added, "And I'm going to class like a good boy."

"Su libros," she reminded him before he got to the door.

"Oh, right," he said, grabbing his briefcase from the table.

John came into class late, which was so usual it was beneath the teacher's notice. He tried lurching over the book of the young woman next to him to see the what page she was on, but she, not wanting to be lurched over, held her book up so he could see. This not-so-subtle move was seen by all, and John quickly buried his face in his book. On the blackboard was a list of verbs ending in -er, -ar, or -ir. John stared at them until they started to blur, and his head dropped. He made himself refocus.

Three types of verbs, huh? John thought. *Not too tough to remember. Glad I got here in time to learn it.*

"Pagina trienta y dos," the teacher called out, and everyone started turning pages. The girl next to him preemptively shoved her book in his face, and John found the chapter. It involved food and dining.

At last, he thought, *something I can use!*

On the page were pictures of foods grouped together to form meals, along with various drinks. John stared at the pictures of items of *desayuno*, breakfast, displayed colorfully on the page. There was *pan tostado*, toast, *huevos*, eggs, *tocina*, bacon, *un vaso de jugo de naranja*, a glass of orange juice, and, of course, *cafe*, coffee. John now regretted leaving without eating breakfast—he could really go for some of Maria's roasted potatoes.

He looked at the clock, but it was only ten thirty; he had an hour and a half to endure until lunch. His hunger made it impossible for him to concentrate on Spanish, especially food in Spanish.

"Los platillos del desayuno," Olivia said, pointing in turn to fried eggs, bacon, toast, and coffee.

The class, all except John, responded in unison with, "Huevos, tocina, pan tostados, y café."

Olivia then proceeded with some simple questions. She selected an eager student and asked, "¿Carlo, tomas café?"

Carlos promptly replied, "Sí, yo tome café." *I take coffee.*

She turned to Chloe and repeated the question.

Chloe gave a different answer. "No, no tome café."

This surprised Olivia, and she questioned her further. "¿Usted no toma café?"

"Me prefiere te," Chloe said. *I prefer tea.*

"Muy bien, Chloe," Olivia replied, but inwardly she thought, *Of course you would have to be different.*

Olivia moved on to the foods of *almuerzo*, lunch. With each savory item of food, John could feel his stomach protest. Before him appeared a sandwich, some fried potatoes, a glass of milk, and a plate of cookies. He checked the clock—it was eleven thirty, so he only had twenty more minutes to endure.

Before John could scarf down the textbook sandwich in his mind, Olivia moved on to *la cena*, dinner. John turned the page and looked down at his book. *La platillos del cena*, dinner food, all in brilliant color. Arrayed before his hungry eyes were *la ensalada*, a salad, *bistec*, steak, *papa hornas*, a baked potato, *guisados*, green beans, and *un vaso de vino tinto*, a glass of red wine. The steak looked particularly tasty to John. He was already in the mood for juicy beef, and this really set him off. He glanced at the clock on the wall—it hadn't moved a minute! He felt his mouth fill with saliva and had to catch it before it ran out.

Olivia was walking around the room with an empty plate and asking the students to respond. At this level, she liked to engage the students, and it also helped her evaluate their progress to ask simple questions concerning the proffered imaginary foods. When possible, she used the Spanish version of their names.

"¿Ramon, ustede quiere ensalada?" *Raymond, do you want salad?*

"Sí, yo quiero la ensalada," he responded.

Olivia extended the empty plate and said, "Aqui lo tiene." *Here it is.*

Olivia repeated this drill with random students, using various food items, until she felt the class had learned them sufficiently. She then employed the slightly harder concept of a verb: to like. Unlike English, in Spanish one does not say one likes something directly. Rather, the verb *gustar* means "to be pleasing," so the object pleases the person, instead of the person liking the object. This concept could be difficult for English speakers, so Olivia tried it out with Chloe—one of the more attentive students—first.

"¿Chloe, le gusta el bistec?" Chloe, is the steak pleasing to you?

Olivia expected Chloe to say, "Me gusta el bistec," meaning she liked steak.

Instead, Chloe looked affronted and said, "No, no me gusta el bistec." *No, the steak does not please me.*

Chloe's syntax and grammar were correct, but Olivia was curious about her answer, so she asked, "¿No? Por que?" *No? Why?*

Chloe was ready and replied with pride, "No, me gusta el bistec. Yo soy vegetariano."

Grammatically and factually correct—Olivia couldn't fault that, so she gave Chloe an enthusiastic, "Muy bien." *Of course you would be*, she thought.

She then turned to John and posed the same question so that he should have an easy response. "Juan," she said. "Le gusta el bistec?"

John was in no mood to talk about imaginary food, and he distinctly disliked being called Juan. He sighed and imitated Chloe quickly so he wouldn't forget.

"No me gusta el bistec." He glanced at the clock; it was ten until noon, and the class should be over.

Still, Olivia pressed him further. "No?"

"No!" he said firmly, finally.

She persisted. "¿Por que?"

John didn't want to play the game anymore. He was hungry, and he wanted out of there. He thought back to the last thing Chloe had said, and used it.

"Uh...uh...vegetarian," he said, not even in Spanish.

Olivia didn't want to end on such a bad note, but it was past time to dismiss the class, so she turned away from John and said in a cheery voice, "Es la hora para almuerzo." *It's lunch time.* "Adios!"

John rushed back and arrived at the house ahead of the others. He paced anxiously while Maria took her time setting the table. Aromas wafted in from the kitchen, and he imagined he smelled beef—just what he had been hoping for. Chloe and Hayden arrived and took their places at the table. The young boy Pepe came in, looking as anxious as John for lunch to begin. Maria took no further action and waited for Lourdes. A few more minutes passed, and Lourdes made her appearance and took her seat at the table. Still, no food had appeared. They all sat, and Maria disappeared. John waited impatiently. When Maria did return, it was only to wheel the Old Señor in and then take great care in putting him in a comfortable position at the head of the table.

Is everyone in on the conspiracy to keep me hungry? John asked himself. But finally all were in place, and the meal could begin. Maria left and came back carrying a platter of roast beef with roasted potatoes, a bowl of steaming green beans, and the usual basket of freshly baked rolls. It was just like in the lesson, a dream come true. John looked up from his death-stare on the roast to find that everyone had bowed their heads.

"When did this start?" he muttered. His belief that they were intentionally depriving him of food was strengthened.

Lourdes led the prayer in Spanish. "Señor…"

John bowed his head but kept one eye on the food. When he heard the words, "En la nombre de Padre, el Hijo y el Espirito Santo," he knew the prayer was over. His head popped up a little too quickly, which seemed to draw everyone's attention, and he tried to act nonchalant about eating.

Then Chloe interrupted the beginning of the meal. "Señora, nuestra leccion in la clase esta manana era la almuerzo." *Our lesson this morning was about lunch.*

"Muy bien!" exclaimed Lourdes. "Entonces podemos tiene la almuerzo todo en espanol, no. ¿Estamos de acuerdo?" *Then we can have lunch all in Spanish. Agreed?*

"Que bueno," exclaimed Hayden, "todo en espanol."

That only left John.

Hayden, with barely concealed spite dripping from his voice, turned to face John and said, "De acuerdo, Juan."

John knew the punk was setting him up, but he was in no position to challenge him in front of everyone and so reluctantly said, "Whatever."

And with that, what should have been a meal turned into a continuation of the Spanish class. It began with Lourdes slicing off a large portion of the roast and offering it to John.

"John, quiere la carne asado."

John eyed the meat hungrily, but before he could even nod his acceptance, Hayden spoke up. "Juan no te gusta la carne."

"No?" Lourdes asked, not sure what was going on. "Es verdad?" she said, looking at John.

Once again, Hayden spoke up. "Sí, Juan es vegetariano."

Lourdes gave John a questioning look, but before he could come up with a reply in Spanish, Chloe chimed in. "Sí, es verdad. Juan dijo Señorita Walker que el es vegetariano."

Hayden had control of the bowl of potatoes and asked John, "Quizas, Juan, le gustas las papas?"

"Yeah, I'd like some potatoes," John said.

"Como? *What*? Perdon, no comprendo Ingles," Hayden said. *I don't understand English.* He withdrew the bowl.

Lourdes knew what was going on but had committed to conducing the meal totally in Spanish. It was the total immersion concept she had always maintained, until John Sanford came along. It would be weak of her not to support it. But she did not approve of Hayden's bullying tactics. Looking at John, she could tell that his hunger had been replaced with anger, and that kind of frustration could get out of control quickly. But was she sure Hayden was being such a bully? It was quite an accusation.

Lourdes withdrew the plate and turned toward Hayden. "Entonces, Hayden te gusta la carne?"

Hayden smiled broadly at the large portion meant for the señor and said, "Sí, me gusta mucho." He helped himself.

Next, Lourdes scanned the table and saw Pepe looking up at her hopefully. She smiled at him and asked gently, "Pepe, te gusta la carne?"

Eagerly, he said, "Sí, me gusta mucho."

She passed the plate past John and into the eager hands of Pepe, who responded, "Gracias, señora."

She hoped things would settle down and she could try again with John, but even Pepe was aware that the joke was on John and wanted to join in the fun. He saw the household dog, Cervantes, watching the meal from a distance, and cut off a small sliver of meat for him.

"Cervantes, te gusta la carne," he said, dangling the piece of roast.

At the sound of his name, Cervantes's ears perked up. He ran to Pepe's side.

"Sí, Cervantes, le gusta la carne," Pepe said, and let Cervantes pick the morsel from between his fingers. After gobbling it, the dog looked at him expectantly, clearly hoping for more.

Hayden placed his hand over his mouth and, in a low, growling voice, answered for Cervantes, "Grrrrrracias."

Everyone at the table started laughing uncontrollably. Chloe had to hold her hand over her mouth to keep from spitting out her food. Hayden maliciously directed his laughter at John. Even Lourdes laughed a little. Then she gave Pepe a piercing look, and he shrunk under the table.

But when she saw the cruel look on Hayden's face, her mild mirth turned to anger, and she shouted out, "Basta!" *Enough!*

The room went completely silent. John used the opportunity to reach across the table and grab an unguarded roll.

Chloe and Hayden quickly finished whatever was on their plates and excused themselves. Hayden felt Lourdes's eyes boring into him, and for once he found nothing attractive about it. Lourdes walked around the table, took John's empty plate, filled it up, and put it back down in front of him.

John looked up at her and mumbled, "Gracias." He ate, although he wasn't very hungry anymore.

Everyone had scattered but the Old Señor and John. Lourdes stood back and looked at the two of them. She was upset with Pepe—it was not proper for a boy to make fun of a man like that. She had taken him in, and he had embarrassed her by offending a guest in her home.

Her strongest contempt she reserved for Hayden. He had shown himself for what he was, a bully. Though Spanish had been his weapon, it was no different from teasing someone like the Old Señor, who could not walk. Maybe Mr. Sanford had brought some of it on himself, but it was still bullying, it reflected badly on her, and she would not allow it in her home. The sooner Hayden and that little flirt were out of her house, the better. She looked at the two men at the table and felt pity for both of them.

19

John, Bill, and Jake were now a regular trio at the Gringo. They were comfortable in one another's company and could kid each other with no offense taken. John had started pacing his drinking to get the most out of their conversations together. About eight o'clock, the three became annoyed when the jukebox blared a little louder than they liked. They tried to ignore it and pick up the conversation, but then the loud music's player made herself too apparent. Bill made a well-worn cringe as his wife, Vivian, slung herself over his shoulders and breathed tequila in his ear. Jake, of course, recognized her, and gave her a luke-warm greeting.

"Good evening, Vivian."

"Evening, Jake," she said, not bothering to look at him. She swerved around, saw John, and paused to give him an overt once-over.

"Bill, there's a new man in town, and you didn't tell me?"

Bill reluctantly introduced his wife. "Vivian, this is John." He looked at John warily. "John, this is my wife, Vivian."

John, trying to be gallant, said, "Bill didn't tell me he had such a lovely wife."

Bill cringed again, knowing how Vivian would react.

"No, he'd just as soon nobody knew." She slurred her words through brightly painted lips.

Without taking her eyes off of John, she yelled to the bartender, "Jose, another margarita!"

Jose sensed trouble and looked to Bill for approval. Bill hesitated, then gave reluctant nod. Jose went to work.

Drink in hand, Vivian turned to John and said, "Now, don't you move." It was an order.

She backed away to the jukebox and made her selection, all the while maintaining eye contact with John. The song "Tequila" blared forth, and Vivian made her way back, swiveling her hips seductively along the way. Her hand beckoned him.

John looked pleadingly at Bill, who set down his glass and forcefully led Vivian out the door—but too slowly to keep the whole bar from hearing her cry out, "Can't I have any fun in this stupid town?"

20

John came down at a reasonable time for breakfast, and took his usual seat next to Chloe, across from Hayden.

"Buenos días, John," Chloe said, fake-cheery.

John lowered his newspaper and replied politely, "Buenas días, Chloe." He pulled the paper back up and waited on Hayden to chime in.

"Buenos días, *Juan*," Hayden said. He was eating another breakfast fit for a lumberjack, while Chloe drank her herbal tea and nibbled on whole wheat toast. Maria had figured out everyone's breakfast habits and cooked to suit them. Chloe watched her weight and ate lightly, concentrating on the fresh fruit. John liked black coffee and the fluffy rolls with strawberry jam.

That morning, John had brought with him a copy of *USA Today* and read it while he sipped his coffee. He could feel Hayden and Chloe reading the part facing them, basking in the English. John finished his coffee and got up, leaving the paper on the table on purpose. As soon as he had left, they both reached for the paper, but before they could get their hands on it, John returned and snatched it away. They looked at each other in embarrassment and turned back to their meals.

John arrived only slightly late and quietly took his seat in the back of the classroom and tried to follow as Olivia made an announcement. "Estudiantes, hoy es el ultimo dia para dos de nuestros estudiantes. Hayden and Chloe. Volveran a los Estadios Unidos manana." *Students, this is the last day for two of our students, Hayden and Chloe. They return to the United States tomorrow.*

John perked up when he heard their names. He looked around and then turned to the young girl at the desk next to him and asked, in English, "What's going on with Chloe and Hayden?"

The girl gave him a dirty look for not even trying to speak Spanish. She answered him quietly, also in English. "They're going home tomorrow."

"No shit?" John said. The girl scowled at him again.

— —

Lourdes would have liked that evening's farewell dinner to be a celebration, but things had not been the same since the bullying incident, and the mood at the table was subdued. John wore a dress shirt, jacket, and smug grin for the occasion. He, at least, was celebrating Hayden's departure. Maria had cooked a special dinner, the kind that had caused Chloe to lose five pounds during her stay. Hayden, on the other hand, looked as if he had gained weight during his month.

Lourdes came down wearing a white blouse, a festive skirt, and her warmest smile. When she entered, Hayden felt it, hard, in his heart. Even though there was never a possibility of anything between them, he regretted that he would never see this magnificent woman again.

"Buenas tardes," she said, cheerful, determined that their stay would end on a high note. She didn't want to be remembered for her outburst at lunch.

Chloe, always entertained by fake emotion, pulled an unconvincing sad face and said, "Estoy muy triste, por que esta es la ultima dia con tu, nosotros madre en Mexico." *I am very sad, because this is our last day with you, our Mexican mother.* If calling her their mother was meant as a slight, it was lost on Lourdes. After all, she was their guardian while they were in her home, and she often referred to them as *ninos.*

Hayden's feelings were very real—he despised the thought of leaving her alone with Sanford.

He wanted to say something memorable, but all he could come up with was, "Gracias, por todo amables a nos durante nos estancia." *Thank you for your kindnesses to us during our stay.* He had bought her a gift—a silver necklace that he hoped would make it impossible to forget him—but he didn't want to present it in front of Chloe or Sanford. The small box stayed in his pocket.

John could read the pain written across his face and almost felt sorry for him. He could see how a young guy like Hayden could have a crush on the older woman. *Too bad, kid. Tomorrow you'll be forgotten,* John thought. John wanted to take a shot at the kid in Spanish while he was down, but he couldn't come up with the right words, so his gloating would have to go unexpressed.

Lourdes could feel the tension in the room rising and was relieved when Maria entered the room carrying brightly painted ceramic pots. The exotic scent of cinnamon and cumin filled the room. Chloe sniffed the air appreciatively, but really thought, *This is the last time I'll be subjected to this culinary torture.* In her mind, she was already planning her first meal back home.

Hayden wasn't so picky. "Mmm," he said, beaming at Maria, "la aroma es muy sabrosa." Maria did not acknowledge his compliment. She was not after the approval of Hayden or Chloe and cooked the way she did out of pride.

Lourdes left the room and returned with a bottle of red wine and four glasses. It was the first alcohol that any of them had seen in the house. She poured four glasses, though she didn't know if Chloe the vegetarian also eschewed alcohol. When everyone had a glass she held hers up and proposed a toast.

"A nuestros paises, Los Estados Unidos y Mexico, buen vecinos siempre." *To our countries, the United States and Mexico—good neighbors always.*

John, in a rare moment of good taste, raised his glass and said, "A Mexico."

"A Los Estados Unidos," Lourdes said, smiling.

Hayden fumed, wishing he'd thought to toast Mexico.

Lourdes took each plate and filled it according to the individual's taste, starting with Hayden; he got an extra-large serving. Chloe, who wasn't going to eat it anyway, only received a nominal portion. For John and herself, she dished out moderate portions.

Hayden always forgot himself around food and began shoveling it in without waiting for anyone. Weight issues loomed in his future. John had an appreciation for a well-prepared meal, but tonight he was distracted, and ate absentmindedly. Chloe used her bread to push food around, and in the end did at least eat the bread. Hayden had seconds of a corn dish similar to Italian polenta, mixing it in with sauce from the chicken. John saw that Hayden's glass was empty and poured him a second. *Let the kid drown his pain in wine,* John thought.

At the end of the main course, Maria brought in a cake with a marzipan filling. It was so delicious, even Chloe had a large portion. Hayden took a second large helping, and John poured the remaining wine into Hayden's glass, trying to bring attention to Hayden's gluttony.

— ⁓

The next morning was a Saturday, and Lourdes waited in the doorway for the driver to take Chloe and Hayden to the airport. She had insisted that Maria be there with her to say goodbye to the students. Chloe came down gushing and feigning sorrow that their wonderful friendship was coming to an end. She spoke fluently in Spanish that she must have composed the night before.

"Lourdes, no puedo nunca agradecer para todo hacer para me. Ha hacienda ambos amiga y madre a me. No voy nunca olividas tu." *I can never thank you for all you have done for me. You have been both a friend and a mother to me. I will never forget you.*

This was probably the most dramatic, and least sincere, of the countless goodbyes Lourdes had been through in her business. She had seen some girls tear up, but never as melodramatically as this. She was relieved when she heard the driver pull up.

Hayden appeared with his bags, proceeded past them, and delivered both his and Chloe's bags to the driver. When he turned back he had a sour look on his face that he did not try to disguise.

Lourdes leaned forward to give him a brief hug, but he pulled her closer and held her tightly, surreptitiously pressing a small box into her hand. Lourdes was caught off-guard and could only mouth a quick thanks to Hayden before secreting the box in her dress pocket.

John broke the moment when he appeared at the bottom of the stairs, although he didn't move to join the group. He stood on the bottom step, casually dressed in tan slacks and a golf shirt.

His manner was as casual as his outfit when he said in English, "So long, kids."

Chloe practically jumped up and down as she waved goodbye. "Adios, John!" she cried.

Hayden, having released Lourdes, turned to face him.

He said as coldly as he could muster, "So long, Sanford." He then turned back to Lourdes, staring at her longer than was comfortable. Eventually he tore his gaze away, and headed for the taxi. "Goodbye, Lourdes," he said in English using her first name. He slid into the back seat of the taxi and resumed his stare at Lourdes through the taxi's window.

Chloe got in after Hayden her arm outside the window moving furiously until the car was out of sight.

Lourdes watched until she saw the car turn the corner. Maria, not caring about either departing boarder, had already left. Lourdes, still in the doorway, found that she had been tightly clutching the door handle, and she let it go, inadvertently letting a long sigh escape her lips.

John went to the table and poured himself a cup of coffee. "It must be a relief to have that pair gone," he said.

Lourdes responded too quickly to be convincing. "No! I found them delightful." Exhausted, she sat at the table and poured herself some coffee, too.

"Are you serious?" he asked incredulously.

She shrugged as if to say, "Why not?"

"They didn't get on your nerves just a little bit? Chloe's phony sweetness?"

Lourdes didn't answer, which John took as a yes.

"Yeah, I thought so," John said. "And the way that kid Hayden was always mooning over you!"

"Mooning?" Lourdes was unfamiliar with the term, but she could infer its meaning. "Please!" she said, indignant.

"You weren't aware?" John leaned back and took an appraising look at her before saying, "No, maybe you weren't, but it was obvious to everyone else." He shook his head in disbelief, and enjoyed a chuckle at Lourdes's obvious discomfort.

Lourdes started to say something in her defense, but thought better of it. "If you'll excuse me," she said, "I have things to do." She ducked into the closest room, the kitchen. Maria looked up to see what she wanted, but Lourdes waved her off and sat down. With her forefinger pressed against her lips and the gift box pressing against her thigh, she tried to think it through.

Maria left Lourdes with her thoughts and, touching the pocket of her apron, remembered the letter she had been given earlier in the morning, before all the goodbyes. It had been delivered by one of the local boys and was addressed to John Sanford, in a woman's handwriting. She took it into the dining room, where she found John lingering over his coffee. She stood before him, and when he looked up, she thrust the letter at him and left without a word.

John held the letter out and looked it over for a while. *Who could this be from?* he wondered. He looked around to assure himself of his privacy and then, taking a butter knife from the table, slit the envelope open and removed a single folded sheet. In a sweeping longhand, it read:

> *John,*
> *I am home, and very much alone, every night after seven. I could use some*
> *attention, how about you?*
> *V*

John put the letter back in the envelope and tapped it against his cheek as he pondered its contents.

21

John entered the Gringo a little after seven and found Bill at his regular stool, which confirmed what Vivian had written. John moved down to the opposite end of the bar, putting as much distance between him and Bill as the place allowed, but Bill looked into the mirror behind the bar and saw John anyway. Bill wondered if John was avoiding him over the embarrassing episode with Vivian and felt it was up to him to say something first. He got up and made his way over to John, who was hunched over his drink, pretending not to notice Bill.

There was an awkward moment between the two men until Bill said, "Sorry. About last night."

"Last night?" John said, playing ignorant.

"You know...with Vivian," Bill said.

"Oh, that?" John said. "That was nothing! Don't give it a second thought." As he spoke, he eyed the clock above the bar; it read 7:20.

"That's kind of you to say," Bill said. "She hasn't always been that way." He paused, reflecting, then continued. "She was my secretary before I retired. I married her after my wife died. I guess I was lonely. It was a mistake to think she would be content down here." He stopped again and then smiled, obviously lost in happy thoughts of the past.

"My first wife and I ran across this place while on a vacation," Bill said. "It became our dream to retire here. We never had children, so there was nothing keeping us back home."

His smile faded. "She died before we ever made it back. I thought I could just substitute Vivian into my plan, but..." He sighed. "You just can't give someone else your dream."

John glanced at the clock again—it was 7:28. He thought about slipping away. Instead, he said, his tone a little harsher than he meant, "No, Bill, it was probably a mistake to try."

Before John could come up with an excuse to leave, Bill picked his narrative again. "There are times, like last night, when I think I should just let her go her own way." He swirled his drink. "But she's made friends, she's making a life for herself. It's just that she's still too young for this life. Too young for me."

John felt bad for him. *It's his fault, though,* he thought. He looked at the clock again. *What am I waiting for?*

"Funny thing," Bill said, and took another drink. "Funny thing is, despite all the problems, I still love her. Very much."

John wished he had left already and not heard that last part. One more time, he looked at the clock, which said it was 7:35.

Bill looked chagrined and said, "John, am I keeping you from something? Got somewhere to be?"

John's guilt won him over. He sighed in resignation, extended his empty glass to Jose, and settled back on his stool. "No, old buddy," he said, "I've got nowhere to go."

"Anyway," Bill said, "John, old boy, I've been meaning to talk to you about something else. Having a little party at my place tomorrow night, mostly Americans. Good chance for you to meet the gringos who haven't passed through here yet."

"Sure, why not? Be nice to talk to someone besides you for a change," he said with a smile.

Bill smiled too, and wrote his address on a bar napkin. "Say, about eight o'clock?" he said.

― ⁓

Monday morning, a school day, John came down for breakfast, and instead of the usual meat and eggs, there were only coffee and rolls. Maria wheeled the Old Señor in and was soon joined by Lourdes.

"Pretty sparse setting for breakfast, now that the kids are gone," John said, just to be troublesome.

Lourdes said, "I'm surprised you even noticed. If there's something more you would like, I'll have Maria prepare it."

"No, coffee and rolls are fine with me. I'm not a growing boy, you know," he said, emphasizing Hayden's absence. "Well, I'm off to class."

Glad to see the last of those two, John thought as he made his way down the street. *Maybe now Lourdes will let up on the total immersion thing.*

He arrived at class, not late for once. He settled into his chair and looked to his right. The snooty girl who didn't like to share answers with him had moved across the room. In her place sat a new girl. She was tall, thin, blond, and looked Scandinavian.

John smiled. She smiled back. Things were really looking up.

― ⁓

Lourdes had received a very polite formal invitation from Bill. They had met at some town meetings where he tended by default to unofficially represent the American community. It was her practice to decline, equally politely, but this time she wavered. For one, she had already heard from Olivia, who wanted her to go. Together they represented the bridge between the American and local community, and that gap seemed at the moment to be growing wider. The two should work together, Olivia had said, and once she put it in the form of a duty, Lourdes found it hard to decline. She should be working toward a greater cultural exchange.

Lourdes was one of the few locals who spoke any social English. The waiters, the shopkeepers, the hotel personnel—all spoke a sort of commercial English, and they spoke it very well, but it was limited in scope to their business needs. Only she and Olivia could speak about abstract thoughts with any proficiency. Not that the conversations would get too deep or philosophical. At most, there could be a discussion of a book or movie popular back in the US.

She would be uncomfortable the entire evening. She had nothing in common with the women who regularly attended these parties. She didn't follow the current American movies, didn't know who the movie stars were, and thought it unlikely they would care about Mexican cinema.

— ⁓

A bare sliver of a moon had made its way above the hilly horizon surrounding San Miguel, casting no light and holding no promises. Lourdes was in an ambivalent mood as she climbed the stairs. She was going to a party tonight, but her concerns were more than just what to wear.

At least it was at Bill Martin's house. She had met him on several occasions, and of all the American residents, she found him the least objectionable. When they spoke, he always complimented her English and apologized for his lack of Spanish. He was considerate and respectful of local ways and made an effort to be part of the community. His wife, Vivian, on the other hand, was shrill and vulgar and everything the locals disliked about Americans. But that was all the more reason to go, to help smooth local-expat relations. Maybe she could reach the woman.

Lourdes crossed the threshold to her bedroom and closed the door quietly behind her. *The things one does for friends,* she thought. She opened the closet door and stood back to consider what to wear. "Ay dios," she sighed, tucking back a strand of hair that had escaped the chignon at the back of her neck and fallen across her eyes. "What to wear?" she muttered.

It wasn't that parties were foreign to her. She went to fiestas at the church and the occasional community celebration in town. But this was a different sort of party. There would be Americans there. She took out the red tiered skirt and embroidered blouse she usually wore to parties but immediately put them back. That was an ensemble she would wear among her friends—her people. The Americans would see that outfit and think that she had on a colorful "costume" and say, "How charming!" She would be the token local color.

She reached in the closet and took out a watercolor sundress of periwinkle and soft aquamarine. Its silk organza skirt flowed when she walked, and when a breeze exhaled in the summer nights, it floated in a cloud around her. The layers of fabric made her look like a dancer in a lyrical ballet and made her feel magical and young again. But the days were getting shorter now, and that dress was for summer. With regret, she hung it back in the closet.

What to wear? she thought, puzzled. The women there would be in their cashmere wraps, palazzo pants, silk blouses, and designer shoes. She would feel like a poor relation—or worse, like a primitive native—next to them. It had been so long since she had occasion to wear anything sophisticated. *When was the last time?* she wondered.

Then she remembered. Several years ago, Ernesto wanted to meet with some men regarding the ranch. He wanted to impress them, so he told her to go out and buy a dress. She knew she was to be shown off like a prize pony, and she wasn't happy about it. But it had been the dress, or suffering the consequences. So she went out and bought a simple black dress. At the time, she thought the dress was a bit dowdy—maybe even matronly, but she didn't care. The dress hadn't been for her. But where was it?

Lourdes pulled clothes aside and almost in the very back, next to some shawls that she kept when her mother passed away, was the dress. She pulled it out of the closet and took off the plastic garment bag that had covered it all these years. She held her breath. It might have fallen apart. Could it possibly still fit? Lourdes lifted the dress up for a close look, and, surprisingly, it was still in excellent shape. She slipped off her blouse and skirt and slid the dress over her head.

The dress was made of black silk crepe, and had a surplice bodice that draped across her breast, forming a lovely V below her neck and giving the slightest glimpse of her cleavage, which had blossomed in the years since the dress was first purchased. The fabric attached at the sides, accenting her waist and flowing smoothly over her hips in a curved line. Perhaps it was slightly snugger than before, but it would still work. The slim sleeves traveled down her arms to her delicate wrists. Somehow, the dress didn't look dated anymore. It seemed to suit the woman she was now more than the woman who had bought it. She had grown into it.

In an ancient box, she found her mother's opal necklace and earrings and put them on. Quickly, Lourdes brushed on some mascara and some ruby lip gloss and stood back. *I hope this will do,* she thought. But something still was not right. Her face looked severe with her hair in the bun. She reached back and pulled the combs from her hair, which fell into a soft cascade of curls and caressed her shoulders. With her fingers, she brushed her thick hair and stood back from the mirror again. *This is better,* she thought, slipping on some heels she had bought last Easter. *Hopefully, I'll fit in and not be noticed.*

That wasn't going to happen. She looked stunning.

— —

John had little to choose from in his sparse wardrobe. He would wear his gray suit with a black, tight-fitting tee. It was a hip, young man's look—too young for him, but he didn't think of himself as middle-aged, nor did he think about how to dress appropriately. He could see it in others, though, especially those who missed the mark by miles.

John had been thinking about age more often these days, mostly regarding the age gulf between him and the women he dated. Different music was part of it, sure, but it was more than that. In truth, he missed the relationship he had had with his ex-wife. It was real, but they had wanted different things. She had eventually gotten what she wanted. He hadn't yet. It had stung, but windows of opportunity don't last long, and he figured she was right to move on. He shook off the still-painful memories and turned back to the problem at hand.

Why am I so worried about how I look? He wondered. *It's just gonna be the crowd from the Gringo.*

He smoothed out his coat and glanced in the mirror as he passed. He considered changing into the white dress shirt he was saving for his return trip. He leaned forward and took another look. He still had it. The T-shirt would stay. He looked good, he reassured himself. His body was still lean and hard, and salt-and-pepper hair wasn't a bad look. *Yeah, you got this,* he thought, giving himself an extra splash of cologne.

Downstairs was quiet. The dinner table had not been set. He did not see Lourdes, either, only the Old Señor and Maria. When Maria saw that he was dressed to go out, she assumed he did not want supper but asked him anyway, speaking very slowly. "¿Quieres algo para la cena?"

John knew the basic verb *querer*, to want. The inflection made it a question, and the context indicated that *cena* meant meal. He smiled at her and the old man and said simply, "No, gracias." He headed for the door and turned back before exiting to say, "Adios."

He had the directions Bill had written out for him at the bar. They started at the Gringo, so John went that direction. The cool night air invigorated him, and he found he enjoyed walking in San Miguel. *Nice to not have to get the car out to go anywhere,* he mused. He stopped in front of the Gringo, reoriented himself, and set out for Bill's house. It was a several-block walk, but still a comfortable walk.

John could hear voices, all speaking English, as he knocked at the front door, which was answered promptly by a middle-aged woman in a low-cut dress that revealed an overly tanned chest and sagging cleavage. She had a drink in her hand, and it was obviously not her first.

She gave John a long look up and down and said, "Come in, handsome."

John, ignoring her come-on, said, "I'm John Sanford, pleased to meet you." He extended his hand and she took it, holding on a bit longer than necessary.

She gave a coy smile and said, "I'm Beverly Watson." John recognized the last name—it belonged to one of the regulars at the Gringo. As gently as he could, he excused himself and entered the house.

He found that Bill's house, a modern reproduction of a traditional Mexican house and constructed to blend in with the rest of the neighborhood, had all up-to-date facilities on the inside. The decorating scheme was more modern art deco than what the traditional Mexican exterior indicated, but it was tastefully done. It was centered around a large patio—its glass doors were open, letting people and evening air flow through the space.

He surveyed the room. The crowd was definitely middle-aged and American. He spied Bill and was headed in his direction when he heard Vivian's drunken cackle. John wanted a drink before he would have to talk to her, but unfortunately she was hovering around the makeshift bar—a countertop that opened into the kitchen. He slipped around to the kitchen side and surveyed the liquors. Tequila, vodka, and medium-grade bourbon, along with bottles of red and white wine—but no scotch. Bourbon was an adequate substitute. As soon as he had it poured over ice, he felt more sociable. He took a long drink and surveyed the room again, less critically this time. Before the ice in his drink had melted, he finished it and made himself a second. Armed with one drink in hand and one in his belly, he ventured into the living room to greet Bill and get talking to Vivian out of the way. He took another drink from his glass, and when he looked up he saw that Olivia Walker had spotted him and was on her way over. She wore a flattering dress, and he realized that, out of the classroom, she really was an attractive woman. But she would insist on him speaking Spanish, so he took another drink and mentally prepared.

"John, buenas noches," she said. "¿Como esta usted?"

John had been expecting that question, and had a response ready. "Muy bien, y ustede?" He immediately put his glass to his face, hoping to cut off further conversation, but she continued as if he were taking a lesson.

"Bien. ¿Tu gustas la fiesta?" *Fine. Are you enjoying the party?*

He answered, "Sí, sí," and left it at that.

He felt like that should be enough, but she did not let up.

"¿Usted conoces Bill and Vivian?" Once again, a question that he could answer.

"Sí." He nodded at her and made to leave, but she placed a hand on his arm, ready to speak again. It was starting to feel like a battle to him, keyed up as he was with the alcohol and tension. He waited for the next verbal assault.

"¿Como los conoces?"

He replayed the short sentence in his head and said some of the words out loud, but he couldn't get it. She stared expectantly at him, which made him angry—he hadn't come here for a lesson. "Aren't you ever off the clock?" he asked. "This is a party, not your Spanish class."

Olivia knew that she had no control over a student outside of class, and with John, little control in class as well. Still, she wanted to make her point.

"John, you should try to speak Spanish all the time while you're here. It's not good to spend too much time with the Americans. Remember, total immersion."

John nodded and said, "Right. Excu-sie *moi*." He walked away.

"That's French!" Olivia yelled at his retreating figure. She sighed, then went to the bar.

John wanted some fresh air and went to the patio. He exhaled and inhaled deeply, the cool night air reviving his spirits. Bill, who had seen but not heard his encounter with Olivia, was on his way over. It was nice to see his familiar, English-speaking face.

"You didn't warn me the schoolmarm was going to be here," John said, gesturing at Olivia.

"Who, Olivia Walker? Lovely lady, don't you think?"

"Yeah, well, you don't know her like I do. Any more surprises? You haven't flown in my mother or ex-wife, have you?"

Bill laughed heartily, though he couldn't understand how he could equate Olivia with his mother. "No, you're safe here," he said. "Relax. Don't wander off, though. There's someone I want you to meet."

Bill moved away and John directed his attention to his drink. He turned away to check out a younger woman in tight-fitting pants, and when he turned back he and Lourdes were shocked to be facing each other.

"John, I'd like you to meet a true native of San Miguel, Lourdes de Madrid," Bill said.

Lourdes did not let on that they knew each other. "Mucho gusto," she said. *Much pleasure.* She didn't offer her hand.

John knew the proper response from class and replied, "El gusto is mio." *The pleasure is mine.*

"Well, you two seem to speak the same language, so I'll just leave you to get acquainted," he said, pleased with his double entendre before moving off.

John, who had just gotten free from one of his female tormentors, was not in the mood for the other. She did look gorgeous, though, which caught him off guard. She saw him looking, and they both stood there, surprised and embarrassed.

They both held their breath until Bill was out of earshot.

"I didn't know you were going to be here," he said, in accusatory tone he did not intend.

"Is there something wrong with me being here?" she asked.

"No, it's just," John said, wondering why he had even said that, "it's just that I never knew you went out." Once again, his words came out wrong. He wished he could take them back, but she cut him off. She had a temper when she felt she had been insulted and was about let him have it.

"Funny thing," she said, "I can't recall seeing you at the dinner table in a while—and that derelict who staggers into the breakfast room for coffee and aspirin in the morning, is that you?"

John was mad but still tried to help the situation. "Okay, I'm probably not the perfect guest," he said, "but I'm used to staying in hotels and not having to please the staff."

"The *staff*!" Lourdes spat the word back at him.

Nitpicking, John thought. He tried again. "Well, maybe not staff, but pleasing my...hostess?"

Lourdes was not mollified. "Please? *Please?* If you ever pleased anybody but yourself. That would be the day."

John, through trying to avoid conflict, said, "Well, I think you know what I mean." He was angry, and her black dress wasn't helping, either. Multiple kinds of passion mixed and churned inside him.

"Yes, unfortunately I know exactly what you mean." Lourdes took a moment to compose herself and noticed some people were staring at her, including Bill, who was on his way over.

"Is everything all right here?" he asked.

"Everything is fine," John spat. "Just having a squabble with the ol' landlady. Didn't I tell you before, Bill? This is the woman I'm living with here in San Miguel."

Lourdes did not care for his wording's implications and felt it necessary to explain. "He is a student staying with us. There are others—well, *were* others, they're gone now, but…"

She turned to John for help, and he gave her a smug smile and finished her sentence. "It's like she says. Just the two of us."

Lourdes gave John a hard stare. When he dared to smile back at her, she turned and left without another word.

"What got into her?" he asked, feigning innocence.

"John, don't you know a classy woman when you meet one?" Bill said, a frown creasing his forehead. "No, maybe you wouldn't."

John rolled his eyes. "Fine. I'll go after her," he said reluctantly.

John wound his way through the guests and was out the front door in time to catch up with Lourdes. Bill followed behind at a distance. In the street, John caught up with Lourdes and grabbed her by the arm. "Lourdes, wait," he said.

She jerked to a stop and looked at his hand on her arm like it was a big, hairy spider. "First," she said, "I would appreciate it very much if you would immediately release my arm."

John did as he was told. Lourdes continued, saying, "Secondly, Señor Sanford, I have not given you permission to address me by my Christian name. In Mexico, we consider manners very important. We take the role of host very seriously. You are a guest in my house, and I will continue to show you every courtesy for the remainder of your stay. But I am through getting you out of bed every morning, seeing that you get to class on time, and that you eat. From now on, if you want, you can stay out all night, sleep all day, and eat junk at that bar you go to."

She folded her arms. "You're never going to learn Spanish anyway, Mister Gringo Businessman. You'll return to the United States as ignorant of our language and as unappreciative of our culture as when you came." She finished and stared at him until he looked away. Only then did she walk away into the night.

When she was down the street, Bill stepped out of the shadows and stood beside John.

"Can you believe that?" John said.

Bill sighed and thought for a moment before saying, "Yeah, I can believe it. It's true. We come down here for the climate, the cost of living, the slower pace of life, but we shun the people and their culture. We don't even bother to learn the language. Only a few people like Olivia Walker can bridge the gap between communities." Bill paused, as if wondering whether to go on. "But, John, I've never insulted anyone here like you've just done, and especially someone like Lourdes de Madrid."

"Oh, so you're taking her side?" John said. "And what do you mean, 'someone like Lourdes de Madrid'?"

Bill didn't wonder whether to talk this time. "Man, if you don't know, I can't tell you." He turned his back and left John standing in the street.

⚊ ⚊

John watched Bill walk away and resolved not to accept further hospitality from him. He returned to the house and set his nearly full drink on a wrought iron porch table and left in the direction of the plaza. He wandered aimlessly, his head down, rehashing events. When he looked up, he found his feet had taken him to the Gringo, which seemed like a refuge.

He found the place devoid of regulars. Scattered around the room, sitting at tables, were what he took to be day tourists. The men wore guayabera shirts and drank bottles of Modelo beer, and their wives drank frozen margaritas out of wide-rimmed glasses lined with salt. At the bar,

John perched himself on a stool. Jose had seen him come in and had a scotch with soda and ice ready for him.

As John took a sip from his drink, Jose said, "Sorry, Mr. Sanford, everyone is at a party tonight." If Jose sensed John's inner turmoil or wondered why John wasn't at the party, he didn't say.

"Good. I prefer it that way," John said.

John didn't know who he was madder at—Lourdes or Bill. No, it was Bill. Bill was supposed to be his friend. *Who is he to lecture me?* John thought. *Couldn't hack it in the US anymore, so he hides in Mexico? Some people just can't handle the pressure. Poor baby.*

And to someone like Bill, this town would be a nice refuge, away from the fast pace and high demands of America. John thought Bill wouldn't last a week in the land of Internet and free trade.

The ice had melted in his drink, making the scotch weak. He decided not to order another and pushed off his stool and made his way out the door. He walked unconsciously, his mind replaying Lourdes's furious tirade against him. He was confused by the mix of emotions it had generated in him. He had felt her unbridled passion and it had felt...? What? What was it he had felt?

It was then that he found himself back at the plaza. He was not sure what had brought him here, but he accepted it without question. He sat on a bench across from the cathedral and became transfixed by a sad sliver of moon as it passed across the black sky. He watched it until it transected the church's cross that pierced the sky. At the point when the two symbols merged, one of nature, the other of the spirit, he felt their combined forces focus on him. He felt powerless as they held him in their grasp. Eventually the moon moved past, and he felt released. But more than that, he felt that he had been forgiven, and that he was permitted to leave.

22

*L*ourdes had not slept well. The horrible scene from the night before had played over and over in her head. After the last dream, she preferred not to fall back asleep. Neither did she wish to get up. She just lay there and thought over the last two weeks.

The fuse had been lit the first night. She couldn't remember the last time she had been so upset, so totally out of control. Then she remembered. It would have been with Ernesto. She did not want to revisit those days, so she pushed herself onto her feet and rose from the bed. Who else but a pig-headed man could get her to act that way?

But this morning, it was not John Sanford she was mad at. It was herself. How had she let things get so out of control? Though she didn't expect much from John Sanford, she set higher standards for herself. She felt ashamed for the first time in many years. He had brought chaos into her ordered life. But it wouldn't last forever—at most, he had two weeks left.

Anyway, she was on her feet. That was a beginning. She did not feel like going downstairs, but she had responsibilities besides her guest. There was Maria, and the Old Señor. She should at least check on them. She put on a robe over her nightgown. She did not bother with makeup and ran the brush through her hair just enough to get it out of her face.

Maybe something good had come out of last night's fiasco. She had put him on notice. There would be no more babysitting him. He was on his own. She would let him sleep all day if he wanted, and if he wanted to return home early, she would gladly refund him the balance of his rent. She had not heard him come in last night, so he would probably be sleeping late. His class attendance would now be Olivia's problem. When she thought about it, it should always have been Olivia's problem.

Lourdes was preoccupied with these thoughts as she made her way down the stairs, her feet flopping in her house shoes. As she passed through the dining room to the kitchen, she stopped in her tracks. John Sanford was sitting at the dining room table, dressed, groomed, and looking up at her. His textbook was open on the table.

She stood motionless for a moment and then reached down to make sure her robe was fully closed. Her hand went to her face and then to her hair, which she tried to brush into some order with her fingers. John looked at her expectantly. She opened her mouth to speak, not sure where she was going to start, but he spoke first.

"Señora, I think—no, I'm sure—I need to apologize for last night," he said.

She was stunned but recovered quickly. "No, señor, it is I who needs to apologize. I had no right to speak as I did to a guest in this house. I hope I did not cause you any embarrassment before your friends."

"No, not all," John said. "I've had some time to think, all night in fact, and I—"

"No, you need not say anymore," Lourdes interrupted. "Please, accept my apology. Excuse me."

John had more to say. "No. Wait, I want to—" but before he could get it out, Lourdes had disappeared into the kitchen. Safely behind the oak door, she finally took a breath. She poured a cup of coffee from the pot on the stove and slumped into a kitchen chair, where she would wait out Señor Sanford. She didn't like feeling trapped in her own house, hiding in the kitchen, and wanted to go back out and regain control, but she simply wasn't up for it. Her disheveled hair and robe put her at a disadvantage, and she promised herself she wouldn't be caught like that again.

John was frustrated not to be able to speak his mind but also knew she needed her space. He closed his book and thought. The Lourdes he just saw looked so different from the woman last night. Her face had a soft gentleness that he had not seen before—that she had not shown before. He had been attracted to, maybe even aroused by, last night's fiery Lourdes, but this morning he felt somehow different about her. His thoughts drifted until he became aware of someone standing over him. It was Maria, with the morning basket of bread, the pot of coffee, and the bowl of fresh fruit. Apparently, despite the drama, the routine would be maintained.

She put down the breakfast and left without saying a word.

John checked his watch. It was still early. Now that the drama had passed, he realized that he had an appetite. He had to admit that Maria made great coffee, and the aroma of fresh bread was irresistible. He poured himself a cup, reached into the bread basket, and extracted a roll with steam still rising from it. He spread butter and jam on it. To say the roll melted in his mouth was not just an expression—it really felt like it did. He did not ordinarily eat fruit, but this morning he tried slices of papaya and mango and found them both delicious. The mango was slightly better. For some reason, everything tasted better today. He finished his coffee and set out early for class.

—   —

When Olivia Walker arrived at the classroom, she, like Lourdes had been earlier, was stunned to find an attentive John Sanford reading his textbook. Remembering the night before, she cautiously greeted him.

"Buenos días, John."

"Buenos días, señora," he said with a smile. She smiled back but kept a wary eye on him as she prepared for class.

Olivia had never had a student quite like John. More than anything, his attitude held him back—in his third week, he should have moved beyond his present level. Always late, always unprepared, always inattentive—but today, he was early. Maybe he was ready for a breakthrough.

The classroom began filling with young men and women, most of whom were American college students, but there were some Europeans working on their third or fourth language. Despite their different backgrounds, they all tended to dress alike: jeans and sweatshirts and sandals with socks because of the cool mornings. And regardless of their first language, they all seemed to understand English, the *lingua franca* of the twenty-first century.

At promptly nine o'clock, Olivia began. "Clase abre su libros a pagina viente y siete." *Class, open your books to page twenty-seven.*

John said the words, "Abre sus libros," under his breath, and looked at the other students. He caught on and turned to page twenty-seven.

When the class had the page, Olivia said, "Bien."

She saw that John was attentive and asked him, "¿Señor, como se llama?" *Sir, what is your name?*

John knew this one. He answered promptly, "John Sanford."

"Muy bien," Olivia said. *Very good.*

She started to move on to another student but changed her mind and took a chance asking him a more difficult question. "Juan, dame los nombres de su familia." *John, give me the names of the members of your family.*

There was a pause while John thought, but he realized it was material he had studied in his textbook the night before. He knew *nombre* meant name, and *familia* was, of course, family.

John was taking his time, which Olivia took to mean he didn't know the answer. She had turned to another student to pose the same question, when John spoke up.

"Mi...padre es John Sanford Senior. Mi madre es Katherine Sanford. Yo tengo un hermano, Roberto Sanford. Yo no tengo esposa. Yo no tengo ninos." *My father is John Sanford Senior. My mother is Katherine Sanford. I have no wife. I have no children.*

"Gracias, Juan. Muy bien!" Olivia said, surprised.

John smiled with satisfaction.

John felt good leaving class. He was in good stead with Olivia, and now he felt confident to try with Lourdes again. He had barely gotten a word in that morning, and he knew he would have to change tactics. His next move was obvious: flowers. They spoke in all languages, and more eloquently than he could. He would let them speak for him.

He went to a flower shop he remembered seeing near the plaza, a small storefront with a large glass window displaying its wares. He stood for a moment, looking in. He never knew what kind of flowers were appropriate for what occasions. Funerals, flowers for hostesses, romances, apologies—they were all different. He would need help choosing.

The shop was so tiny, he couldn't enter without being noticed. A small woman greeted him immediately.

"Buenos días, señorita," he said to her with a smile.

"Buenas tardes," the woman said.

John corrected himself. "Buenas tardes." He composed his next sentence in his head, and spoke hesitantly. "¿Ustede tiene los flores?" *Do you have flowers?*

She looked at him quizzically for a moment and then spread her arms wide to indicate that the shop was full of flowers. "Claro!" she said. *Of course.*

John realized how ridiculous his question sounded but pressed on. "Right, uh...yo quiero los flores." *I want flowers.*

The attendant saw he was struggling and said, "I speak English."

This caught John by surprise. She was just a little shopkeeper, but she spoke English.

"No, no," he said, "let's stay with Spanish." He was determined to at least try.

She shrugged her shoulders and said, "Bien."

John looked around until he found a small bunch of roses wrapped in shiny paper and picked them up. He spoke again in his elementary Spanish. "Yo quiero estos flores." *I want these flowers.*

She took the flowers from John's hand, wrapped them in tissue paper, and handed them back, during which time John mentally composed his next sentence. "Cuanto cuesta?" *How much do they cost?*

"Ciento cincuenta pesos," she said slowly and distinctly.

John knew *ciento* was one hundred. The other figure he was less sure of. He ran the numbers in his head until he got to *cincuenta*, which he realized was fifty. He took out his wallet, got out his pesos, and meticulously counted out 150. Handing them to her, he said, "Aqui lo tiene." *Here you have it.*

She replied, "Gracias, Señor."

"De nada," he said, happy to know the proper response. *You're welcome.* He had completed the entire transaction in Spanish and was very proud of himself.

John entered the house, scribbled a message on the card that went with the flowers, and left them on the dining room table in plain sight. He started to leave but saw that the Old Señor was in the room and had been observing him. John didn't want to ignore him like a piece of furniture, as he had in the past. He didn't know if the Old Señor could comprehend anything, let alone English, but he felt he should say something.

"Made a bit of an ass of myself last night," John said leaning over to make level eye contact. "But flowers always work. You know how it is," he said, winking at the Old Señor like they were buddies, two men of the world.

John wanted to walk away, but he saw the old man was agitated and struggling to say something. His lips trembled, he emitted a short burst of breath and some specks of spittle, but John couldn't make out any words.

He waited impatiently for the old man to stop sputtering, then patted him on the shoulder and said, "Yeah, I knew you would understand," and departed without looking back.

Lourdes returned home after shopping and saw the flowers. She paused, although it wouldn't have been unusual for Maria to leave flowers on the table. But these weren't in a vase, and, even more unusual, they were roses. She looked around to see if anyone was watching her, then bent over to inspect the flowers.

There was a card nestled between the blooms. She snatched it up and read it in a glance. It was only three words: *I'm sorry.—John.* Feeling startled, she grabbed them and hurriedly carried them upstairs to her room, where she found a vase full of day-old flowers. She discarded them and replaced them with the roses. She took the card and sat down on the bed to read it again.

— —

John came in the front door after his afternoon class. He was about to sprint up the stairs—taking it easy on the booze had made him feel better and younger—when he saw that his flowers were gone and bowl of fresh fruit was on the dining room table. Maria had always put fresh fruit there, but John was starting to really appreciate how her little touches brought the house to life.

He surveyed the arrangement and selected a juicy bunch of grapes. He ate them, relishing their sweet, fresh flavor. There had always been fruit out but only now were they part of his newfound appreciation for life.

Then he spied the old man through the half-open French doors, sitting partially in the shade, his face turned toward the afternoon sun. He often occupied this spot on the patio. John considered him. Of all the people in the household, he appeared to be of the least consequence, but due to his sex, and, more particularly, his age, he held a position of deference. John had not given him much consideration before now—but then there was a lot that slipped by him. The Old Señor had always seemed to John like a picture on the wall—not quite gone, but not quite there, either. A living portrait, not hanging on the wall, but sitting in a wheelchair. But a portrait of what? Not a father, but maybe an uncle? Maybe he was the landlord. Who knew?

He sat in his wheelchair, seemingly oblivious to anyone and anything but the sun warming his face. A blanket kept his legs warm. He seemed to personify old age itself. White hair, a face shaven clean daily, but surely not by himself. His stout figure occupied a seat, his throne on four wheels.

John wondered what that stage of life would be like. The waiting—the daily, weekly, monthly, yearly waiting. No ambition, no hope, but then again maybe no worries. The Old Señor seemed content with himself most of the time. But was he really peaceful? John had witnessed a frustrated rage yesterday behind his broad, placid face. What had those eyes seen in a lifetime? Did he have regrets? Was he replaying his life over and over in his mind, regretting his mistakes, lamenting his lost opportunities? John could only speculate. Old age would not be the same for any two people.

The Old Señor represented everything that John feared: old age, helplessness, and worst of all, pity. But at least he had someone to look after him. Even if it was Lourdes. Did she let him drink the occasional glass of wine? Smoke the occasional cigarette? She was his nurse, or maybe his warden, but what else?

John shook his head, ate a few grapes, and thought, *Well, he's not my problem.*

Someday, if he lived that long, would he be that man? No, he would not. He had no family that would outlive him, except maybe his brother, but that was not the same. No, John really had no one. He had his business, a 401k, and some real estate ventures, but it was probably too late to start a family. He wondered when that time had passed. It was not any single moment, but a series of moments that ran before you while you were busy thinking about something else.

John did not like where his thoughts were taking him. He was no longer wondering about someone else, some figure in a wheelchair. The old man was him. As sure as he had gone from child to teenager to young man, from young man to the man he was today, he would someday be the old man. The thought scared him. You could run, drink to forget, but you couldn't avoid time. It would find you, whoever you were, wherever you went, whatever you did.

And what was he doing? Was he ever in control? What series of events had led him to this place, this moment, these thoughts? He was as afraid as he had ever been before. Before, all his fears revolved around success or failure, measured by money. Dollars could buy you comfort and physical security, but they did not protect you from loneliness.

What did the old man have? Did he have money? Was he financially secure, did he know, did he care? Was he blessed by the gift of oblivion?

John suddenly realized he had been served up a life lesson. But what had he learned? He wasn't sure, but he had been given a gift. He just had to unwrap it. The Old Señor was a vision of the future. John just hoped he'd seen it in time.

— —

John came down at seven o'clock for dinner, right on time. Lourdes arrived soon after, and then Maria wheeled in the Old Señor. New flowers had replaced the bowl and John wondered what had become of his flowers.

Maria brought in a platter of chicken cooked with olives. The meal passed awkwardly. John made a point of trying to carry on polite conversation in Spanish, mainly complimenting the dishes Maria had prepared. Lourdes corrected his Spanish when necessary, but other than that she contributed little to the conversation. The Old Señor ate little, and after a while Maria gave up on him and wheeled him away, leaving John and Lourdes smiling uncomfortably at each other.

John planned on staying in that night and working in his Spanish workbook, not going to The Gringo. He thought of using the table on the patio and decided to take a cup of coffee with him. He reached for the pot, noticed that Lourdes's cup was empty, and offered it to her using a simple Spanish phrase. "¿Mas café?" *More coffee?*

She appreciated his new attitude toward Spanish but was skeptical of his motives. "Gracias," she replied. Venturing further, she added, "Usted es muy amable." *You are very kind.*

John understood she said he was *amable*. But what was *amable*? "I'm what?" he asked.

"Polite," Lourdes replied.

John smiled. "Sí, yo estoy amable," he said.

He had used the wrong verb form, so Lourdes corrected him. "No, yo *soy* amable."

"Okay," John said. "Yo soy amable." Realizing he had her attention, he launched into what had really been on his mind. "Look, what I really want to tell you is that, since I came here, I know I've been—"

Lourdes cut him off. "No, Señor Sanford, that is all behind us. You need not mention it again."

John disagreed, but before he could say any more, Lourdes left the room. He took his cup of coffee, went out to the patio, and opened his workbook, but he was too distracted to study. He was tempted to head down to the Gringo, but facing Bill was even less appealing than his Spanish homework.

He thought about Lourdes. She would always talk to him, if it was in Spanish. Spanish was the key. He had to make more of an effort. He looked down at his workbook. The exercise was sheer repetition. Pen and paper. Writing the same phrase over and over, changing the verb ending to reflect the person and number. He took a sip of coffee and began the grueling process.

23

The next afternoon, John sat on the patio once again and studied. After a while, he paused, glanced down once more at his textbook, and then went to the kitchen where he knew he would find Maria. Maria was surprised and then irritated to see him in her kitchen. This was her space and not part open to the household guests. Did he want an afternoon snack? He looked like he was about to speak Spanish. She spoke preemptively.

"¿Quiere algo para comer?" *Do you want something to eat?*

"¿Comer?" he said, remembering that it meant to eat. "Comer, no," he said. "No, no comer aqui este noche."

Maria thought he meant he was not going to eat here tonight, which made no difference to her. She never knew his plans anyway. "Bien," she said.

John realized he hadn't said what he wanted to. He tried again. "La señora y yo no comimos aqui este noche." *The lady and I will not eat here tonight.*

"No!" Maria exclaimed. "¿Por que no?" *Why not?*

John had run out of prepared text. He tried to ad-lib.

"No cocino...uh," he said. *I no cook.* The sentence didn't make much sense, but Maria thought she knew where he was headed and did not like it. It was not a good idea, but it was not for her to decide. Still, she was not going to give in easily, she said, "¿Como?" *What?*

John, desperate and out of words, grabbed a black skillet off the gas range and began moving it vigorously back and forth over the unlit burner. "No cook, no cook," he said, feeling like an idiot.

"Sí, sí," Maria said. Anything to get him out of her kitchen.

Satisfied that he had gotten his message across to Maria, John set off to find Lourdes.

She was at her desk in a small alcove off the main room, paying bills. An old-fashioned ledger book was open before her, and he suddenly realized they were both businesspeople. They had something in common. She wore reading glasses and had a different look about her. John found it strange how she could look so different depending on the setting, although she was always beautiful. He wondered, given the time, how many other different looks he could experience.

"Sí, Señor?" Lourdes said, expectantly. He must have been staring too long.

John tried to collect his thoughts. She looked impatient.

"Buenas tardes," he said.

She replied, "Buenas tardes," but she knew he must have more to say than that.

John recited his prepared text. "Este noche, yo quiero...tomar ustede a la cena." *Tonight, I want to take you to dinner.* He thought he'd done well.

She smiled at him, grateful for the invitation and appreciative of his Spanish. Still, she declined. "Gracias, pero no, Maria ya cociñio la cena." *Thank you, but Maria has already cooked dinner.*

John, who knew she would say that, said, "No, Maria no...cocina esta noche." *No, Maria is not cooking tonight.*

Lourdes started to speak, but John interrupted her. "Por favor." *Please?*

Reluctantly, she replied, "Bien."

"Muy bueno. A las siete?" *Good. About seven?*

She struggled to find a better answer but in the end she just gave up and said, "Sí,"

— ⁃

At seven o'clock, John waited downstairs wearing his dress suit, although with a starched shirt instead of a tee. At ten after, Lourdes appeared and, once again, seemed to look completely different.

John had already picked out a place to eat and knew the way. He extended his arm to her, thinking it courtly—the kind of thing a classy woman like Lourdes would appreciate. She reluctantly took it, but only until they reached the plaza where she gently slipped it out. She felt that all eyes were on her, but it was really just people going about their own business.

They arrived at a colorful, touristy place called The Restaurant, its name in English. Lourdes would not have picked it herself, but it was a first-class restaurant, and one where she was unlikely to see anyone she knew. She had never been there before, although she had heard of its chef, who was known to be top notch. It had probably recommended to John by the Americans as a place to impress a woman.

The decor managed to be ultrachic and colonial at the same time. A wood-burning fireplace gave off a comfortable warmth and a forest of potted plants dotted the room. The room's chicness was enhanced by its simplicity. Instead of starched white linen, the tables had bare, white enameled surfaces, each topped with a single votive candle in a glass etched with twigs. In the background, a jazz piano whispered a familiar tune. To Lourdes, it was a place that tried too hard to impress. She preferred more natural charm. John was surprised that a small town like San Miguel could have a place so elegant. He believed he had chosen well.

A white-coated waiter seated them. "Would you like a drink before dinner?" he said to John in perfect English.

"Sí, scotch," John said automatically, but then changed his mind. "No, a margarita, por favor." He thought something Mexican would be more appropriate for the evening.

The waiter turned to Lourdes, switching easily into Spanish. "¿La Señorita quisera cocktel?"

"No, gracias," she said, "Agua mineral, por favor." She wanted a mineral water.

The waiter disappeared, then returned with their drink and menus. John studied the menu. The left side was in Spanish, with an English translation on the right side. Under Starters, he recognized the Caesar salad, which he chose by default. For an entrée, he picked a roasted chicken breast when he found that there was no steak.

He addressed waiter in Spanish. "Ensalada de Caesar and un Pollo rosado, por favor."

"Muy bien," the waiter said enthusiastically, both congratulating John on his Spanish and angling for a big tip.

He then turned to Lourdes, who said, "Ensalada de arugula y el champinon, por favor." It was the lightest thing on the menu—an organic arugula salad with Manchego cheese, caramelized walnuts, and a cider vinaigrette, and herb-roasted mushrooms with polenta and ricotta cheese in white truffle oil.

For wine, John ordered a 2011 Casa Madero Chardonnay from Parras, Mexico—the oldest winery in North America, dating back to 1597.

John took a sip of the margarita, which was too sweet and fruity for his taste. He had liked them in Cancun, but here it felt out of place. He set it down on the table and did not pick it up again.

There was little talk during dinner, John not wanting to start an argument during a good meal, and Lourdes not having much to say in the first place. But once the plates had been cleared away, John started to really talk.

"Señora," he began, but she cut him off.

"I know it is not your custom to be so formal," Lourdes said. "Please, I would like you to call me Lourdes."

John felt this put them off to a good start. "Lourdes, what I have been wanting to say for days is—"

Lourdes raised her hand to cut him off again, but he didn't let it stop him.

"You can't walk away this time," he said. "You're going to have to listen."

Lourdes was trapped. Although most of the people in the restaurant were only tourists, she didn't want to cause a scene.

John didn't know how to say what he wanted, so he asked. "Lourdes," he said, "como se dice, I'm sorry'?"

"Lo siento," she said.

John said, "Lo siento, Lourdes."

"Gracias, John." She was relieved that was all he had to say.

They left the restaurant and strolled back to the house. The streets were deserted, and Lourdes felt more relaxed. She was almost enjoying the evening out, but when they reached the front door her discomfort returned. As she reached for the doorknob, she felt John's hand reach for hers. He turned her to face him.

She smiled at him and said, "Please John, it's late."

"Right, it's a school night," he said jokingly. But he did not release her arm.

She looked up and quietly but firmly said, "Please."

"All right, I understand," he said. "I won't say another word. But if you would like me to kiss you, just blink."

Lourdes immediately felt compelled to blink, but she forced her eyes to stay open. John waited intensely for his opportunity. When her eyes started to water, she leaned over and kissed him on the cheek. They both laughed, he released her arm, and the moment passed. She opened the door.

"Muchas gracias, y buenas noches," Lourdes said, and headed up the stairs. John watched her leave, then went to his own room, where he got in bed and tried to study Spanish. But he was too distracted, replaying dinner in his head, and he gave up. He turned the lights out, visions of Lourdes still playing in his mind.

Like John, Lourdes tried and failed to read. She laid the book across her chest and saw the flowers on her table. She thought about kissing his cheek and let out a small laugh but caught herself. She turned out her light.

24

John came down to the dining room full of joy, anxiously looking forward to seeing Lourdes. He was disappointed to find the room empty.

When Maria appeared with his coffee and bread, he asked immediately, "¿Donde esta la Señora?" *Where is the lady?*

Maria replied brusquely, "Se fue." *She left.* She did not really know where Lourdes was, but who was he to inquire about her whereabouts? She knew, of course, that they had gone to dinner the night before, but that did not mean he had any say in her life. She was suspicious of the American. He was—he was a man, and that was all she had to know.

John left for class and followed his usual course, which took him through the plaza. He stopped, thought back to the night of the party, and found the bench on which he had sat that night. He looked back to the cathedral, same as he had that nigh. He remembered how the slim moon had perched itself on top of the church steeple like an ornament. It, of course, was no longer there, but the feeling he had experienced was still with him.

Had he ever had a feeling like that before, like the universe was trying to tell him something? He had been moved once before, enough to commit to marriage. What had he felt then? He allowed his mind to wander back in time and space to a place very different from here, where he was younger—but not so young that he didn't know what he was doing. He closed his eyes and tried to envision Nicole, his ex-wife.

At the time, he believed she had it all, and maybe she did: perfect face, blond, blue-eyed, a slim figure. And she came from the right family. That was important to a young businessman on the rise. He didn't work for her father, which would have made advancement easy, but he worked for a company he had enough control over to get him a good position and a clear path. He had an MBA. It wasn't as if John wasn't good at what he did, but being married to Nicole did help. And he had worked hard—probably too hard. Between his long hours and her social life and charity work, they didn't have much time for each other.

There was no affair or anything, because neither had the time or energy. There was no defining moment that he could pinpoint, nothing like what he had experienced that night in the plaza, just an ever-widening gulf between them.

But there must have been more, he thought to himself. She was intelligent, more educated about the finer things than he was, and had a hectic social life that consumed most of her energy and time. *She never really knew me,* he thought. *But then I didn't know myself, either. There really wasn't that much to know.*

She was the first to admit that something was wrong between them. They didn't even have the passion to fight about it. There were no accusations, just the sad recognition that they had made a mistake. They talked about being friends afterward, but he hadn't talked to her since. Their lives just went in different directions. He knew she had remarried and had two children. Her face seemed to have disappeared from the society page of the Houston newspaper. She had apparently found what she was looking for.

He, on the other hand, had replaced her, not with a person but with a business. He left the company with which he had had such a promising career, cashed in his pension, and started his own business with the funds. If he had worked hard for his employer, he worked even harder for himself and he had been successful. Each day was filled until it flowed into the next, leaving no time for regrets, no time to reflect on his life, his choices, until now.

He had never had these thoughts before, drunk or sober. Would he still not be having them had he not come here? Was this a good thing or a bad thing? Could he go back to being the person he was before? Would the person he was becoming be tough enough to survive in the jungle he had left behind? That thought scared him more than anything, scared him to his very core. Here he was in a strange country, sitting in the midday sun, completely sober, and examining, not just his life, but his very soul.

—— ⁓

Lourdes had left early to go to her church. Its magnificence was lost on her this morning. Her somber clothes matched her mood as she sat in the confessional booth.

"En el nombre del Padre, del hijo y de Espirito santo. Bendigame Padre porque ha pecado tengo una semana de no confesarme," she said. *In the name of the Father, Son, and Holy Spirit. Bless me, Father, for I have sinned. It has been one week since my last confession.*

¿Tan pronto asi? The priest thought. So soon. One week and now she's back?

"Sí, Padre, a noche bese a un hombre que no es mi marido," she said. *Last night, I kissed a man who is not my husband.*

"¿Sientes que has cometido un pecado?" *Do you feel you have committed a sin?* The priest wondered if there were more she was concealing.

"Sí, Padre."

"Veinte y cinco Santa Marias." *Twenty-five Hail Marys.*

"Sí, padre."

"¿Algo mas?" *Nothing more?* He said gently probing for more of her strange confession of a such a benign event.

"Nada mas." *No more.* She spoke it with a certainty that did not invite future discussion so the priest merely answered, "Vete en paz." *Go in peace.*

25

John entered the class with new reasons to learn. Spanish was a way to communicate with Lourdes, to understand her, to reach her. Trying to learn a language to get even with some potential business partners hadn't been motivation enough. Now he worked hard and participated eagerly in class.

When he returned to the house for lunch, Lourdes still was not there. His appetite, and the bouncy feeling he'd had that morning, waned, and he returned to his afternoon dialogue class with little enthusiasm. After class he strolled slowly through the town, his thoughts on what might have changed since the night before. He realized he was near the Gringo and went to it, opening its door just far enough to see who was inside. He didn't want to be tempted to drink.

He saw the back of Bill at the bar and hesitated. He hadn't seen Bill since the night of the party and hoped there were no hard feelings. John knew that guys like him and Bill would rather pretend something never happened than to confront it, but he was ready to apologize if necessary.

He went in toward Bill, who saw his reflection in the mirror and turned to greet him with a broad smile. John knew immediately that all had been forgiven.

"John, old boy, where have you been keeping yourself?" he said, showing no sign of the trouble that had passed between them.

"Just trying to see a little more of the town than these four walls," John said jokingly.

"How about a drink on me?" Bill said, trying to keep John from leaving.

"No, gracias," John said automatically.

"Remember, no Spanish here," Bill said, trying to keep the conversation light.

John sat, but didn't say anything. An uncomfortable silence grew. Bill could tell that John was mulling something over, trying to decide whether he wanted to talk about it with the only friend he had in town. Bill sat and waited patiently.

John finally swiveled on his stool toward Bill, and said softly so as not to be overheard, "Bill, what do you know about Lourdes De Madrid?"

Bill thought for a moment. "So that's what this is about? I thought I saw sparks fly that night. Well, good luck getting anywhere with that woman. She's not known to go out with men."

John looked at him expectantly.

"To answer your question," Bill said, "not much. She's a very private person."

"Oh," said John.

Bill, seeing the disappointment in John's face, added, "If you really want to know, there might be one person."

"Really? Who?"

"Olivia Walker."

"It would be her!" John cried, throwing his hands up.

— ⁓

Olivia had noticed the more prepared and attentive version of John Sanford in class. She was no longer afraid to call on him for an answer—occasionally he would even volunteer one, and a smile would work its way across his face. He didn't have that bleary-eyed look he used to show up with, either. *He might learn some Spanish after all,* she thought.

That day after class let out, he hung back until everyone else had gone. Olivia wondered what he had on his mind. He approached her, and she could see he was trying to process something in his mind.

"¿Juan, ustede quiere algo?" she said slowly. *You want something?*

After John translated the question, he said, "Sí, es un pregunta muy personal." *Yes, it is a very personal question.*

Olivia could tell he was very concerned about something beyond his ability to express in Spanish. She looked around to make sure there were no other students within earshot, and said, "John, tell me what it is. You may speak in English."

John was relieved at first, but he couldn't really find the words for his problem in English, either.

"Um...Olivia, I, uh...I need to speak to someone." He paused, wondering if this was the right thing to do, and the right person to do it with. "But you probably don't care too much for me."

Olivia saw his point. He had been a pain in everyone's side since he arrived. But now he seemed so vulnerable. "John," she said, "I'm concerned for my own reasons."

John wasn't quite sure what she meant by that, but he took it as permission to continue. Still, it was awkward. Pouring his heart out to a stranger was not his style. He wished he had never begun the conversation and was trying to think of a graceful way of exiting it when Olivia spoke.

"John, let me tell you my story first," she said. "We all have one, you know."

John listened, surprised that she was willing to open up to him.

"Years ago, when I was a student at Iowa State, I signed up, much to my parents' disapproval, for a summer course at the University of Guanajuato. It was my first time out of the Midwest. That summer I fell in love with a language, a country, a culture, and a young Mexican student. I suppose he was attracted to my white skin and blond hair. We married hastily. It lasted only a few years, but I never returned to the States. I continued my studies here. One morning, I woke and realized that I had dreamed in Spanish. Then I noticed I was no longer translating into English and back to Spanish. I was thinking in Spanish. I know more about the language, culture and history than almost any native. But, John, I'll never know how it feels to be a Mexican." She gave him a minute to process what she'd said. "Can you ask your question now?"

John felt emboldened by her story, and ready to talk. "It's about Lourdes," he said.

This confirmed what Olivia suspected, and had once hoped for, but she feigned surprise.

"Oh," she said softly.

"Yeah. Um...Olivia, what can you tell me about her? She's such a mystery. I try to get to know her better, but as soon as I think we're getting somewhere I feel her pull back. Do you know what I mean?" He looked at his shoes and rubbed his hand absentmindedly across his mouth, wondering if he had revealed too much.

"I do know what you mean," Olivia said. "I've known her for..." She did some mental calculation but then just said, "a very long time." She looked him up and down, as if deciding if he was worth more information.

"Well," she said, "she had a very bad marriage." Quickly, she added, "Not her fault. They lived on a very large ranch north of town. I know he kept a mistress in town. The very house you're staying in."

John wondered what kind of man could be married to Lourdes and still keep a mistress. *Have to be something wrong with one of them,* he thought.

Olivia continued. "The stroke that took him was a blessing, as far as I'm concerned." She sighed. "That's really all I know. She doesn't confide in me," Olivia admitted.

With more questions raised than answered, John thanked her and rose to leave.

"Oh, John," Olivia said.

He turned back and said, "Yes?"

"Buena suerte." *Good luck.*

26

ohn walked the streets of San Miguel, his thoughts not on his destination. On a wall he spied a poster for a bullfight. Although he'd seen the arena, it seemed strange that this quiet town would actually have them. It seemed too rough for such a cultured place.

Maybe it's for the tourists, he thought. Bill had never mentioned bullfighting. He read the poster and realized that the fight was in two days.

As he was mulling it over, a small boy approached him and said, "Boletos, señor?" *Tickets, mister?*

John spoke to the boy in Spanish. "¿Estos boletos son buenos?" *Are these good tickets?*

"Sí, estos boletos son buenos," the boy reassured him.

"¿*Muy* buenos?" John asked.

The boy sized him up and, apparently finding him worthy, flipped through his tickets again and selected two. "Estos boletos son muy buenos," he said. *These are very good tickets.*

John recalled his encounter with the shoeshine boy. He still had to take a kid's word for it, but it was a wonder how much speaking the same language let him feel more in control.

"Bien. ¿Cuanto cuestan?" *Good. How much are they?*

"Twenty dollars US," the boy said.

"Aqui lo tiene," John said, handing the boy a twenty-dollar bill. *Here they are.*

"Gracias, Señor," the boy said, and gave John the tickets and moved on to find a new customer.

John had a plan. He would compose a pitch, in Spanish, and get Lourdes to go with him. It would be part of the cultural experience, he would say, and it would be her duty to accompany him, no matter how distasteful she might find the spectacle.

When he found her, he launched into his prepared sentence. "Lourdes, yo tengo dos boletos para la corrida. Va conmigo. Los boletos son muy bueno." *Lourdes, I have two tickets for the bullfight. Go with me. The tickets are very good.*

To his surprise, she did not question his intentions, but turned her full attention to the two bits of paper he held in his hands. "¿Puedo ver-los?" *May I see them?*

John passed the tickets to her. She only needed a moment to assess their quality.

"Hmm..." she said critically, her eyebrows furrowed. "Estan en el sol." *They're in the sun.*

"¿Como?" *What?*

"Lleva un sombrero," she said brusquely. *Take a hat.*

—● ●—

The next day was Sunday, and, after Mass and a light lunch, they set out on foot for the arena. Lourdes was wearing tight-fitting black slacks, a tan blouse with a black waist-length jacket, and, of course, a hat. John thought she looked a little bit like a bullfighter herself. John wore tan slacks and a black pullover. He thought he and Lourdes looked good together in their color-coordinated outfits.

The arena was only a couple of miles past the plaza, but he had never made the effort to visit it. They made their way down the street, merging with others headed in the same direction. John scanned the crowd and saw only locals. He guessed the Americans were home watching NFL football by satellite.

At the entrance, John took out his tickets and tried to figure out where their seats would be. Lourdes took his elbow and directed him to the other side. Apparently she was very familiar with the arena. Before they entered, Lourdes stopped at a vendor's stand and bought a large sombrero, which she carried in. They emerged from a tunnel into the bright afternoon sun. John looked around and saw everyone on their side of the arena was wearing a hat. Tickets in hand, Lourdes guided John down to their seats, which were very close to the action.

"See? I told you," John said. "Estos boletos son muy buenos." *The tickets are very good*. He turned, and the glaring sun struck him directly in the eyes.

"And I told *you*," Lourdes said, "you'd want a hat." She handed him the large brimmed sombrero.

John felt silly with the large hat, but when he placed the hat on his head, the glare receded.

"There will be some preliminary fights," Lourdes said, "and I will use them to instruct you on the proceedings. But when the main event begins, I will be too busy to talk to you. My eyes will be on El Glison entirely."

Like I'm gonna be jealous of some swivel-hipped matador, John thought.

"Preliminaries before the main bout, like a boxing match?" John asked.

"Yes," Lourdes replied, "but without the weight classifications to equalize. Some of these bulls can weigh up to 1,300 pounds."

"How does anybody win?" John asked.

"The bull is outnumbered," Lourdes said. "Each matador has a team of assistants."

"Well, that pretty much stacks the odds against the bull," John said.

Lourdes shrugged and said, "Remember, John, at the end it is only the bull and the matador." For a few moments, she let John take the place in. He saw a circular arena but without grass. Then she said, "Now, John, it's time for a little Spanish." She pointed to the arena's floor.

"The floor of the arena," she said, "is not packed dirt, but a layer of sand. The Spanish word for sand is *arena*. The reason for the sand will become apparent later."

She looked back at him. "John, from what word do we get the word *matador*?"

"*Matar*, I guess," John said.

"Muy bien! And what does *matar* mean?"

"To fight?"

"Close, but it's actually to kill. Take your English word *decimate*. It is made up of two Latin words: *deci*, meaning ten, as in decimal, and *matar*, to kill. Literally, to kill every tenth man, not to kill almost all. It is always misused in English. It comes from the Romans," Lourdes said, clearly relishing her role as storyteller. "When the troops performed badly in battle, it was their practice that the commander would line them up and kill every tenth man. It was cruel and wasteful, but they conquered the world."

John cringed, not only at the thought of a man counting down to his own arbitrary death, but the way Lourdes savored the story. She was a complex woman.

A blast of trumpets ended the lesson, and men and horses paraded around the arena. John watched the pageantry unfold, but without an appreciation of its history, which went back all the way to Andalusian Spain. He was sure every part meant something, but there was no way Lourdes could have explained it all right then, so she let it unfold without comment.

When, at last, the first bull entered, Lourdes restarted the lesson. "The matador is sizing up the bull, looking for any peculiarities in his vision, his movements, or his manner." In this case, she noticed that the bull was territorial and had staked out a section of the arena. She explained to John that this type was actually more dangerous than an offensive bull that focused on the man.

The picadors came in on their padded and blindfolded horses, stabbing the bull with lances. It was the first blood of the afternoon.

"Is that fair?" John asked.

"It has a purpose," Lourdes assured him. "The lances are placed in the neck muscle so the bull's head will be lowered."

That didn't address John's question. It still seemed unfair.

Next, three *banderilleros* entered on foot and, after being chased around the ring by the bull, succeeded in planting two *banderillas,* little flags on barbed sticks, in strategic positions on the bull's neck and shoulders. Lourdes explained, working in Spanish terms whenever possible, that these were meant to further weaken the bull.

So it was an exhausted and blood-depleted bull that awaited the matador. John decided he was firmly on the side of the bull, who didn't seem to understand why he was being tormented by these men and was obviously ready to exact revenge on the small, lone man in the ring. This was where the artistry, if the spectator was inclined to find any, occurred.

Lourdes was entranced by the spectacle, literally on the edge of her seat, as close to the action as she could get. She weaved in her seat with each pass of the bull, telling John the name or distinction of each, and she joined the crowd in shouting *ole* after each successful pass.

Her face glowed with an ardor John hadn't seen before, almost as if she were sexually aroused. He would rather have watched her face rather than the action in the arena, but when she caught him staring, she turned his head so that he faced the arena.

John watched the remainder of the fight and winced when the matador thrust his sword between the bull's shoulders. It wasn't a clean kill, and the bull staggered around, blood flowing from its still-pumping heart. The crowd was aware of the bungled *estocada* and showed their disapproval by shouting. John did not understand the words, though the sentiment behind them was clear. Lourdes wasn't shouting, but the look of disgust on her face was obvious.

A second blow cut the bull's spinal cord, and the animal went to the ground, to everyone's relief. The point of the sand became clear to John as workers appeared with shovels and a wheelbarrow, taking away any sand soaked with blood. Mules dragged the bull carcass away.

John finally caught his breath and turned to Lourdes. In an effort not to seem weak or squeamish, he smiled and said, "Well. That was really something."

"I am sorry you had to see that," Lourdes said. John thought she meant the gory bullfight and was surprised when she said, "A poor kill like that dishonors both the matador and the bull. Let's hope the next one is better. It should be. It's El Glison."

That was twice she had spoken of the matador by name, and with reverence. Who was this El Glison? John felt a pang of jealousy and sighed as he sank back in his seat, preparing himself for more.

After more fanfare, El Glison finally appeared. The crowd, including Lourdes, chanted his name. John marveled at Lourdes, usually so reserved, becoming one with such a common crowd. John looked across the ring and sized up the matador. He was small in stature but carried himself with grace. Despite his size, he was imposing.

John took an instant dislike to him. He would be pulling silently for the bull. The matador walked the arena's perimeter, bowing to the crowd. When he passed close to them, John could see he wore a metal brace around his left knee. So, he'd been hurt in a match, patched up, and sent back out. That earned no sympathy from John. The fight was still unfair.

When the bull entered the ring, it made a beeline for the stands, close to John and Lourdes. John recoiled—it was larger than the last one and snorting defiantly, spraying hot snot, striding around like he owned the arena. John liked his attitude. If the bull had had a name, he would have chanted it.

When the picadors were through with him, his head was bloodied, his neck was bowed, but he had not lost his will to fight. Unlike the territorial bull that focused on defending an area of the arena, this one focused solely on El Glison, who played to the crowd, ignoring the bull. The bull stamped and pawed the ground, snorting his outrage.

Finally, El Glison turned his attention to the bull and waved his cape at him—but then it was the bull's turn to be contrary. Instead of charging, the bull held his ground, pawing at the ground with his front hoof in invitation. The matador had no choice but to approach, whipping his cape as he went. The bull, seeming to enjoy his power over the man, waited patiently, until El Glison was in his range. He charged, but the matador was ready, and executed a smooth pass. Everyone in the crowd cheered, except John.

El Glison turned, advancing toward the bull in an effort to make him charge again. The bull loped toward him at a leisurely pace, but after passing the cape he suddenly made a sharp turn toward the matador, catching him off guard.

John did a quick fist-pump and cried, "Yes!" His yell was lost in the gasps of the rest of the crowd. Despite their fears, El Glison didn't panic and avoided the bull's sudden charge, though without his usual grace. He showed himself to the crowd so they would know he had not been hurt, but that meant his back was also to the bull, which couldn't resist such a prime target.

It was a trick, of course, and the matador turned skillfully, avoiding the bull's charge. The bull flew past him. This was what the crowd had come to see, and they shouted their approval.

John's attention, however, was on the bull. He imagined he was the only one siding with the beast.

El Glison returned to his tactic of waving his cape and shouting at the bull to draw him out. The bull held his ground, but he looked fatigued and seemed to be conserving the strength he had left for the right moment.

When the distance had been closed and the bull was still not drawn in, the matador meekly knelt on the ground, making himself an irresistible target to the bull. John looked to Lourdes for an explanation, but she was intently focused on the scene, watching, appraising, still drawn into the frenzy.

Her eyes widened, and John looked back to see what she'd seen. The bull was on the move, charging hard, gobbling up the distance between himself and the matador. He was spending the last of his strength on the charge.

El Glison did not stand up smoothly, either because he misjudged the bull's speed, or, more likely, because the brace on his left knee held him back. He staggered a few steps and fought to regain his balance. He was on the defensive, although not defenseless, considering his training.

The crowd knew the danger was real, and that there would be no graceful exit from this predicament. They held their collective breath. Picadors scrambled to get into the ring and distract the bull. John screamed out a futile warning in English. Seeing a human in danger caused John to immediately side with his own species.

El Glison had regained his feet, but was not in a proper stance.

"If he stays in the center," Lourdes said, not taking her eyes off the arena, "he could miss the horns. But he can't escape the bull entirely!"

John watched in bewilderment as the man stood his ground, attempting no last-minute moves. Instead, he blinded the bull with his cape and smothered the animal as best he could.

The matador positioned himself in the middle and fought to keep the sharp horns from his chest while the picadors worked to get the bull off of him. Enraged, the bull raised his head to gore them all, and El Glison used the opportunity to escape. The picadors returned his sword and cape to him, and he assumed a proper, aloof stance, as if nothing had happened.

Seeing the man still standing, the bull bellowed and made one final, fatal charge. El Glison was ready and stood on his toes to send his sword swiftly, mercifully, directly into the bull's heart. It was as clean a kill as anyone there had ever seen. El Glison stood over the bull, not in triumph, but in admiration. When he bowed his head to the beast, the crowd roared.

Lourdes was on her feet, cheering as loud as any man there. John's heart was still racing from his first vicarious encounter with death. When he had gotten his breathing under control, he turned to look at her and saw not fear but passion flowing through her, and he wondered how the two sides of her could coexist in the same body.

The matador toured the arena, bowing to the crowd. When he passed before John and Lourdes, John could not help but acknowledge the man's courage and took his hat off as a token. Lourdes snatched it out of his hand and sent it sailing into the ring.

"Hey," John said, bewildered, "I was beginning to like that hat."

— ~

John left the arena feeling emotionally drained, as if he had been to hell and back. He had turned his back on humanity, only to learn that, for better or worse, in the end people come first. He felt one with the mass of Mexican people pressing against him. They all shared the same humanity. He had always thought of the workers at the *maquiladora* as drones, to be exploited for profit. It would be hard to look at them that way again.

John and Lourdes let the flow of the crowd carry them out of the arena and sweep them into the streets. They continued on, directionless, until John felt a tug on his arm. Lourdes separated him from the crowd and led him to a side street he hadn't been on before. At the end of the street, John saw, under an awning, a group of tables gleaming in the fading afternoon sun. Lourdes went straight to the first one and sat down without a word. She did sigh, however, glad to be away from the commotion.

John checked the place out. The tables were wooden, with flattened metal beer signs nailed to their tops, forming crude, but colorful, surfaces. It was a working man's bar—not one he would have chosen for her. But it was now clear to him that, since they had left the house, Lourdes had been in charge.

John took his seat and looked at Lourdes. She was a different person from the one he had left with three hours earlier, her gentility replaced with robustness, her face glowing with spent energy. The long black curls she usually kept primly behind her ears were now plastered to her cheek.

He tried to avert his eyes, but they were drawn back to her chest as it rose and fell, without modesty, under the stretched taupe cotton blouse that had seemed so demure before. He took deep breaths to try to bring his emotions under control. He would initiate nothing today. She would lead him, and he would follow.

She caught the waiter's eye and made a gesture that resulted in two sweaty beers landing on their table, unaccompanied by glasses or napkins. John's tension increased with Lourdes's every inhalation and, despite his decision to let the scene play itself out, he took the initiative back. He thrust the wet beer bottle in front of him, holding it out for a toast.

"To El Glison."

But before he could drink to the matador, Lourdes said, "Al toro."

After reflecting for a moment, they took long-awaited gulps. John had forgotten how good a well-placed beer could feel washing over his palate, like a foamy, hoppy wave of refreshment. Lourdes drank deeply and felt the welcome, cold, refreshing liquid revive her. The strong, pungent smell of the beer brought back memories of her days on the ranch, but she forced them back.

She placed the bottle back on the table and turned to John, who had just taken a second deep draw and was savoring its feel. He saw her looking at him and reluctantly put the bottle down.

"This El Glison—is he from around here?" he asked innocently.

"Don't be silly, he's a world-famous bullfighter," Lourdes said. "It was very special to have him here. That's was why I was so thrilled when you got the tickets."

John felt jealousy rise again as he realized he was not the reason she agreed to come. A hurt look passed across his face.

Lourdes realized her mistake and said, "I enjoyed sharing the experience with you."

That helped, but he still worried about enjoying a human's near-death experience. American football was violent, but rarely fatal. This was more like auto racing, where the thrill came from knowing that any turn could produce a fatal crash. He had been guilty of this himself. It kept coming back to him—no matter how different their cultures seemed, it was really only a difference in form, not substance.

"Well, I noticed that you toasted the bull," he said, redirecting the subject.

"Yes, why shouldn't we? He was magnificent. It was a great day for him, too."

"Also his last," John said.

"Remember, John, it is sometimes the man who dies." Lourdes thought for a moment. "John, I know it is hard to understand your first bullfight. But it is a...what is the word..." She searched her mind, then said, "A metaphor, a metaphor for life."

"Life? You mean death, don't you?"

"Yes, death, too. But death is a part of life," she said emphatically. Then she frowned and said, "But that's another subject." She paused, took a sip of her beer while she organized her thoughts, and then started again. "In the bullfight, you saw only the bull's struggle and death. You do not understand a fighting bull's glorious life."

"No, can't say that I do," John said.

"Have you ever been on a ranch?"

"Hey, I *am* from Texas," John said, as if that answered it. In truth, he'd only driven past them.

"Well, then you know the difference between a bull and a steer."

"Yeah, and I don't think I like where you're headed," he said, when, in fact, he had no clue what she was talking about.

"As usual, John, you see only part of the picture," Lourdes said. "When a male calf is born, he is destined to be either a steer or a bull. If he is a steer, he ends up on your plate." Her voice rose with enthusiasm as she continued. "But if he is a fighting bull, he is allowed to grow up never seeing a man until the day he enters the ring. His due is forty-five minutes of hot passion, and if he has fought well, the admiration of all. That is what you saw today."

"'A life without passion isn't worth living,' is that it?"

"Remember, John, we are still talking about bulls."

27

That night in bed, Lourdes replayed the day's events in her head. Strange how just the smell and taste of beer had transported her back years and miles to the ranch—a place she had both hated and loved.

She remembered that, within days of their horrible honeymoon in Acapulco, she had found herself on that monstrously large tract of barren land in the north of Mexico. Fortunately, her new husband hadn't stayed long—just made a cursory look at the books, checked with the foreman, and left for Mexico City. Lourdes spent the first few days exploring the rambling ranch house, with its many patios, courtyards, and balconies. She tried to talk to the staff, but all they did was agree with her. The place was beautiful, or could have been with a few personal touches. But she hadn't felt it was her place to change things.

After a week, she went to the foreman and asked him to help her select a horse. He showed her several gentle mares, but she asked about a large stallion. Wisely, he advised her that she was not ready for him. She agreed, and he saddled up an older gelding. To teach her how to handle a horse, he turned Lourdes over to the stable boy, who seemed to be as afraid of her as she was afraid of her husband. She treated the boy like a skittish, young horse, the kind that needs some patience.

He helped her on once, then she dismounted and tried to climb up on her own. She was determined not to seem weak or lazy, but the tired old gelding sensed Lourdes was a beginner and decided to have some fun. The horse was stubborn and would respond to none of Lourdes's commands.

Eventually, the stable boy, who barely came up to the gelding's nostrils, jumped off his mount and swatted Lourdes's horse across the nose. The horse began to obey. Lourdes was surprised how quickly the boy resorted to violence, but she had just stepped into the ranch life and was not going to judge. Perhaps brutality was necessary here.

She continued her lessons, then rode on her own. When she was confident, she insisted she would do her own saddling and care for the horse. The horse gave her the freedom to explore any part of the ranch within a day's ride.

After a month, she asked for the stallion. By then she had some horse smarts and understood their mentality. The foreman was reluctant—she might get hurt, and he would be blamed—but she was the mistress, and he couldn't refuse her.

Going from the gelding to the stallion was like going from a station wagon to a sports car. The power and spirit the horse exuded was exhilarating, and she could feel it as it moved up her loins. She insisted on bathing, brushing, and feeding him herself, and she could tell he appreciated the personal attention. She found herself talking to him as she worked, and he seemed to understand. Whenever she entered the stable, he seemed glad to see her and eager for her to take him out.

With a horse capable of keeping up, she investigated the cattle-raising business. Early mornings, she would ride and watch the cowboys at work. She knew her presence made them uncomfortable, but she thought that since her husband wasn't visible to them, at least she could be. She watched as they expertly herded the cattle into separate corrals for tattooing or shots. Another corral held only juvenile bulls, and activity there seemed more frenzied.

One day she dismounted and was walking toward the juvenile corral when the foreman stopped her and said she, as a lady, shouldn't watch.

Lourdes gently moved past him and looked over the cowboy's shoulders at the young bull held in the metal chute. The cowboy's hand was bloody, clutching the calf's severed scrotum, which he placed in a blood-filled bucket.

Her stomach rose to her throat, but she did not look away. She did not want them to see her disgust. This was part of the business she found herself in, and she was not going to pretend otherwise. She gathered herself, turned back to the worried foreman, gave a slight nod of approval, and slowly moved off.

After that, the cowboys came to accept her presence. She tried to do each task at least once, so she would know what was involved. Her effort was appreciated, but never really taken seriously until the day she took the knife from the boy's hand and used it on a young bull. From then on, she was a woman to be reckoned with. At dinner that night, by tradition, she dined on her trophy. A strong red wine helped get her through it.

Her passion for life found an outlet on the ranch. She could go from nursing a sick calf, to gelding its father, to driving its mother to market. The constant flow of life, from birth, to maturity, to death, all played out there in compressed time.

Her husband, when he was there, dressed as a *caballero,* although he'd long since traded horses for pickup trucks, and even then someone else drove. The cowboys tipped their hats to him, but he only spoke to the foreman.

Lourdes's jeans started feeling like a second skin, and her legs grew stronger. Her face tanned to match the workers around her. She was a woman in full blossom, and any man would have adored her. Any man but her husband. He was older, but not yet old, and had a bearing that would attract any woman. But he was used to women he could treat with disdain and who would take it. He viewed her no differently from his bought women—after all, she had brought no property into the marriage. She was beautiful, yes, educated, but she still carried some Indian blood, while he was pure Castilian. She was beneath him, and he thought she needed to remember it.

He needed violence and insults as a prelude to sex. The others had learned to accept it, and so would she, he thought. At first she was willing to give herself to him, but when he called her names and spat on her, she told him he would never touch her again.

He took delight in insulting her before the servants. This did not bother her. She knew they detested him, too, so he was only humiliating himself. And then one night, after heavy drinking, he went beyond words and, for the first time, struck her across the face in front of the entire household. Harder than a slap, the open-handed blow sent her reeling. She slumped toward the floor but did not touch it. Time stood still, the servants looking on helplessly, Lourdes suspended with one knee inches from the floor. A slight tremble worked its way across her. Then it passed, and strength flowed from her thighs to her heart, and she raised herself to her full height. She stepped toward him as he glowered back, his fist raised to finish what he had started.

She took him down like a roped calf. He hit the floor hard, his breath forced from his lungs, and she came down on him in one fluid motion, her knee pressed to his throat. His face turned red, and everyone was afraid she would kill him. But no one moved. Eventually she rose and stood over him as he gasped for air on the floor. He didn't attempt to get up until she had left the room.

After that, he changed tactics. He started drinking more and talking loudly about her to the servants, behind her back. She was stinking Indian, he'd say, she was frigid, she was a lesbian, she was a whore, she was prude, she had no heart, she had no vagina. He meant to shame her, but he only shamed himself. One night, during one of his more virulent rants, he collapsed and fell to the floor.

<hr/>

The bankers from Mexico City soon started calling on her. There were heavy payments due. *On what?* She wondered. The ranch had passed to her husband by inheritance. It was part of an original Spanish land grant from the King of Spain. Who could be owed payments on that? The bank, she was informed.

The well-dressed gentlemen sat across from her and spoke in soothing tones. The banker from Mexico City she knew already, but this time he had brought along a lawyer. She knew that the profits from the ranch were routinely deposited in his bank. What she didn't know about were the loans.

Her husband had accumulated large debts on the land, she was told. But what had the money been for? She demanded to know. The gentlemen became uncomfortable with the questions. The banker looked to his lawyer, who answered for him.

He looked down and muttered something about expenses.

"What expenses?" she demanded.

The lawyer tried to phrase it nicely. "Well, there was...some entertainment."

This came as no surprise to her. Since he no longer came to her bedroom, she assumed there were others. But it seemed to concern the banker more than her, and that puzzled her.

"You can't throw away that much money on women!" she exclaimed.

The lawyer grimaced. "He liked to gamble. And he wasn't very good at it."

"All of it?" she asked.

"Yes," he said. "All of it."

When did this happen? Why wasn't I informed? Could I have done something? These thoughts filled her head.

"He had to give it up some time ago," the man said. "Our bank cut off his credit two years ago."

Two years ago. The bastard had gone through with the wedding, knowing he was broke. She collapsed into the chair. She was trying so hard to think, that she barely heard the next words from the lawyer.

"It's not much, but there's still the property in San Miguel."

28

In Houston, John never walked. He went from his high-rise condo parking garage to his high-rise office parking garage without his feet ever touching the street. He lived his life at a constant, artificial seventy-two degrees Fahrenheit, 45 percent humidity. It never varied, despite the season, despite the weather outdoors. When he golfed—which was becoming more and more seldom—he rode a golf cart, and then his golf outings were really just business meetings conducted over eighteen holes. At those times, in golf carts with no air conditioning, he was reminded just what a pit Houston could be.

Here, he walked everywhere. He felt the bracing chill of the morning, and the warm sun on his face in the afternoon. He became aware of his surroundings. He read the Spanish words on every sign he passed along the street and learned from them. He was learning, not by drills, but by living. He had an idea and went back to the house to test it.

Lourdes came down and was surprised to see John still in the house. "¿John, por que no va a su leccion de conversacion?" she asked him pointedly. *Why aren't you in conversation class?*

"No necessita va a clase cuando ustede esta aqui. Yo puedo tiene un conversacion con ustede," John said. *It is not necessary to go to class when I can have a conversation with you.*

"No, no soy su maestro, John." *I'm not your teacher.*

"¿Por que, no?" *Why not?*

She looked at him and thought, *¿Por que, no?*

"Lourdes, aprenderme," John said. *Lourdes, teach me.*

She immediately corrected him. "Enséñame."

"Bien. Usted esta enseñarme, ahora mismo." *You are teaching me now.*

Lourdes sensed the trap he was setting for her, but she wanted to walk into it. She had always woven lessons into her day-to-day contact with residents. Why not teach a lesson? She'd always wanted to, and it wasn't as if she was stealing one of Olivia's prize students. This was John Sanford. He needed individual attention.

John was looking hopefully at her.

Reluctantly, she said, "Bueno." She realized that she had accepted before she had fully thought it out. She would develop a lesson plan later, but for now, she would have to improvise.

She headed for the patio, and John followed. She took a seat at the wrought iron table, and John sat down across from her. Lourdes took a deep breath. She had committed to this, and now she must see it through. And she could impose her will now. If he was serious, he would do it her way.

She put on her best teacher's face, looked back at him, and announced, "La leccion empieza, ahora," stressing the word *ahora*. *The lesson starts now.*

John knew what she said, and replied, "Sí, Señora."

"Durante la leccion habla espanol, totalamente," she said firmly.

He nodded and said softly, "Sí, sí."

"John, digame los días de la semana." *Tell me the days of the week.*

"Hmmm....let's see there's," he caught himself speaking English and began again. Los dias de la semana son lunes, mares, mericoles, jueves ....,"

She prompted him, "Viernes."

"Sí, Viernes...sabado and domingo," he finished with flourish.

"Bien," she said passively. "Ahora, digame los meses del ano." *Now tell me the months of the year.*

This time John was able to rattle them off in perfect order, "Enero, febrero, marzo, abril, mayo, junio, julio, augusto, septiembre, octubre, noviembre y deciembre," once again he beamed as if this were a great achievement.

And once again Lourdes only rewarded him with a simple "bien". After all he had been here weeks he should know these words.

"Just bien," John said with disappointment.

Lourdes wasn't going to pamper his feeling and pressed on. "John, digame la fecha hoy. *Tell me today's date.*

"Let's see …. La fecha es octubre ….vient ocho," he said ending with a quiver in his voice.

Lourdes sensed something was wrong and spoke to him in English, "John, what's the matter."

"The month. It's almost over. I can't believe it," he said the pain evident in his voice Lourdes refused to be distracted and continued, "John, digame…."

After an hour of intense and steady instruction a tired but satisfied Lourdes laid down the textbook with a sigh and allowed some light conversation in English, "Muy bien, John. You can learn if you want to. I once went through it, too."

"I've often wondered how you acquired your English."

"I had a year of boarding school in Vermont."

"How was it?"

"Muy frio," she said partly in jest.

"The weather?" he said probing for more information.

"Everything." She said surprising herself with her own willingness to talk about the past with this man. "Mine was the only brown face in the school." She paused and he could see her expression change as her mind turned back in time. When she began again her tone had lost its sentimentality, "We all had to take Latin and since I already knew Spanish it came quite easily and I won the Latin award, but that's not what I was most proud of. It was my English. Any mistakes I made drew laughs from the girls. I took that grammar book and locked myself away with it. And while the others would occasionally use the wrong pronoun, I was flawless as only someone who learned from a text book could be. I still had my accent but I soon lost it too," she ended with a triumphant finality.

John once again felt inadequate before her but encouraged by her openness he changed the subject and dared to go further. "¿Lourdes, quien es, no not es," he realized he hadn't used the right verb form.

"Fue," she corrected him.

John started again, "¿Quien fue Señor Madrid?" *Who was Señor Madrid."*

"Ernesto de Madrid fue mi esposo." *Ernesto de Madrid was my husband.* She answered brusquely not wanting to pursue this subject but pursue it John did.

"Sí, yo se. ¿ Pero que clase de hombre? *Yes, I know but what kind of man?*

Lourdes spoke with undisguised contempt, "Un viejo, un borrocho y un jugador." *An old man, a drunk and a gambler."* There was more but she felt she had said enough.

"¿Por que caso el?" *Why did you marry him?*

"Ustede no puede comprender." *You can't understand.*

But John persisted, "Digame, digame, por favor."

Lourdes reluctantly answered in English to hurry up the unpleasant subject, "To please my mother. She thought we both needed someone like Ernesto."

This made no sense to John. "¿Por que?"

"Ernesto fue muy rico," she said flatly. *Ernesto was very rich.*

"Lo siento, Lourdes."

There was more, much more but Lourdes has already said more than she intended and turned the conversation back to John. "¿Y usted?"

That Lourdes would be interested in his life both surprised and flattered him. "Me?" He paused and reflected back before beginning. "There's no way I can tell this with me coming out looking good."

"I'm not here to judge you, John."

"Well," he began again, "she was beautiful, smart and kind. I really married above myself," he laughed in a self-deprecating manner but then continued in a more serious vein, "but I was more interested in me, my career, financial success, making a name for myself. I didn't make time for my marriage. She turned to social and charitable work. She became quite the figure in Houston society. When we divorced it was just so much paper work, no emotion."

Lourdes thought he was through and said, "Lo siento." But John had more.

"The thing is..." he paused to gather his thoughts and began again as if his feelings were still fresh and raw. "I saw her one day. I didn't let her see me. She was at a shopping mall getting out of a SUV. She was wearing jeans and a t-shirt, with no makeup, no jewelry. She was struggling with two small children but she seemed so natural at it. Still beautiful but a completely different person than the one I had known. Like she had found her real self. Not at all the woman she had been with me." The next words he spoke came with a deep regret. "Her experience with me was probably as bad as yours with Ernesto."

"I doubt that," Lourdes shot back.

29

The next day at two o'clock, Lourdes left her household duties and, after stopping at her desk for her book and writing pad, proceeded to the patio. She found John already seated at the wrought iron table. Lourdes sat down and, without greeting or small talk, launched into the day's lesson.

"Hoy, vas a aprender un verbo muy útil, hacer." *Today you are going to learn a very useful verb,* hacer.

This word, *hacer,* seemed to have too many uses to suit John. Basically, it could mean to do or to make, but it was used to form many incongruous idioms, like to make a line, or to have weather. This was something John would need time to get his mind around. After a while, he had made progress with the utilitarian verb, but it was dull and dry, and his butt was starting to feel the imprints of his chair's crisscross pattern. Lourdes seemed comfortable, but then her frame afforded more padding.

Lourdes saw his squirming and asked, "John, ¿tiene una problema?" *Do you have a problem?*

Not wishing to discuss his posterior, he said, "¿Ustede quiere tomar un paseo?" *Do you want to take a walk?*

He expected her to immediately decline, but instead she gave him a critical look and said, "Estudiamos durante el camino, ¿verdad?" *We study while we walk, right?*

"Sí, sí."

She gave him a long, stern look that said she meant business, and he reassured her further, saying, "Sí, sí."

Finally, when she was content that it would not be a wasted exercise, she warmed to the idea. They could get out of the house, and learn by dealing with real situations. It could work. "¿Quisiera un tour del pueblo?" she said. *Would you like a tour of the city?*

He replied, "Sí, sí."

"No me digas, 'sí, sí.' Contestame in frasces completa." *Don't 'sí, sí,' me. Answer in complete sentences.*

John started to say, "Sí, sí," but caught himself and, speaking slowly and deliberately, said, "Yo quisero un tour de su puebla." *I would like a tour of your town.*

"Bueno," she said, grabbing her sweater from its hook as she headed for the door.

Once on the street, she paused with her hands on her hips and announced, "Empiezamos donde empieza." *We begin at the beginning.* She strode in the direction of the plaza. From the vigor with which she strode, John knew he was in for a long day.

As they walked, her pace slackened and then came to a full stop. "El nombre del pueblo es San Miguel de Allende. San Miguel para el santo Miguel y Allende para Ignacio Allende. ¿Comprende?" *The town is named for Saint Michael and Ignacio Allende.*

John had followed carefully and was able to truthfully answer, "Yo comprendo."

Satisfied that he did, she continued. "Ignacio Allende nacio aqui. Was born." She looked at him and he nodded, so she kept on. "El murió en la Guerra de la Indepedencia." *He died in the War of Independence.*

He repeated, "El murió en la Guerra de la Indepedencia."

"Muy bien," she said, then thought about how to explain the next part in simple terms. At that point, the story was as important as the lesson. "Despues de la Guerra, el pueblo San Miguel fue muy pobre. Pobre, Poor." John nodded, so she continued. "Otros pueblos se crecenn, San Miguel, no." *Other towns grew, San Miguel did not.* She hadn't expect John to follow, but he did. He was picking it up by hearing it in context and learning as he went. Just the thing he was supposed to have done when he arrived but was too stubborn to accept.

"San Miguel," he started, but he didn't have the words to say what he wanted, and instead gestured, pulling his hands in toward each other. The town shrunk.

Lourdes understood. "Es la simila exacto asi fue en mil ocho cientos viente sies." *It is exactly as it was in 1826.*

"The same as it was in 1826?" John asked in English after translating in his head. Lourdes nodded. John looked around the buildings. They looked like a town would have in 1826. Like colonial Williamsburg, but real and alive.

They reached the town square, and John's eyes were drawn to the beautiful, towering Parroquia de San Miguel, an obvious next topic for conversation.

"¿Como se llama este cathedral?" John asked.

Lourdes smiled. "Se llama Parroquia de San Miguel," she said, pronouncing each syllable slowly. But he was mistaken about one thing, and she corrected him. "No es cathedral, exactamente. Es solo un iglesia." *It's not exactly a cathedral. It's only a church.*

John didn't grasp the distinction. She knew he based his assumption on size and grandeur, not on church authority. But it was too complex to get into, so she just said, "Es grandioso, pero no es catedral."

He seemed content with her answer, so she continued. "Es design es Gotico. Entiende Gotico?"

"Sí, yo entiendo Gotico," John said. I understand.

Lourdes had often thought she would be a good language instructor, and she wanted to succeed where others had failed. John Sanford was a challenge. She realized she could not treat him the same as a college student and get results. He had to be let go, so the language would come to him. It was her job to engage him in the process.

The town was built on hilly terrain, and any stroll, even a leisurely one, required much climbing. If John had set out to find a place that was the exact opposite of Houston, he couldn't have done much better. Walking in the cool, crisp air had given him a sharp appetite. Back home, lunch was a sandwich and another cup of coffee at his desk. When goaded by Margie to get out and join the others, he would respond, "Lunch is for wimps," and keep working. But now, he very much wanted a long lunch.

It was not quite two o'clock—early by Mexican standards—when he asked Lourdes, "¿Podemos tener almuerzo?" *Can we have lunch?*

She looked at his anxious face. "Claro, sigame," she said. *Of course, follow me.*

It involved more climbing, but when they reached the hotel on top of one of the many hills, John could see it was well worth the effort. The dining room was on a terrace with a magnificent view.

When they were seated, she let him know that he was still in the movable lesson by saying, "Usted vas ordenar." *You will order.*

She sat back and watched as the waiter handed them large menus. While John studied his, holding it up so she couldn't see his face, she kept her eyes on the table.

The hotel had created the menu with tourists in mind. On the left side, the dishes were listed in Spanish, and on the right they were translated into English. He settled on a roast beef sandwich with fried potatoes for himself, and for Lourdes he selected a rather elaborate salad with chicken and artichokes.

When the waiter returned, Lourdes avoided eye contact with him, and he addressed John. "El Señor, esta listo para ordenar."

John took a deep breath, exhaled, and began, "Trigame un bocadillo de res con papas fritas, y para la señora, un ensalada con pollo y una bottela de aqua mineral y dos vasos de vino blanco." *Bring me roast beef sandwich with french fries, and for the lady, chicken salad, a bottle of mineral water, and two glasses of white wine.*

John looked at Lourdes and asked, "¿Algo mas?" *Anything else?*

Lourdes was astonished. He'd gotten everything right. "Muy bien, no nada mas," she said.

She was about to hand back her menu to the hovering waiter when it struck her. She had only to glance inside to confirm her suspicions. "Yo pense eso," she said. *I thought so.*

She leaned across the table and playfully slapped the menu across the top of John's head before handing it to the waiter.

"No es mi culpa!" *Not my fault.* John stifled a smile.

30

$\mathcal{I}$t was not the familiar morning sun that brought Lourdes out of her sleep, but a rush of emotions. Her eyes came open abruptly and she stared at the ceiling. She was filled with ambivalence. One part of her wanted to close her eyes and return to the dream, and the other was greatly disturbed by it. The rush of the dream was fading, leaving her feeling empty. She closed her eyes and began to replay the dream before it dissolved forever into that inaccessible place dreams go.

Let it go, let it go, be gone forever, she thought, cursing herself for wanting to hold on to it at all. The more she tried to escape it, the harder it pursued her. She reached for something to distract her mind. She turned on the bedside table lamp, hoping that the harsh light would chase away her lingering feelings. The Barbara Kingsolver book lay closest, and she picked it up and started to read from it, but every word she read led her back to the dream.

Not enough that he haunts my days, now he's invaded my nights, when I'm vulnerable. It was a mistake to befriend him. This is what happens when you let a man get close. It was still dark outside—the rays of the sun had not yet crested the hills and reached her window sill. Her bedside clock read 6:12. There was too much time before her daily routine could kick in and blot out the night's aberration. She used the time to reason with herself.

It was just a dream. *No one should feel responsible for their dreams.* She tried to treat it like an outside invader, not something that came from her. Dreams were made up of random bits of memory that the mind spooled together without any glue of logic. There it was, done and over with, she reasoned. She had absolved herself of any responsibility. She felt better. It was foolish of her to have felt guilty.

She got of bed, went into the bathroom and stood over the sink and ran bracing, cold water over her face. She hurried back to her warm bed, pulled up the covers, and relaxed a little. Then she remembered what her first reaction had been. She had wanted to return to the dream—she had wanted to return to him.

She knew what she had to do.

⤙ ⤚

Once again, Lourdes left the house early to avoid seeing John at breakfast. She wandered down to the plaza and sat on a park bench, trying to get control over the emotions pulsating through her body and mind. The church stood before her, as always an oasis of calm and repose. She could confess, and at least get it out of her system. *Yes,* she thought, *I can always turn to the church.* She entered and went to the confessional, not knowing what to say, but confident the words would come to her. They always had before.

She did not have long to wait before the priest entered. He was young—too young, not much more than a boy, really. Nevertheless, she started, with no idea where it was going.

"Perdoname, Padre..." She stopped, no idea what to say next.

The priest waited, then prompted her. "Sí, mia nina," he said patiently.

She was old enough to be his mother, yet in this setting he was the parent, and she was the child. She began again, but with even less confidence. "Perdoname, Padre, yo...yo..."

She couldn't speak to him about her feelings. He was a man—no, not even a man, a boy. How could he understand? It was a mistake to have come, she realized.

"Digame hija mia. ¿Que pasa?" he said. *Tell me, my daughter. What is it?* He sounded sincerely concerned.

She felt trapped in the tiny booth and craved flight, not from the eyes of God, but from the boy priest who, at that moment, represented the male oppression of the church. She cried out, "Perdoname...no puedo!" *Sorry, I can't!* She fled the booth.

She burst into the harsh daylight of the plaza, which was filling with people. She looked into their faces. There was no solace to be found. Each had their own life and carried their own burdens. She momentarily lowered her face into her hands, but then raised her head and set off with resolve.

Lourdes was waiting by Olivia's front door when Olivia returned home from running errands. Olivia knew something of the upset John had caused in her household and was prepared for Lourdes's wrath. Instead, what she found was a shaken woman.

"Lourdes, how good to see you," Olivia said. She had never seen her friend so distraught. When Lourdes didn't say anything, Olivia took her by the arm and guided her inside. Olivia wondered if she should speak English, as they often did, or if Spanish might be better if Lourdes was upset. She decided to wait and let her friend decide.

She guided her to a seat and sat down across from her. Still, Lourdes failed to speak, and Olivia saw that she gripped her left hand with her right so strongly that it turned white.

Finally, Olivia arose and said, "Lourdes, I'm going to get a glass of *jerez* for myself, and I'm bringing one for you, too."

Lourdes did not say no, which was the same as a yes. This spoke volumes to Olivia. She returned with the two glasses and extended one to Lourdes, who accepted and clenched it tightly in both hands. When the glass stopped trembling, Olivia knew her friend was ready to speak. Olivia sat in a chair opposite her friend and leaned toward her in a clandestine manner, even though they were the only two in the house. Olivia took a sip of her drink and watched as Lourdes took her own sip and then opened her mouth to speak. Lourdes looked like she'd had needed to talk for a very long time.

"My life was fine. It was fine the way it was. I was..."

"Happy?" Olivia said for her. "Were you going to say you were happy?"

Lourdes paused and considered the accusation. "Well, if I wasn't happy, I did not know it."

"Can't miss what you never had, is it that it?" Olivia shot back.

"Well, why not?" Lourdes said, without any real conviction behind her words.

"Because you can't go through life that way," Olivia said. "You should want more. You *deserve* more."

"We get what we deserve in this life," Lourdes said.

Olivia rolled her eyes at her friend's religious fatalism. "You get what you *accept* in life. You have to take a chance if you want to experience all life has to offer."

"Well, I can't," Lourdes said.

"You can't? Or you won't?"

"If only things were different," Lourdes said so softly Olivia could barely hear her.

Olivia watched as Lourdes got up slowly and made her way to the door. She knew better than to try and stop her.

31

The morning rain made way for a sunny afternoon. This was the time of day when John and Lourdes had their conversational lesson. John had coaxed her out of the house again and into the beautiful weather. On the plaza, they found a vacant bench.

Lourdes began with a simple question to test John's memory. Pointing to the imposing edifice of the cathedral, she asked, "¿Que es eso?" *What is that?*

He started to say cathedral but then remembered and said, "Es un iglesia Gothica."

"Muy bien," Lourdes said. "¿Mire alrededor?" she opened her arm out to demonstrate. "John, digame que lo ve." *Tell me what you see.*

John surveyed his surrounding and then began. "Hmmm...un banco, una tienda, un café," When John eyes made their way back to the table they met with Lourdes and he boldly finished with "y tu." This elicited only an uncomfortable silence from Lourdes. An impatient John now spoke up emphatically, "Yo quiero mas. La idioma, claro, pero tambien la cultura, la gente, y tu. Puedo llamarte con tu?" *I want to learn more. The language, of course, but also the culture, the people—and you. Can I use the familiar form with you?*

Lourdes was surprised. John had strung together an impressive string of sentences, with only a few minor mistakes. He had also used the familiar form to refer to her. They were way past speaking in the formal tense, but he had asked anyway and she appreciated that.

She laughed. "Sí, pero solomente sí tu lo usas correcto." *Yes, but only if you use it correctly.*

John did not catch the joke but was happy to hear her laugh. It was not a girlish giggle but the deep sincere laugh of a woman.

But his remark about learning the culture troubled her a little. Was he serious, or just trying to impress her?

"¿Digame, que es nuestra cultura?" *Tell me, what is our culture?* When speaking to John in Spanish, she had to keep the sentences simple, especially when dealing with abstract terms, but she felt she had gotten her meaning across.

John was stuck. He didn't really know anything about the culture, and his Spanish limited him even further. He said, hesitantly, "¿Su cultura? Uhmm...es romantic, es feliz, uh...you know," he finished awkwardly.

"No, no se, digame," she said, keeping him on the spot.

John looked around the plaza and saw people simply going about their business. He was at a loss, so he just blurted out words he associated with Mexico. "La comida, *the food*," he said. "Uh...margaritas, siestas..." He was grasping at straws and knew he hadn't helped his cause.

"Eat tacos, drink margaritas, and sleep in the afternoon—is that what you think we are all about?" Lourdes said in disgust.

John didn't miss the significance of her using English. She was making a point. He looked sheepishly at her and said, "I'm in trouble again, aren't I?"

"No, mi quierdo gringo." *No, my dear gringo.* She placed a hand on his shoulder and said softly, "Well, maybe just a little."

"Well, I'm happy here. Muy alegre."

Lourdes considered his words and then spoke boldly, directly and with a tinge of impatience in her voice. "John, tu sabes nada. Manana, voy ensañarte mi cultura." *John, you know nothing. Tomorrow, I'll show you our culture.*

They left the plaza, John wondering what tomorrow held.

～　～

John knew that this day was known as Day of the Dead so when he came down early, he was dressed in his gray traveling suit pants and a dark dress shirt, an outfit he thought appropriate for such a somber occasion. When he entered the dining room, he did not smell the fresh roasted coffee he had come to expect, and instead of the familiar silver coffee pot, there was a decorative ceramic pitcher painted yellow, red, and blue. John tentatively poured a small amount of the thick, brown liquid into his cup. Its texture was almost muddy, and it smelled strongly of chocolate. He gave it a taste. It was very sweet and chocolaty, with a hint of licorice. It was no substitute for the black coffee he craved, but he accepted it as part of the experience.

When he pulled back a cloth covering a basket on the table, he was horrified to see a loaf of bread baked in the shape of a skull, its teeth made of white icing. He quickly replaced the cloth and looked away. It was one thing to make skeletons out of papier-mâché, but food?

Then he remembered his boyhood communion, and how a wafer and a sip of grape juice could represent the body and blood of Christ. He also remembered something his father had once said to him when he was a teenager: "All sports are silly, all religions are weird, but we need them both." He did have a way of mixing the absurd with the profound.

He was still reminiscing at the table, sipping his cocoa, when Lourdes came down. He had expected her to wear some long, black dress, as if for a funeral. Instead, she wore black pants and a white ruffled blouse. The combination of the black and white clothing, her raven hair, and her dark eyes, was striking in its simplicity. She looked too stunning for such a solemn day.

She seemed to be her usual, businesslike self, but she also seemed to be cheerful as if she was looking forward to the day's activities. She went straight to the table, poured a full cup of the cocoa, and sat down. She took a sip before looking at John.

"John, you need not look so somber. This is not your funeral we're going to," she said with a smile.

John was at a loss, but he'd decided that if he was going to err today—and he inevitably would—it would be on the side of respectfulness.

Lourdes reached across the table and pulled back the cloth covering the basket. She smiled in amusement at the grisly, skull-shaped bread. She glanced at John and caught his wary expression.

"Oh, Maria really gets into this," she said, unceremoniously tearing off the eye socket of the skull and taking a large bite. Only then did John reach out and pull apart a large section of jaw, studded with sugary teeth. He took a large bite and washed it down with cocoa.

"You had better go easy on the *pan de muerto* and the *champurrado*," she cautioned. "They're full of sugar." She looked at a clock on the wall. "We have some time before Maria returns. She has her own family to attend to. I would like to give you some background on this holiday."

John leaned back, ready for the lesson.

Lourdes adopted her teacher's voice and began. "Dia de los Muertos goes on for two days—November 1 and 2. It is related to the Catholic holiday of All Saints Day."

"Like Halloween," John interjected.

Lourdes gave him her now familiar look of frustration and spoke with undisguised contempt. "No, John, not like your Halloween, with little girls dressing up like Disney princesses." She instantly regretted snapping at John. It was not his fault the United States commercialized every holiday. She proceeded cautiously. "Actually, it predates the Catholic observance by as much as a thousand years. Before Cortés, before Columbus, the Aztecs had a goddess named the Lady of Death. You may have seen her portrayed around town. She is called Catrina now."

John nodded. "I saw a skeleton of a woman in a dress, carrying flowers."

"That's her," Lourdes said.

"So, it's some sort of mix of Catholicism and Aztec paganism?" John asked.

"Yes, as Judaism was mixed with Greek and Roman mythology to create Roman Catholicism. Most religious holidays are created when a new religion supplants the old. They just change the holiday to fit the new religion. Basic rule of any new religion: never take away a people's holiday, just convert it."

John seemed interested in what she was saying, and for that she was glad, but she had a lot to cover. "But that's another subject," she said. "Today is about death, but we deal with it by making it a happy occasion. It is believed that last night, at midnight, the gates of heaven were opened, and the souls of all deceased children, or *angelitos*, as they are sometime called, are allowed to come to earth to reunite with their loved ones for one day. So today is actually Dia de los Innocentes, and tomorrow it is the turn for the souls of the adults."

"Just when I thought it couldn't get any sadder," John said. Lourdes was about to respond when the front door opened, and Maria entered. Maria did not stop but went straight to the Old Señor's ground-floor bedroom. Lourdes rose from the table, disappeared into the kitchen, and returned carrying what looked to be a picnic basket.

So strange, thought John. *So very strange.* But he was determined to set aside prejudices for the day.

"Estas listas?" Lourdes said. *Are you ready?*

John only had to think for a moment before responding, "Estoy listo."

She still had much to say to John, but it was a long walk to the cemetery, and she would have time to talk on the way. Lourdes strode purposefully, and John hurried to keep up. When he saw she was wearing athletic shoes, not dress shoes like his, he realized they were in for a long walk.

"We'll be spending the morning in the cemetery. You may find this a bit..." She searched for the right word. John could see in her face the moment it appeared in her mind. "Macabre."

John was impressed. She did everything, including speaking a second language, well and with grace. *Better than I would have come up with,* he thought. *I probably would have said "creepy." Her English is better than mine! She must think I'm an idiot. I can make money, but that's it.*

Lourdes continued. "Dia de los Muertos, more than anything, distinguishes us from you."

Her words stung John. She saw them as being on opposite sides, when he wanted her on his side. Or maybe he was willing to join her on hers. *All the more reason to pay attention,* he thought.

"This holiday typifies all that makes us Mexican—our character, our religion, our superstitions, our love of life, our obsession with death." She paused to let her words sink in and then said as solemnly as he had ever heard her speak, "This is the real Mexico, John. This is not for tourists."

John felt the crushing weight of her words on his soul. This was a challenge to everything that had made him who he was. He knew he would have to let go of all his pride and prejudices if he were to follow her on this path.

"Lourdes," he said, "I'm no longer a tourist. I want to do this."

Along the way, unnoticed by John, they had merged with other townspeople heading in the same direction. He now looked around at the people surrounding him. They were the humble common stock that John had always been surrounded by both here and in Houston. But today it was as if he were seeing then for the first time. Unlike Lourdes they wore colorful garb but the women all carried baskets similar to Lourdes's.

The gates of the cemetery ahead caused a bottleneck, and everyone fell into a natural line. When it was their turn to pass under the iron arches, John moved slowly forward. Despite the midmorning's sunny sky, John felt as if he was entering a long, dark passage to another world with other condemned souls.

Lourdes must have sensed his insecurity, because she reached out and took his hand. The light touch sent a wave of positive energy through him, and John felt he could go through. As the naked flesh of her palm caressed his, he felt a shiver of delight more subtle and distinct from the first sensation. When they cleared the crowd, she withdrew her hand, taking the sensation with her.

Lourdes walked ahead, and John followed a few steps behind. They passed families sitting on blankets around decorated grave sites. Some had brought food and were picnicking. John found this strange but was determined to observe without judging. He saw that Lourdes had reached her destination and was kneeling down in the grass beside a headstone and had placed a few ordinary wildflowers at its base. John feared for the knees of his dress pants but knelt beside her in the grass anyway. He did not know if he had intruded on her praying. Her head was not bowed but facing the headstone. John followed her eyes to a small, untarnished, oval-framed picture of a young boy, smiling as broadly as his mouth would allow. The smile made it even sadder. After a while, she looked up at him but did not speak. She went to her basket and pulled out a cup-cake and even stranger a comic book with a caped figure spread across its cover. She did not believe in the child literally receiving the gifts, but she believed strongly in the beneficial effect of remembrance. It was better than trying to suppress the memory. Once a year, you celebrated the life of a loved one and revisited your own pain and then let it go for a year.

Of course, she had no children of her own, and being a surrogate mother to orphaned children was not the same. She did what she could for them, but her love was limited and she did not pretend otherwise. There was no one in her life she could say she truly loved, not as others used the word. She could only give what she had to give—acts of kindness.

She looked back at John, who was kneeling a respectful distance away. Unlike herself, he had not developed the ability to conceal his feelings. She could read every one that crossed his mind, because they were vividly displayed across his face. In some ways, he was no different emotion-ally from the orphaned children she nurtured—his childish behavior, his need for attention, his stubborn insistence on getting his way. He was crying out for something that his life had failed to provide. *Oh well,* she thought. *He'll be gone in a week and be someone else's problem.*

She then remembered what she what she was supposed to be doing and chided herself for being distracted by thoughts of John on this day. She placed the gifts on the grave under the boy's picture. John did not dare speak but watched her for a sign.

Then it was over. Had he witnessed some silent ceremony conducted before him, but not with him?

She let out a small sigh, turned to him, and said, "This child I knew at the orphanage. I must be here for him today, as he has no one else." She paused, considering whether she should burden John with this and then decided maybe he needed it too. "This year he would have been a teenager. Had he not been sick, he would have walked the *paseo* hoping to meet a girl, tried to grow a mustache, maybe sneaked a drink of *pulque*. Instead, he will always love cakes and comic books. He will never know work, worries, or heartache. He is eternally a child. One of the innocents."

She looked up at John, but he had turned away so she wouldn't see the tears welling up in his eyes. He hadn't given it much thought before, but now he fully realized that the very child they were discussing lay under his feet in eternal repose. Could it actually be a blessing to die so young? Before you knew the world and all its misery? These were thoughts he did not want to have—would not have had, but for her. Did he appreciate her for it, or resent her? He did not know. This was a part of her that he had to accept. He cleared his throat and turned back to her. She had already risen and brushed the grass from her knees, holding the basket at her side.

She saw he had composed himself and spoke to him brusquely. "Come, we have many more to visit."

"Will we visit Ernesto?" John asked innocently.

"No," she said her voice turning cold, "I told you, this is not his day."

32

On November 3, after the two-day observance of the Day of the Dead, John went into town and visited the car rental office. He emerged with the keys for a subcompact for the next day. He found that, when trying to convince Lourdes to break her schedule, it was better to present her with a *fait accompli* than discuss it with her.

The following morning, John appeared at the breakfast table with a sly grin. He seemed anxious, and definitely had something on his mind. Lourdes finally confronted him with it.

"¿Que piensa, John Sanford?" *What's on your mind, John Sanford?*

He had practiced the phrase all morning and said it in near perfect Spanish. "Se aquila una coche para hoy." *I have rented a car for today.* He felt he was more likely to persuade her if he spoke Spanish.

"Como?" she said. *What?* The sentence had been beyond his skill level, so she knew he'd composed it beforehand and appreciated the effort.

John said slowly, "Vamos a la Guanajuato."

After a stressful Day of the Dead, the idea of getting out of town for the day appealed to Lourdes. Still, she was hesitant. "Pues..." she said. *Well...*

"Por favor," John said.

"No creo que—" *I don't think that—*

John then played his trump card. "I did spend an entire day with you in a cemetery."

She had to give him credit. *Maybe it will be all right,* she thought. She began, "Necesito—"

John, sensing an excuse, interrupted. "There is nothing you need more than a day away from this town."

Lourdes smiled and answered him in plain English. "I was going to say I need to change if we're going out."

John smiled back.

Lourdes returned wearing slacks and a jacket. When they traded the town's cobblestones for smooth pavement, John hit the accelerator, leaving the town and all its concerns behind. Lourdes leaned back and relaxed a little. She was leaving the present to return to Guanajuato and her past. John could not have guessed that he was taking Lourdes back to her hometown, a place of memories and ghosts.

A few miles before the town, they passed under a giant statute of Jesus on a half dome topping a hillside. As they did so, John asked, "¿Que es eso?"

Lourdes only stated the obvious. "Se llama Cristo el Rey." *Christ the king.* She did not go into any more explanation. As the figure looked down on them, John felt tension fill the car, and he decided not to stop like the other cars unless specifically instructed. As it faded into the distance, so did the tension.

They approached Guanajuato from the hills above, and John pulled the car over at a scenic spot to take it in. Although San Miguel and Guanajuato were similar in size and population, geographically they were exact opposites. San Miguel was perched on top of a hill, while Guanajuato was wedged into a valley. The first things that caught John's attention were the bright colors of its buildings. Brilliant red, soft turquoise, and vivid green spotted the landscape. Ornate buildings climbed the hillside on either side of the narrow valley. With Lourdes directing, they descended into the valley. She guided him to a central area where he could park the car. Unlike other towns its size, Guanajuato did not have a large central plaza. Its steep valley did not provide any area with a broad, flat plain. Instead, the town had El Jardin de la Union as its central gathering place. The Jardin, or garden, was long and narrow, and worked its way past zigzagging streets. It was lined with aged Indian laurel trees that provided a shady canopy. John sought out a bench, but Lourdes had other plans.

Indicating the bench, she said, "We'll return here, but now we have much to see. A lot of history took place here—and you said you were interested in the history." John looked down and saw she was wearing the same walking shoes she had worn to the cemetery, and he knew he was in for another long day.

"This is a town best seen by foot," Lourdes said.

They crossed the street, and John was immediately confronted with the elegant Teatro Juarez, the famous baroque-style opera house.

"Its opening was a performance of *Aida,* attended by its composer, Verdi," Lourdes proudly informed him.

"Verdi, really," John said, nodding his appreciation. He did not know opera, but even he had heard of Verdi.

Next they visited the fountain of the Baratillo. Lourdes told him how it had been commissioned by the Emperor Maximilian and had been made in Italy. With Maximilian's fall from power, it had been moved to a less conspicuous spot but still retained its beauty. Lourdes did not tell that part to John. The role of Maximilian and the French in Mexican history was only a slightly less sensitive subject than Cortés and his five hundred Spaniards.

They climbed up and down paved steps and walked down a street so narrow it was said that, at one spot, neighbors could lean out their windows to kiss. The narrow cobblestone streets seemed, to John, reminiscent of the medieval Italian villages in Tuscany he had visited with his ex-wife, but he didn't mention it. He did not wish to bring the past into the present. They stopped for lunch at a small sidewalk café named Mestizo. The exertion gave a glow of health to Lourdes's skin, and John thought again what a magnificent women she was. The menu consisted of simple, local dishes, and John let Lourdes order for him. She chose the *paella*—it was light enough not to slow them down later and for drinks she allowed only mineral water.

The next stop was the University of Guanajuato, a place of special meaning to Lourdes. Had they lingered, her memories surely would have overwhelmed her, but she only mentioned its reputation and moved quickly on.

At the Museo Alhondigas, Lourdes stopped to explain its unsavory role in Mexico's history. Originally built as a granary, it later served as a prison. While it presently held a museum and a gallery, Lourdes felt it would be disingenuous not to point out that the hooks on the wall once displayed the bloody heads of the rebel heroes of the failed revolution. She chose not to show John the Museo de Mummies, one of the most macabre sites anywhere in the world. Actual dried cadavers, without wrapping, were displayed behind glass. They were victims of eviction, after their families had failed to keep up payments for their burial crypt. After putting John through the two-day ordeal of the Day of the Dead, Lourdes thought he could be spared that sight.

They returned late in the afternoon to the exact bench John had reluctantly left five hours ago. He was fatigued but determined not to show it. He saw a street vendor and returned with cups of sparkling fruit soda in shaved ice.

The sipped their drinks without speaking and watched the last of day slip away. There were still children running and playing, their parents nearby. Lourdes looked about, absorbing the emotions in the air.

"¿Que piensa?" John said. *What are you thinking about?*

"Nada," Lourdes said.

"No, digame."

She rolled her head until she faced him. "Why do you care?"

She said it directly, and John took it as an opportunity to express his feelings. She had asked, and he was going to answer.

"I want to know anything that concerns you," John said. "I care about you." He looked down into his drink. "Were you thinking about us?"

She sighed, realizing she had opened the door for that sort of response. "No," she said. "If you really want to know, I was remembering long ago. I came to this park as a child with my parents. I remember how happy and secure I was that day."

John looked around at the children. He picked out a cute little girl with a dirty face, playing roughly with boys, probably her brothers.

"You were like that child," he said.

Lourdes looked at the child and then at her parents. The man had on a T-shirt, and his large belly overlapped his belt. The woman was overweight, too, and wore a tattered sweater over her dress. Lourdes laughed and gave John a look that said, *You're hopeless.*

"No, John, I was not like that. I wore a starched dress when I went for walks with my parents." She closed her eyes to remember them better. "They were always dressed elegantly. My mother carried a parasol to protect herself from the sun. She was fair-skinned and proud of it. She was of pure Spanish descent. My father had some Indian blood. I know that doesn't mean much to you, but these things are still very important to us here. Maybe it shouldn't be, but it is. My father would always dress in a suit, even to go to the park. He had a neatly trimmed mustache and carried a cane for walks. Like my mother's parasol, it was mainly for show."

John felt the happiness of the day sinking with the sun and changed topics quickly. "I'm hungry. Let's have dinner before we leave—I'm sure you know a place."

— ~

She did know a place, a place that had been one of her favorites. She had not been back in many years, but she knew it would not have changed. In this part of the world, nothing changed overnight. By the time John got back to Houston, restaurants would have come and gone, and he would not have noticed or cared. But in a town like Guanajuato, it would be noticed. She hesitated. She had not told John they were in her hometown, that her parents were buried here, that one day she would join them there. That every street held a memory, and that around every corner lurked a ghost.

She felt a certain liberation outside San Miguel. She felt emboldened, and didn't want to return yet, so she said, "Yes, I know a place. I
think you'll like it."

She rose with vigor, and John got up, careful not to let out any moans.
She led him confidently up more steps and down a few narrow streets,
which were quickly being filled with shadows. Halfway down the block, she
stopped in front of an old oak door with the restaurant's name, La Taula,
painted above. There was nothing about the outside to distinguish it from
many others they had passed, but the inside had a certain ambiance. The
plaster walls were a warm ochre color, and the furniture was oak and heavy.
It was a place of genuineness, of understated elegance, a place where many
generations of family had eaten, friends had drunk, and lovers had met. It
was an early weeknight, so the restaurant was not crowded.

Although Lourdes led him in, it was John the waiter approached. A
veteran server, he had sized John up correctly as American, and spoke in
perfect English.

"Good evening, sir."

John had learned a little dining-out dialogue and answered him back
in Spanish. "Somos dos." *We are two.*

This garnered a smile from Lourdes and a hearty, "Muy bien!" from
the waiter, who was already angling for a large tip from the American.

The waiter led them to a table and asked for their drink orders. John's
last margarita had been a mistake, so he went with his usual scotch.
Lourdes was happy to see John being himself and ordering what he liked.
She followed suit and ordered, *vino tinto,* red wine, the drink of her youth.

The waiter returned with their drinks and menus. Lourdes surprised
him when she set the menu facedown without opening it and ordered one
of the restaurant's signature dishes, tapas, a sampler of the chef's spe-
cialty items served with their homemade bread. The waiter looked at her
curiously. He had been there twelve years, but he could not remember
seeing her before—and hers was not a face one would quickly forget.

"You've been here before?" he asked in English for John's benefit.

"Sí, muchas vezes, muchas anos pasados." *Yes, many times, many years ago.*

"Bienviendo," he said. *Welcome back.*

John got the gist of her answer and looked at her questioningly. He had thought of her as only existing in San Miguel, and always in that house. But, of course, there had to be more. He wanted to know it all. But for the moment, he vowed to be patient and let her tell it in her own time. Even if time was not something he had much of.

With each sip of the deep-red wine, her face seemed to grow darker and more mysterious. Once again, he was amazed at how she could look so altered in different settings. He wondered if others saw this, too, or if it was a special power of his, or if he was just imagining it. An inner turmoil seemed to be playing itself out across her face, but he dared not disturb it.

She, of course, had been to this restaurant with her parents on many occasions. There had also been many evenings with Alejandro, her boy-friend at the University of Guanajuato, holding hands and planning their future. He would drink the local beer, she would drink red wine, and they would share an oven-baked pizza. Their thoughts were of their future, of making a life together. But they were children. What did they know?

She had gone to a girls' prep school in the United States, but instead of going to college in the States as well, her parents had called her back to attend the renowned, local University de Guanajuato. She didn't mind—she had never really adjusted emotionally to the United States. She was always the brown one, never openly discriminated against, but never truly accepted either.

At the university, she had met Alejandro. He was two years older than her and was studying economics, the accepted subject for those on the fast track to government service. In the United States, it would have been law, but in Mexico, the ambitious focused on the dismal subject of the movement of money.

In a town as small as Guanajuato, of course, their families knew each other, and each approved of such a match. The young lovers made plans. They thought they were in charge of their lives. They would soon learn otherwise.

Lourdes's father's family had grown wealthy over several generations from a silver-mining operation in the hills outside of Guanajuato. They had never diversified, always putting the earnings back into the mines. While Lourdes was at prep school, the mines started playing out. By the time she was in college, her family was in dire straits.

On her twenty-first birthday her father had booked the entire restaurant. There were fifty guests, including Alejandro and his family. Her father had paid the check in cash, gone home, and shot himself in the head. Her mother mourned the loss of her husband and wondered how she would live out her remaining years. She sold some jewelry to bribe the priest to overlook the suicide and allow him to be buried in the family plot. Lourdes eventually returned to the university, but Alejandro's family no longer approved of their match because of her family's disgrace. Alejandro finished his studies and moved to the capital to work for the government. Lourdes's mother set out to find an acceptable husband for her daughter, one who was not so particular, who would be able to support both of them. Ernesto de Madrid appeared to be such a man.

Lourdes finished her wine and the waiter appeared out of nowhere to refill it. John looked at her and saw a different woman from the matronly landlady who had greeted him that first night, which now seemed so long ago. She looked strong and vibrant as the red wine surged through her. It was then that a multitude of small white plates began appearing with everything from olives to beef tongue. She insisted that John sample a little of each. He did even reluctantly trying a small bite of the tongue, while she savored the remaining portion.

She had come back to this town, to this very place, and had confronted its ghosts for the first time. Maybe John's presence had given her the courage to do it. She looked back at him and smiled. He smiled back but did not understand what he was seeing in her face. She seemed very determined, but about what?

Finally, as he looked on, she seemed to return to the present. She looked up at him and gave him an encouraging smile. This emboldened him to explore his feelings.

"Lourdes, do you remember your first impression of me?"

"Vividly!" she said emphatically, but with a smile. "You no longer seem like the same person."

John took a deep breath. "Thank you...I think. But, you see, I don't clearly remember you. I didn't pay any attention. I don't really remember anything clearly until that night at the party. I think that was the first time I really looked at you. After you left, I wandered around the town. I finally ended up at the church. I didn't go in, just sat outside and thought. I realized that you were a person, and that I had intentionally hurt you. I wondered why I had done it. I think now that it was because I was afraid of you."

"Afraid of me?" Lourdes said, genuinely amazed.

"Yes," John said, "afraid of anyone getting close to me. It's a defense mechanism I've used since my divorce to keep people from getting too close to me. I think I was afraid it was about to happen again."

"John, I think I understand. Maybe I'm afraid, too."

Their conversation had wandered into territory that was uncomfortable for both of them. Lourdes changed the subject. "So John, are you rich?" she asked in a jovial tone.

He chuckled at her brazen question. "I'm on my way," he said with a smile. In truth, after last year his net worth stood at around two million—but in Houston, that didn't get you in the front door.

She surprised him by saying, "As a child I was rich, but I didn't realize it. You just think that's how one lives." She paused, and said more seriously, "There are children in the orphanage who have nothing. When they dress in the morning, it's in clothes that I or others have donated. When they eat, they believe the food came from heaven. They believe that their support is literally a God-given right. When they turn sixteen, they lose all of that. And they realize, for the first time, that they have nothing."

She looked at John directly. "When my father lost his money, he ceased to exist as a person. John, don't let that happen to you if your fountain of money ever stops flowing. Don't ever let money be the essence of who you are."

She had not meant to lecture him and regretted ending such a lovely day on a sour note. "Ya esta muy tarde," she said. *It's very late already.* "We should start back."

They left and retraced their steps through the deserted streets until they reached the car. John walked around and unlocked the door.

Lourdes stepped forward, but John did not move aside, and she walked into his arms. In the moonlight, her face no longer had that dark intensity but seemed illuminated, taking on an angelic appearance. The thoughts John had entertained in the restaurant no longer seemed appropriate, but he tried anyway. He held her tight and kissed her. She allowed the kiss, and then responded, her breath coming fast.

He pulled back and said, "Es muy tarde, pero...we could stay the night."

His words brought Lourdes back to her senses, and she responded gently, but firmly. "Lo siento John, pero no puedo." *I'm sorry, John, I can't.*

They rode back in silence. Lourdes turned her head away and watched the three quarter moon lead them back to San Miguel.

33

John came downstairs wondering which Lourdes he would meet, but he found only Maria, ready with his breakfast.

"Donde esta la Señora?" he said. *Where is the lady?*

Maria's response was no help at all. "Se fue," she said. *She left.*

John was used to this kind of treatment from Maria. He didn't take it too personally—Maria was very protective when it came to her lady, and she had a general suspicion of men.

Lourdes arrived early to the confessional. She couldn't undo last night, but she could confess. The priest entered his side of the booth and spoke to her through the screen.

"¿Que tienes, mi hija?" *What is it, my child?*

"Perdoname, Padre, de haber pecado. Hace dos días de no confesarme." *Forgive me, Father, I have sinned. It has been two days since I have confessed.*

The priest remembered her from earlier in the week. "Bien, dime," he said. *I will hear your confession.*

She took in a breath and then began. "Sí, Padre a noche bese a un hombre que no es mi marido." *Yes, father. I kissed a man last night who was not my husband.*

"Viente y cinco Santa Marias," the priest said. Twenty-five Hail Marys. He thought there must be more on her mind or conscience than a kiss, so he prompted her, saying, "Algo mas, mi hija?"

"No, es todo." *No, that's all.*

The priest crossed himself, signaling that Lourdes's time was up, and she rose and exited the booth, her feelings still unresolved. On a park bench in the still-deserted plaza, she sorted through them. On another bench a few feet away, she saw a young couple holding hands. They leaned together and met in a kiss. Lourdes watched as the young man placed his hand on the girl's thigh and moved his hand up her skirt. Lourdes tried to turn away but felt her own thigh warm up and her face flush with blood. The young woman looked up and caught Lourdes's gaze. She reached down, pushed the young man's hand away, and tilted her head toward Lourdes, giving her a look of disgust.

Lourdes fled back into the church and reentered the confessional booth. Without prompting, she started. "Perdoname Padre de haber pecado." She looked down at her watch and continued. "Hace viente minutos que no me confieso." *It's been twenty minutes since my last confession.*

—— ~

John returned that afternoon to find Lourdes sitting on the patio reading a book. She was dressed in a skirt, blouse, and sweater against the impending chill of the late afternoon. Once again, her looks seemed to match the setting and the mood. In her reading glasses, she had a gentle, studious look. She looked definitely middle aged but middle age had never looked so good to John. Shadows were beginning to make their way across the tile floor, and based on their location, John could see he had less than an hour to work. Without saying anything, he set about studying his book, occasionally peering over it. Finally, he put it down and looked longingly at her. She could no longer ignore his presence and knew he had something on his mind that she would have to deal with. She would tread carefully with him this time.

"What are you doing, John?"

"Counting the differences," he said.

"Finding many?" she asked accusingly.

"Plenty. We come from different countries, different cultures, different backgrounds, different languages, religions—is that enough for you?" He waited for her to respond.

"Does my Mexican heritage test your Anglo prejudices?" Lourdes wasn't sure where he was going with that. Was he trying to tell her he was giving up? She would be relieved, but there would be disappointment mixed in.

He surprised her with a simple, "Yes."

"Well don't expect me to apologize for being who I am," she said, with a combination of pain and anger.

"Please, Lourdes, let's not take that step backward," John said pleadingly. "We've never been anything but honest with each other. And, Lourdes, despite the differences, I've never felt closer to anyone in my life. I never realized it before, but now I know I've been lonely my whole life. Now, for the first time, I don't feel alone. You've done that for me."

Lourdes had to set John straight. "John, there are things I can do for you, but there will be things you need that I can't give you. Do you still think you understand?"

"I think so. You've already given me more than I have reason to expect, and I know I'm going to miss you terribly when I'm gone."

Gone. There it was, said and out in the open. There was an ending date, and it was beginning to loom larger with every passing day. One day, he would be gone, and someone else would move into his room. Many had come before him, so many she could no longer even recall all their names or faces. But there would only be one John. No one else would come along to take his place, but he had to leave, for both their sakes.

~ ~

The next day was Sunday morning, and Lourdes had already left to attend Mass. John came downstairs to find the usual breakfast of fruit, bread, and coffee. The Old Señor sat in his chair facing the window. John could not tell if he was awake, asleep, or in the twilight he often went into. John did not relish sitting with him alone, so, after having a quick coffee, he went back upstairs to put on his newly purchased Nike shoes. He had come to enjoy walking, and the weather was certainly suitable. Now that he thought about it, the weather always seemed to be perfect in San Miguel. The mornings were like a perpetual fall, the afternoons were perpetual spring, and the nights were a bit of winter. It was like spending a whole year each day, except there was no summer. That suited him fine—Houston, where summers lasted half the year, had given him his fill. He could now see why Bill and the other Americans had picked this place. Now that he had stopped his heavy drinking, he noticed how much better he felt. Better weather, better food, no pollution, no traffic—but then again, no jobs. *Maybe I could buy a condo here, for vacations,* he thought. He had picked up some brochures from a real estate office earlier in the week and thought this would be a good time to check out the neighborhoods.

As he went out the door, he picked out a sweater he had recently bought at the market, hand-woven wool that felt good wrapped around his chest. He had not packed appropriately for San Miguel. In his ignorance, he had imagined San Miguel as being tropical. He brought along with him lots of touristy shorts and shirts that he had picked up in Cancun with the Corona beer logo emblazoned on them. Now he was ashamed of them, his ignorance, and how little he paid attention to anything that was not business-related. Business. The word stuck in his mind. Since his call to Houston the first week, he had not given his business a thought. If the deal with the Mexicans went through, as he wanted, the savings would increase his profit margin significantly. They would run the assembly on the border town, and he would benefit from the third world's lower labor costs. He had offered to make them partners. It was a bold move for him, but one that had to be done. If he pulled it off, it would give him an even greater incentive to learn Spanish. He could return again, and this time do it right.

He realized he had been walking without direction, and stopped to get his bearings. He still knew the way to Bill's house and would check out that neighborhood first. He noticed that even the newer developments adhered to the eighteenth-century Spanish architecture style. The homes were built with little setback from the street. No yards, but all had patios, balconies, and large potted plants—much more sensible than the suburban sprawl of the United States, with its mandated St. Augustine grass that had to be maintained despite environments very unlike its native Florida.

John matched a townhouse with one in the brochure. At $399,000, it was doable. Real estate was always a good investment in the long run, he reasoned. In truth, he wanted a toehold on this spot of the earth. He wanted this feeling to go on past his allotted month. He took a steep street and climbed it until he reached the end, where he could look out across the valley. He felt the ever-present cool breeze on his face tempered by the warm sun. In the distance, he could see clouds rolling in and he smelled the scent that preceded the rain. He wanted to hold on to that feeling. He wanted to be part of it. He did not want to go back home to Houston. He accepted that, but the next thought he could not accept as easily. He wanted her, he needed her—he loved her. He couldn't stay here without her, because without her, none of it mattered. He did not know if he could go on without her. He looked at his watch. She would be home now. John both longed for and dreaded seeing her.

What was it about her that he craved? She was definitely a handsome woman, but he had certainly known more beautiful women. But her beauty was patient. It didn't strike you immediately but grew slowly, and it seemed like he could never see it all at once. It was a beauty that couldn't be frozen by a camera. Her face was a sea of never-ending waves, driven by emotions that could range from ripples, to whitecaps, to crashing waves—anything but sameness. She was not young, although he did not know her exact age. She had black hair, black eyes, and light brown skin, but so did almost every other Mexican woman. He closed his eyes and tried to imagine her but couldn't. There was something intangible that he couldn't describe, even to himself. There was an underlying physical attraction, but that was not what drove him. It was something more. He did not want to admit it to himself, but it was more spiritual.

He remembered Bill's prophetic words to him at the party: "If you don't know, I can't tell you."

He now understood what he meant. Even now, he couldn't find the words to tell himself. But she made him a better man. He had only one more day left in his month. Then where would he be? There was no time left to think. His mind was made up. He had to face her and he would not leave without an answer.

He looked up at the sky, and ahead of the advancing storm he viewed a white glint before a blue sky. An airliner headed south, probably to Mexico City from the United States, maybe even from Houston, its contrail forming a wispy link between her world and his. Only two hours by air, but worlds apart. It was not like him to think abstractly like that. The wispy contrail was breaking up and he felt cut off from that life that lay waiting for him in the north.

He turned from the sight and started back down the hill, a cool, moist breeze at his back telling him rain was sweeping the valley. The energy it carried invigorated him, and he would have loved to stay and watch it from his vantage point, but it would be lunch by the time he got back, and Lourdes would be there.

34

That night John sat across from Lourdes at the dinner table. Neither had shown much interest in their food. They stared at each other but did not speak. It was John's last night, and that hung over the evening like a death sentence. The tension grew heavier with every tick of the clock. He was determined that tonight his question would not go unanswered. He would have a resolution, whether by words or action. He looked at Lourdes across the table. She did not look away. They both knew they would eventually have to deal with the issue.

Lourdes felt responsible that it had come this far. She had lost control of the situation, and now it was her duty to deal with it openly and directly. She saw words start to form on John's lips, only to fade away. He started again, but the words continually failed to form.

Finally, she could stand the strain no longer. She would have to initiate things.

"John, what is it?" she asked impatiently.

John pondered how to tactfully advance his cause. He had tried out different approaches all afternoon, but they all felt disingenuous. He was determined that, whatever he said, the statement would not go unanswered. There would be a resolution. He *needed* to know, he *had* to know, he *would* know. He would speak to her in her own language, in words that would leave no doubt.

In a quiet voice that carried great weight, he said, "Te amo." *I love you.*

There. It was said, out in the open, done. There was no going back from those words. He would live the rest of his life with whatever happened next.

She knew it and had known it for some time. She felt he deserved the truth and had planned to tell him, but she had not prepared for the effect those two words would have on her.

So instead of giving him an honest answer, she replied glibly, "Do you know what that means?"

Although she meant to question his knowledge of Spanish, she realized her question had a more complex meaning, too.

John had wanted a yes or no. He was prepared for either, but instead he got a question. Nothing had been decided. It made him angry.

"Yes," he said, "but I wonder if you do." It was the perfect exit line. He could leave with some dignity. He got up from the table and backed away, his eyes still locked on hers. He turned his back and began to walk away slowly, giving her a chance to speak. But still she said nothing. He still struggled for some type of closure. She had not said yes; she had not said no. She had left him hanging and he craved a final resolution. Words had not been enough, so it was time for action.

He stopped and with his back still turned to her, he spoke, "Lourdes, this may be our last night together, or only the beginning. Tonight, when the house is quiet, I will come to you. If you do not wish to see me, put on your latch, and I won't disturb you. Goodnight."

He left immediately. He did not wish it discussed. She called out to his retreating figure, "John...John..." But for him, the time for words had passed.

～ ～

Maria, unaware of the drama unfolding in the house, finished cleaning up the kitchen and turned off the water. Through an open window in his bedroom, John watched as the full moon rose over the surrounding hills. He sat up in bed anxiously and looked out to the moon. Its light filled his room and cast long shadows across it. The house grew ominously quiet as the sound of running water stilled. John remembered what he'd said, *when the house was quiet.* Now the house was quiet. He wished he hadn't put everything on the line, but what other choice did he have? Now he just wanted this night over with.

Lourdes was lying in her bed anxiously. She, like John, had heard the water stop, and now she waited. She looked to the latch she had purposely left undone. She looked toward the crucifix on the wall, but it lay hidden in the darkness of a long shadow cast by a curtain. She looked toward the window and stared into the face of the full moon that seemed to lurk just outside.

John sat in bed. The house had become quiet, eerily quiet. He got up and left his room to face his future.

Lourdes lay on her side, facing away from the door, her eyes transfixed on the moon. She heard a door creak, and footsteps slowly approaching. She turned back and looked at the latch, then the crucifix, then the moon. She heard the footsteps stop, and she quickly got out of bed and silently made her way to the door. She stood at the door and watched the knob as it began to slowly turn. As it completed its turn, she reached for the latch and lowered it, just as the door started to move. It met with the resistance of the latch, paused, and then slowly drew back. Footfalls could be heard in retreat.

Only then did she let out her breath, and say softly to herself, "No, John."

John returned to his bed and stared at the ceiling, his expression not one of anger, but of sad resignation. Across the room, his suitcases sat packed, ready for a morning departure. His eyes slowly closed, and as the moon made its transit across the room, he began to nod off.

Something had happened that caused John to open his eyes slightly. The room was bathed in an eerie moonlight that played tricks on his eyes. In the white haze, he believed he saw a ghost in a flowing gown standing in the doorway. Then it started to move toward him and slowly came into focus. It was Lourdes. He waited for her to speak, but she said nothing, as she stood over him. Only when he sat up did she move toward him and lower herself into his arms. John started to speak, but she put her lips to his mouth before he could get a word out, pressing hard. The untied straps allowed her silky gown to slip from her shoulders revealing her breasts. John took in the sight of her dark areoles and pointed tips, like two dark eyes staring back at him in defiance. He rose to meet them, and soon she was moaning softly at his gentle kisses and the soft tugs of his lips against her firm pointed nipples. He then engulfed one with his entire mouth, and she swooned. He felt that he could stay there forever, but she wanted more, and she slid down until their faces came together for a deep kiss. Her tongue plunged down into his mouth and met with his. He did not need to think what to do—she had come to him. It would happen on her terms.

Lourdes slid back until she was poised over him and then lowered herself onto him. Their bodies meshed, and all barriers between them disappeared. They became as one moving in a synchronized motion until her body convulsed in a silent shudder followed by his. He watched as her face moved from aroused, to frenzied, to serene. She slid off him and, without shame, wrapped her wet leg around his and laid her head on his heaving chest. He stayed as still as his heaving chest would allow, not wishing to disturb the moment, but feeling like he needed to speak.

Finally he cleared his throat and began, "Lourdes…"

But she placed a warning finger on his lips and held it firm. He nodded. Only then did she put her head back on his bare chest.

35

John awoke with a burst of joy. He laid his head back down on the pillow and wondered if the night before had all been a dream. It seemed like a dream, it felt like a dream, but he had never had a dream like that before. He leaned to his left and smelled the pillow. It was her scent. Strangely, that was the most real evidence of the night. He leaned back and replayed the surrealistic memory. It had seemed so strange, so unreal, but he knew he did not possess the imagination to have created such a scene.

He felt happier than he could ever remember feeling. It was a new day, a new life, a new John. No longer would he dull his feelings with alcohol—he would take life head on. With her by his side, he could face anything. He would see her every day, he would learn her every expression, and they would share with each other their every thought. He would draw from her fountain of strength, and he would reward her with everything he possessed.

This was day one of his new life and the hope that knew no boundaries. He stopped and said a short prayer for himself and the future. He dressed quickly and bounded down the stairs.

When John entered the dining room, he found Lourdes standing by the Old Señor, feeding him small bites of scrambled eggs. John moved quickly toward her, but she rushed to meet him and held him off at arm's length.

John leaned toward her to kiss her, but she turned her head and said, "John, no, please."

Her head turned back to the table and to the Old Señor, who was straining forward in his chair to see what was happening.

John looked at her in bewilderment and asked, "Lourdes, what is it, what's wrong?"

She acted as if she didn't know what he was talking about and instead spoke of his impending departure. "Please, Señor," she said, "you must get ready. Your driver will be here soon to take you to the airport."

"Airport?" he said in astonishment. "I'm not going to the airport or anywhere else. I'm staying with you. We belong together."

"No, John," she said, dropping the pretense of calling him señor, "it won't work. It can't work."

"I love you, Lourdes, and what's more, I know you love me. You could never have come to me last night if you didn't. That much I know," he said indisputably.

Without denying what had happened, she answered, "That doesn't matter, John."

"Doesn't matter?! Love doesn't matter? It's all that matters! What doesn't matter is everything else. Where we live, who lives with us, what we do. What matters is that we're together!" He had to pause as a wave of dizziness swept over him.

"I told you all along it wouldn't work," she said. "You should have listened to me. Now, you must! You must!"

John's head spun. He couldn't believe what he was hearing. It was as if another entity possessed her body. But he was not ready to give up.

He continued in a pleading voice. "We'll make it work. You want to leave here? We'll move to Houston. You want to stay here? I'll sell my business and move here with you. We can all stay together—Maria, Pepe, the Old Señor." He smiled reassuringly at the Old Señor, who seemed to be trying in vain to raise himself out of his chair.

Lourdes just shook her head. "Believe me, John. We can't."

John, in desperation, found himself speaking franticly in Spanish. "Por que? Por que? Diga me! Diga me!" *Why? Why? Tell me! Tell me!*

Lourdes turned away from him and attempted to flee the room, but John grabbed her by both arms spun her around and forced her to look him in the eye.

She started to shake, and then to cry, but John held her tightly and demanded, "Tell me!"

Shaking, trembling, and sobbing, she finally shouted out for all to hear, "The Old Señor is Ernesto!"

John released her, his hands falling to his side. She moved quickly away and hurried to Ernesto's side. The old man's eyes had lost their anger and were now moist with tears. He pitifully looked up at John, who could not bear to meet his gaze and looked at the floor instead.

Lourdes knelt by the old man, holding his head to her chest and sobbing. Saying repeatedly, "Perdoname, Ernesto. Perdoname."

John was rooted to the spot, not wanting to watch, but unable to escape the tragedy he had wrought.

Lourdes turned back to look at him, and in a voice now devoid of emotion said, "John, please leave us."

⌐ ⌐

A little while later a driver pulled up to the front of the house. John had been waiting by the gate and now moved toward the car. The driver got out and took John's bags. John took a seat in the back and rode away without a backward glance.

On the bed where they had spent their last night, Lourdes sat hugging his pillow to her chest. When she heard the car pull up, she hurried to the window in time to see John enter the cab and depart.

She watched it until it disappeared and then said to herself and heaven, "Lo siento."

El fin

www.ingramcontent.com/pod-product-compliance
Lightning Source LLC
Chambersburg PA
CBHW070623130626
46556CB00001B/451